The Woman Who Saved His Christmas

STAND-ALONE NOVEL

A Christian Historical Romance Book

by

Chloe Carley

RUBEDIA
PUBLISHING

Disclaimer & Copyright

This is a work of fiction. Names, characters, places, and incidents either are products of the author's imagination or are used fictitiously. Any resemblance to actual events or locales or persons, living or dead, is entirely coincidental.

Copyright© 2025 by Chloe Carley

All Rights Reserved.

No part of this book may be reproduced, duplicated, transmitted, or recorded in any form—electronic or printed—without the prior written permission of the publisher. Unauthorized storage or distribution of this document is strictly prohibited.

Table of Contents

The Woman Who Saved His Christmas	1
Disclaimer & Copyright	2
Table of Contents	3
Letter from Chloe Carley	5
Chapter One	6
Chapter Two	19
Chapter Three	30
Chapter Four	40
Chapter Five	49
Chapter Six	58
Chapter Seven	67
Chapter Eight	76
Chapter Nine	85
Chapter Ten	92
Chapter Eleven	101
Chapter Twelve	112
Chapter Thirteen	123
Chapter Fourteen	133
Chapter Fifteen	142
Chapter Sixteen	152
Chapter Seventeen	162
Chapter Eighteen	170
Chapter Nineteen	179
Chapter Twenty	188

Chapter Twenty-One	197
Chapter Twenty-Two	207
Chapter Twenty-Three	215
Chapter Twenty-Four	224
Chapter Twenty-Five	230
Chapter Twenty-Six	238
Chapter Twenty-Seven	248
Chapter Twenty-Eight	258
Chapter Twenty-Nine	267
Chapter Thirty	278
Chapter Thirty-One	288
Chapter Thirty-Two	295
Chapter Thirty-Three	302
Chapter Thirty-Four	310
Chapter Thirty-Five	318
Epilogue	326
Also by Chloe Carley	333

Letter from Chloe Carley

"Once upon a time..."

...my best childhood nights had started with this beautiful phrase!

Ever since I can remember, I have loved a good story!

It all started thanks to my beloved grandfather! He used to read to my sister and me stories of mighty princes and horrifying dragons! Even now, sometimes I miss those cold winters in front of the fireplace in my hometown, Texas!

My best stories, though, were the ones from the Bible! Such is the spiritual connection that a sense of warmth passes through my body every time I hear a biblical story!

My childhood memories were not all roses, but I knew He would always be there for me, my most robust shelter!

Years passed by, and little Chloe grew up reading all kinds of stories! It was no surprise that I had this urge to write my own stories and share them with the world!

If God has given me a purpose on Earth, I think it is to spread His love and wisdom through my stories!

Brightest Blessings,

Chloe Carley

Chapter One

Wintervale, Wyoming 1884

The other passengers on the train stared at Isabelle Heart with narrowed eyes and pinched lips as she shuffled her way down the aisle toward the open door, suitcases in each hand. With only six weeks left until Christmas, the weather had turned, and the air outside was cold and biting. The cold seemed to have taken up residence inside the train, too.

The truth was, she didn't blame them for their anger. It still hurt, though. Her cheeks flamed. A lock of dark brown hair spilled loose from her bun and she gave her head a vigorous shake to get it out of her face. She forced herself to keep her head high and her eyes fixed straight ahead. She couldn't let herself look at anyone around her or she might break down.

Baby Abby, strapped to her front, let out a wail, provoking more grumbling from the passengers as Isabelle walked past them.

If she wasn't my baby, I would be angry about all the yelling too.

But then, Abby *wasn't* Isabelle's baby. Not really.

Abby was howling like this because she was hungry. They'd been stalled on the tracks for hours thanks to the snowstorm, and Isabelle had missed her guess when it came to how much milk she'd need to pack for the journey. There would be nothing more for Abby until they reached their final destination—the home of the man who was to be her new husband.

She shivered with anxiety at the thought of it.

She was stabbed with guilt, as well, with a thought she'd had several times since she'd taken responsibility for the baby—that she could never be a proper mother to Abby. Not really.

She would always take care of her best friend's daughter. She would raise Abby as her own and love her as her own. But if there was one thing this journey had made abundantly clear, it was that there were some things only a biological mother could provide.

If Vivienne had been here, she would have been able to give Abby the milk she needed and Abby wouldn't be screaming with hunger right now.

A porter took her luggage from her and helped her to step down from the train and onto the platform. He gave her a sympathetic look as he handed her bags back to her, but said nothing, and Isabelle felt sure he was glad to be rid of her too. He must have had complaints about the baby. Abby had been crying for hours.

At least the air here was warmer than it had been in Hearthstone, where she'd boarded the train. It still had the crisp bite of winter, but it didn't sting her skin in the same way it had back home. There was a layer of snow on the ground, but it wasn't the deep snow she'd left behind. It didn't rise above the tops of her boots and sink in, wetting her feet. Instead, it was a fine powder, barely deep enough to record the impression of her footprints.

Someone had gone to the trouble of tying a wreath to the signpost at the edge of the tracks. If Isabelle hadn't been so frightened and alone, that might have seemed festive.

She looked around as the train pulled away. Wintervale was a small town, and only two other people had disembarked here. Both of them were men and both of them were walking away from Isabelle, leaving her standing alone in the gathering darkness.

She shivered.

The man she was supposed to meet—Cameron Mercer—should be here. She had fully expected that he would be waiting to pick her up. What kind of man *wouldn't* be waiting to pick up the bride he had sent away for by mail? What kind of man would leave a woman standing alone at dusk like this?

She jostled up and down to try to stop Abby from crying but it was no use. The baby wouldn't be comforted until she had something to eat.

"It's all right," she said quietly, her voice breaking a little. "It's all right, Abby. We'll be at our new home soon and there will be something for you there. I promise." She adjusted her grip on her bags. Isabelle was short and slight, and having the baby strapped to her made it hard to balance.

"Isabelle? Are you Isabelle?"

The voice didn't belong to a man but Isabelle was so relieved at the sound of her name that she hardly noticed. She turned to see a woman, perhaps in her early thirties, with sandy brown hair in a sensible bun and a welcoming smile on her face.

The smile faded almost immediately.

"Whose baby is that?" the woman demanded.

Isabelle took a step backward, releasing one of her suitcases so that she could bring an arm up to shield Abby. "Who are you?" she countered.

"You're Isabelle Heart, aren't you?"

"I am…"

The woman sighed. "You never said you were bringing a baby with you."

"You still haven't told me who you are." Isabelle shivered with the cold and the strangeness of this conversation. "How do you know my name?"

"I'm the one you've been writing to," the woman said. "My name is Eloise Mercer. I'm Cameron Mercer's older sister."

A chill passed through Isabelle, and this time it had nothing to do with the cold. "The letters were signed *Cameron*."

"Yes, well, God will have to forgive my brother for his stubborn nature. He would never have agreed to a mail-order bride," Eloise said.

"You mean… he doesn't know I'm coming?"

"Don't worry. I know you're coming and that ought to be good enough. I have a room prepared for you and everything. Though I *do* wish you'd told me you had a *baby*! That's going to make all this *so* much more difficult."

"I assumed you knew," Isabelle said. "The baby is Vivienne's, not mine. I assumed you must have talked about it with her when you made your initial arrangements. Or maybe you did and you didn't realize that her baby had survived when she died?"

"I never knew that Vivienne was expecting a child," Eloise said slowly. "Was she married before?"

Isabelle pressed her lips together. There was no flattering way to tell that story, and she wasn't going to risk painting her best friend in a bad light. Not to this woman she had only just met. 'The point is," she said, "I'm here, and so is Abby, and unless you're going to put us on a train back to Hearthstone, we'd like to get somewhere warm."

"Yes, yes, let's get you out of the cold," Eloise agreed. "Oh, I'm going to be having words with Sheriff Grayson about this one, you can bet on that."

Isabelle had no idea what the sheriff could possibly have to do with anything, but she didn't care, because Eloise came to her and picked up both of her suitcases. For the first time in a long time, her hands were free to tend to the baby. She wrapped her arms around Abby and pressed a kiss to the top of her head.

"It's all right, sweetheart," she murmured. "We're going to find our new home. Everything's going to be just fine."

***

By the time they reached the ranch, the snow had begun to fall vigorously again, and the mild weather on the train platform seemed like something Isabelle had imagined.

Isabelle wished she could get a better look at the place, but the darkness made that impossible. She only knew they'd arrived at all because Eloise brought the wagon to a halt. "Wait here," Eloise said. "Cameron will come and help you with your things."

Cameron. She had whispered the name to herself dozens of times over the last few weeks, but the man himself was still a mystery. She was glad of the chance to stay where she was, to just observe for the moment.

Eloise clearly knew her way in the dark. After only a few moments, a rectangle of warm light split the night as a door was opened and a man stepped out.

He had the same sandy brown hair as Eloise and Isabelle heard his voice rise in volume as the two of them conversed, though she couldn't make out what was being said.

There had been no conversation on the ride here. Eloise had muttered under her breath a few times and Isabelle had thought she'd caught the word *baby*, but there had been no attempt to actually discuss that matter. For Isabelle's part, she had been too preoccupied with trying to quiet Abby's cries, a job that seemed even more important now than it had when they'd been on the train. To know that she was irritating people she'd never see again in her life was one thing, but to make a bad impression on the people who were going to be her new family… that was something else altogether, especially when they clearly hadn't known that Abby was going to be coming at all.

You're a good baby. Show them what a good baby you are. It isn't your fault you've had nothing to eat for hours, but if their first experience of you is listening to this wailing, they're going to get the wrong idea. They're going to feel the way the people on the train felt.

She stared out at the man she was sure was Cameron Mercer. He was the right age and he looked enough like Eloise that he had to be her brother.

I wonder why he needed to send away for a mail-order bride. He was handsome enough, tall and muscular with broad shoulders and a square jaw. If he wanted a wife, surely he could have found himself one on his own?

She had expected that she'd be happy if the man she was to marry turned out to be handsome. Instead, it made her uneasy. *His looks are no obstacle at all… so I wonder what the obstacle is?*

Maybe it was just that there were no eligible women around. Isabelle had gotten no impression at all of the town of Wintervale because it was so dark outside, but Cameron Mercer was carrying a lantern and it allowed her to see the house behind him. It didn't look well-tended. There was a pile of lumber in front of the door and a broom leaning against the side of the house. What a broom might be doing outside, she couldn't imagine.

Seeing the mess gave her the strength she had been lacking. She wrapped one arm around Abby to secure her and climbed down from the wagon.

Cameron noticed her right away, looking over at her and sizing her up. His gaze softened for a moment at the sight of her… then his eyes fixed on the baby.

His lips parted slightly and he breathed in. He hadn't expected a baby, of course. Eloise had made that clear. But he didn't seem angry or upset. Shocked, yes, but the way his eyes had gone wide and his palms had turned upward, as if he might reach out and take Abby into his arms...

She took another step forward, emboldened by that response. "Good evening," she managed. "I'm Isabelle. Isabelle Heart."

His mouth closed. Isabelle took a few steps forward, allowing him to see her better. She wanted to see him better, too.

For a moment, they stood face to face, gazing at one another. His dark eyes seemed like a continuation of the night all around them, except that the sky was cold and empty. Cameron's eyes were full of warmth. Was he going to reach out to her? Offer her a hand to shake? An embrace would be far too forward, and yet there *was* something tense and binding between the two of them already...

Then he turned away.

"You're interfering," Cameron said, turning back to Eloise without saying a single word to Isabelle. "Interfering again, just like you always do."

"A man like you needs someone to interfere, or he'd rot," Eloise said smoothly.

"Eloise, this is no fit place for a baby! Even you must see that."

"May I say something?" Isabelle interjected.

They both turned to look at her, eyebrows raised, as if they were surprised she had anything to contribute to this conversation at all. As if it hadn't occurred to either one of them that she might take an interest in what was being discussed.

She bristled. Was this what it was going to be like here? Would she be treated as if she didn't exist?

Not if I can help it.

"I think we can agree," she said, "that this is not going to be resolved tonight. Is that a fair assumption?"

"She has a crying baby, Cameron," Eloise said. "You're not going to turn her away."

"It's not my fault you brought a woman with a crying baby here," Cameron growled.

"She's hungry," Isabelle explained. "Is there any milk? She hasn't eaten in hours."

"I'll go fix you something," Eloise said. "We have bottles that we use to nurse the livestock."

"No, I have one," Isabelle said quickly. She reached into her handbag and pulled out the bottle she had been using on the train, which had been empty for hours. She handed it to Eloise.

Eloise nodded. "I'll get this ready for you. Cameron, get her into the house, for goodness' sake. It's cold out here."

Eloise went into the house and Isabelle and Cameron were left face to face with Abby fussing fretfully between them.

"You'd better come inside," Cameron said. "This weather is only getting worse."

At least he was letting her into the house. Isabelle closed her eyes briefly, thankful for small mercies, then bent to pick up her two suitcases.

"I'll do that," Cameron said. He grabbed the cases, turned, and went into the house, leaving the door open. She assumed he'd done it so she would know that she was welcome to follow.

Isabelle wrapped her arms tightly around Abby and went in. The door opened on a small front room that featured a worn settee, an armchair, and a rocking chair. All the furnishings looked as if they were older than Cameron himself. There was a fireplace in which a fire had been lit, and that was homey and welcoming, but the room itself was a mess. Dirty shirts were strewn over various surfaces. There was a fine layer of dust covering everything. Books and newspapers lay on every table. *Has this room ever been cleaned?*

It should have bothered her, but instead, it made her feel something like hope, a fragile bubble rising up in her chest. She turned to face Cameron.

"Mr. Mercer," she said, "I believe you need a woman's help around here."

"That's what my sister said," he replied with a frown, eyebrows furrowing. "Did the two of you cook this up together?"

"I thought I was exchanging letters with you. It wasn't my intention to trick you."

"You didn't know a woman's handwriting when you saw it?"

"The letters had your name. I assumed I was being dealt with honestly," she said, her tone sharp. "If you want to be angry with someone, then by all means do so. But I'm not the person you're angry with. I boarded a train today because I was told there was a man here who wanted to marry me, to care for me and this baby and to have me care for him in return. If that isn't the truth, then you and I have both been tricked."

He sighed. "My sister has always thought she has the right to take a heavy hand in my life," he murmured, raking a hand through his hair. "I'm sorry you were brought here under false pretenses, Miss Heart, but I had nothing to do with it."

She looked up at him. For a moment, there was a spark of the same connection she had felt when they had first met outside, when she had still believed he might welcome her.

Maybe he doesn't want me here. But I'm here for a reason. God has brought me here.

She didn't want to leave. Even though she had known him for less than half an hour, being in the same room with him lit her up in a way nothing had for a very long time. He was exciting.

I have things I can offer to him.

"If she truly believes you need help turning this place into a home, she might have made a good decision. I'm someone who can help you with that," she said. "I can clean for you. I'm a good cook. You'll be glad you have me around if you give me a chance."

Eloise came back into the room with a bottle in hand and gave it to Isabelle, who nodded gratefully and offered it to Abby. After a moment of protest, the baby accepted it and suckled greedily, and the sound of her cries faded for the first time in hours.

Isabelle closed her eyes and let out a deep sigh. She had almost forgotten how blessed silence could be.

"Is that baby always like that?" Cameron asked. His tone was mild, but Isabelle's nerves were frayed. She had been stared at for hours by people on the train and she was failing as a mother. How could this man who had just met them presume to ask her what Abby was like?

"She was hungry," Isabelle said defensively. "The train was delayed, and she had almost nothing to eat." She hesitated. "Mr. Mercer, whatever you decide, please don't put us back on another train tonight. She needs to rest and take nourishment."

"Of course I'm not sending the two of you back out into this snowstorm," Cameron said, as if the very idea was preposterous. "At the very least, you'll have to stay until the weather clears. Eloise, I trust you have a room prepared for her?"

"Of course," Eloise said. "You can think whatever you'd like about all this, Cameron, but I would never have done it without making preparations." She smiled at Isabelle. "Let's get you settled in. Cameron…"

Cameron turned without another word to either of them and strode from the room.

Isabelle let out a long sigh. "He doesn't want anything to do with me, does he?"

"He's going to get used to the idea. I always knew it would take him some time," Eloise said. "And until then, you'll have me. I have my own house here on the ranch, so you'll see me all the time."

That was scant comfort. After all, Eloise was the one who had gotten Isabelle into this mess. *If she had told me the truth about what to expect when I got here, I don't think I would have come in the first place.*

Maybe that was why she hadn't told.

Eloise had been in for a surprise herself. It was obvious that she was still trying to decide what to think about Abby's presence. Vivienne had kept that to herself.

Everyone has been keeping secrets, Isabelle thought, her heart heavy. *And now I'm the one who is going to have to pay the price.*

Chapter Two

"She's weak. The bleeding isn't stopping."

The doctor's voice seemed to come from a long way away. The only thing Isabelle could focus on was her best friend's face. Vivienne had gone bone white.

Isabelle knelt on the hardwood floor beside her bed, clutching her hand. The posture should have hurt her knees, left her stiff, but she couldn't think about that either. "Hold on, Vivienne. Your baby needs you now."

Vivienne's eyes closed. "Please take care of her, Isabelle."

The words were like ice in Isabelle's veins. "You're going to be the one to care for her," she insisted.

"No," Vivienne whispered. "I don't think I am."

"She needs her mother."

"There's a man."

"What?" Was Vivienne hallucinating? The only man in the room was the doctor.

"There's…" Vivienne gasped in pain, and Isabelle gripped her hand more tightly. "There's a letter. In my dresser. A man. He was going to marry me. Care for us. Go to him, Isabelle. He'll help you."

"Don't talk like this, Vivienne! You have to fight. You have to stay with me. You have to stay with your baby!"

Isabelle's voice was frantic, but Vivienne's hand had gone limp in hers, and then there were strong hands on her shoulders, drawing her back, pulling her away. She fought to free herself, but the hands held her, and the doctor's voice murmured in her ear, "She's gone…"

***

The sound of Abby's cries were the first thing Isabelle heard when she woke in the morning. Not only that, they followed her around all day long.

There had been no sign of Eloise or Cameron. She had woken to an empty house, apart from herself and Abby. She'd gone straight to the kitchen to look for more milk, but there had been none to be found.

The first hour of the day was spent in a whirlwind of anger. How could they have left her alone like this, with nothing to give to Abby? Even if they hadn't been prepared for a baby, they knew there was one now. They should be doing all they could to help care for her, and that wasn't happening. Where *was* everyone?

All Isabelle could do was go about her business and hope they would return soon. She'd tried to lose herself in the chores she had assigned herself. She had cleaned all the surfaces in the kitchen and tidied the living room. These were the two main rooms of the house—the living room at the front, and the kitchen at the back, connected by a small hallway. There was a second hall that led off to Cameron's study and his bedroom, neither of which Isabelle felt she ought to touch. She hadn't even been inside them. As for her own room, which was located off the kitchen, it was neat as a pin and had been from the moment she had arrived.

Surely someone would come back any minute, she had told herself. When they did, she would demand milk for Abby.

But no one had come and now it had been two hours since they had woken.

Abby had to eat.

She went to the tiny bedroom she had shared with the baby. She suspected this room might have been a pantry once—there was barely room to move around now that her bed and the milk crate she was using as a makeshift cradle had been placed within it. Her suitcases had been stowed under her bed, and without a wardrobe to speak of, she was living out of them for the moment.

Isabelle pulled Abby from the cradle up into her arms. Abby's little body tensed against her and Isabelle's guilt threatened to overwhelm her. Sometimes she was sure Abby knew she wasn't with her mother. She must sense that Isabelle was nothing more than a replacement. No matter how hard she tried to fill Vivienne's shoes, she would never be Abby's mother in the same way Vivienne would have been.

If Vivienne was here, Abby wouldn't be hungry right now.

Abby let out another yell.

The righteous cry out, and the Lord hears them; he delivers them from all their troubles. It was her favorite Psalm, a reminder that God would always hear her when she called out to him. Sometimes, like now, she needed reminding. When Abby cried, it was easy to believe that no one at all was listening.

I may not be able to understand His plan for us, but I have to trust that He has one.

She sighed. Perhaps this was her own fault. Perhaps she should have made sure to speak to Cameron about their needs last night. At the very least, she might have talked to Eloise about it. Eloise seemed to care for them more than Cameron did. She would want to know how to provide for Abby.

Just one more example of me failing as a mother. I'm sure Vivienne would have gotten it right.

"All right," Isabelle said under her breath, determination solidifying within her. "God has put this challenge before me, and I'm going to succeed. Don't you worry, Abby. You and I are going to manage, whatever it takes."

She wrapped a warm blanket around the both of them and stepped outside into the snow. Almost at once, her feet were wet, the high drifts rising above her boots, but that didn't matter now. She had to get to the barn. That milk she'd been given last night had come from somewhere and if Cameron wasn't going to take the trouble to provide it for her, she was going to have to go and get it herself.

She high-stepped across the yard between the house and the barn, thankful for the fact that it was fairly close and that the snow had, at least, stopped falling. Once she was inside, she shook herself off and looked around.

She'd hoped for cows, but instead, all she saw was a lone goat in a stall. But the goat, if it was a female, would be able to give milk... she walked over and peered down. Yes, those were udders. Her heart lifted slightly, though she wasn't sure she knew what needed to be done. She had never milked anything before in her life. With a frown, she sat down on the stool next to the goat, wondering whether it would even be possible to do this and hold Abby at the same time. She quickly deduced that it wouldn't. She needed to be able to lean over to reach the udders. She spread the blanket on the floor and laid Abby down on it. Abby continued to scream with frustrated hunger and Isabelle's guilt sickened her. Hopefully, she would have milk to give before long.

She spotted a pail and pulled it over to her side, positioned it under the goat, reached for the udders, and began to squeeze.

Nothing happened.

Was there no milk to be had? Maybe she was doing it wrong. But if she was, she didn't know how to correct herself. Isabelle thought back, trying to remember the techniques she had seen when she'd watched people milk animals in the past, but nothing came to her.

Abby let out a particularly woeful scream, and this time, Isabelle was so distressed that she cried out in fear and frustration herself.

Abby actually silenced for a moment, startled by Isabelle's outburst. Isabelle's spirits sunk even lower. All she wanted was to make a safe and happy home for her friend's child and she failed at every turn. Now it was clear that there was to be no milk this morning. Isabelle went to the blanket, sat down, and picked Abby up. She tried rocking the baby, bouncing her lightly, but Abby took no comfort from the gesture. Of course she didn't. She wasn't crying because she was unhappy. She was *hungry*. The only thing that was going to soothe her was being fed.

Filled with frustration, beyond the point of rational thought, Isabelle opened the top few buttons of her dress and tucked the baby to her breast. She felt like a mother to Abby. She wanted to be a mother to Abby. Perhaps God would step in and give her a miracle.

She knew even as she tried that it was too much to hope for. Abby tried to suckle, but Isabelle had nothing to give. It was painful, and she joined the infant in crying. She would do this as long as it took if there was even a chance it might work. But she knew that there was no chance. If God had intended to give her milk, He would have done so. He wouldn't have waited until now.

Still, she prayed. *Help me. I can't do this on my own,* she pleaded. *I wasn't ready to become a mother. I don't know how to be a mother. I want to be what Abby needs. Help us. Please.*

She thought of her Psalm, but it was scant comfort right now. If God was listening—she was sure that He must be—He wasn't answering. He wasn't giving her any reason to feel that she was going to be provided for.

I just have to trust.

Isabelle closed her eyes, finally allowing the tears that had been threatening for days to stream down her face.

She was good at trusting God. Her faith had always been strong. She had always been able to look beyond her circumstances and trust that God had a plan.

With a life like hers, a history of tragedy and loss like she had experienced, a person had to be able to trust.

Isabelle couldn't remember a time when her life hadn't been marked by tragedy. The earliest images in her mind were of standing before the mirror in her parents' house and looking at the scars on her face and on her shoulder. Her parents had assured her that they would fade over time, and they had. But Isabelle had always seen those scars first when she had looked at her own reflection. Before she had noticed her cornflower-blue eyes, her high cheekbones, the gloss of her dark hair, she had seen scars. Flaws.

Then her parents had been killed when she was nineteen years old, and she had been on her own. All alone, except for Vivienne, her best friend... and now she was gone too, less than two months ago, her loss still a fresh wound.

Throughout it all, she had put her faith in God. No matter what she was going through, she had known that He was on her side.

But it was different now, because she wasn't only asking God to watch out for her. She needed Him to watch out for Abby, too. Her own life might have been hard but Abby's had been nothing *but* hardship. If Abby was to have any chance at all of a good and happy life, she would need both God and Isabelle to provide for her.

Isabelle knew that she was coming up short.

The door began to open and she gasped, hurrying to right her dress and fasten up the buttons. She had barely managed to do it when the door was flung open. A burst of cold air came in and along with it, Cameron Mercer.

It was her first good look at him, her first look at him in daylight. Had she been on her feet, he would still have towered over her—but then, most men did. Even most *women* were taller than Isabelle. He had broad shoulders and a weathered face that suggested a lot of time spent outdoors. Right now, that face wore a pinched scowl that made her heart beat faster, as if she had been caught doing something she shouldn't.

"Why are you out here?" he demanded. "It's freezing."

His eyes darted briefly to her dress. She looked down—she'd missed a button. Her heart rate accelerated, and she adjusted it quickly.

"I needed milk," she explained. "I thought maybe…" she gestured to the goat.

"You need milk a lot," he observed.

"I have a baby," she pointed out sharply, getting to her feet. "She has to be fed. I… I didn't know, when I came here, that you didn't know about her. I thought you would be prepared for her needs."

"I'll milk the goat," he said. "You go into the house. And take that baby with you, for goodness' sake. That crying is only distressing the animal."

She stepped forward, frowning. His face was unfamiliar, and the way his hair hung had disguised at first what she was noticing now—a cut on his forehead, disappearing into his hairline. "You're hurt," she said, her stomach clenching at the sight of it.

"I'm fine," he told her.

"You're bleeding," she protested. "Won't you let me look at it, at least?"

"No," he said firmly. "Go in the house, and I'll milk the goat for you."

He turned away from her and sat down on the stool.

Isabelle lingered for a moment, Abby in her arms. Vivienne had always told her that her empathy was her weakness. Isabelle herself thought of it as a strength, but there was no denying that it could cause her trouble when it was directed toward people who didn't want it. Cameron had made it clear that he had no interest in being cared for.

He's getting us milk and that's what matters.

Still, as he reached down to begin milking, she saw him wince. He rotated his shoulder. He was in pain, there was no doubting that.

He doesn't want me to care. He doesn't care about me. He doesn't care about Abby. He's only doing anything for us because he feels obligated and he's probably going to send us away as soon as the weather clears.

She tucked Abby into her arms and made her way back up to the house to sit in the kitchen and wait.

The kitchen was dark and cold—there was no fire here—but at least it was clean, after the work she had put in this morning. When Cameron finally arrived, he didn't seem to take any notice of that fact. He didn't even look at the surfaces she'd spent such a long time scouring this morning. He placed the bucket of milk in the center of the table and walked out of the room without saying a word.

Isabelle stood up and looked in. Her heart sank at what she saw.

The goat must not be a reliable source of milk, for she was looking at a shockingly small amount. It might be enough to fill the bottle, but she wasn't confident about that. They would have to milk several times a day if they were to meet Abby's needs, and how was she ever going to ask Cameron for that when she couldn't get him to sit down and have a conversation with her?

I'm going to have to search the grounds for Eloise's home... but how will I do that when we're surrounded by piles of snow and I have to take Abby everywhere I go?

She'd hoped so desperately that when she got here, she would have someone to help her parent this baby. That she wouldn't be doing it on her own.

So much for that idea.

She transferred the milk to the bottle and put it in a pan of water on the stove to warm, feeling that it couldn't possibly heat up fast enough. Finally, it was ready, and she removed it from the heat and gave it to Abby, who began to suckle greedily.

Isabelle knew she couldn't afford to let Abby eat too quickly after having been hungry for so long, so every minute or so, she took the bottle away. Every time she did it, she despised herself, for Abby would immediately begin to whimper again. Isabelle would force herself to count to five as slowly as she could and would then return the bottle.

She wished things were easier here. Even though she didn't know what her life would look like, even though sometimes she didn't think she had any good options before her, there had to be some hope for her and for her baby.

God would provide. She just had to keep faith.

Chapter Three

"Is your shoulder still bothering you?" Adam asked.

"Shoulder's fine," Cameron grunted, not bothering to look at his red-headed ranch foreman. Adam was the best horse wrangler in Wyoming, in Cameron's opinion, but he asked too many personal questions. He was the sort of man who always wanted to talk about everything. He was never content to keep quiet, to let things lie when they weren't any of his business.

The two men stood in the stable, the hay crunching under their feet as they tended to the horses. Even though it was still snowing outside, it was warm in here, the lantern giving off heat and the walls shielding them from the worst of the weather. The air smelled of horse, musky and earthy, and Cameron closed his eyes and breathed it in. He was more at home here than anywhere in the world.

"I saw the stallion give you a wrench into the barn door yesterday," Adam said. "I worried you'd dislocated it."

"Well, I haven't." Cameron raised and lowered his shoulder a few times to prove the point. "See? Perfectly fine. Now, let's get these horses fed so that we can get inside."

"You've been spending less time inside over the past two days than I usually see from you," Adam said. "If I didn't know better, I'd think you were avoiding the house."

"I guess it's a good thing you do know better, then." Cameron turned away from his foreman and saw his black Labrador, Bear, pawing at a bucket. "Bear, get away from that."

He went over and picked up the bucket. It contained leftover oats for the horses. He held it up so that Adam could see. "What's this doing sitting around on the floor?"

"I don't know, and don't look at me like that," Adam said. "You know as well as I do who's usually to blame when there's a mess around here."

It was true—of the two of them, Adam was unquestionably the tidier one, and that point couldn't be argued. Still, Cameron wanted to blame his friend, even though he knew that was both incorrect and mean-spirited.

I suppose I just want to blame somebody for something. And that seems completely understandable. There's been a lot of blameworthy behavior of late!

He hadn't even spoken to Eloise since she had delivered Isabelle and her baby to his house. His sister seemed to have decided she would be best served by going into hiding for a while and she'd disappeared into her own house. Ordinarily, with the weather being what it was, Cameron would have made a point of going over at least once a day to check on her. Right now, the thought of her made his blood boil. She was going to have to be the one to make the first move when she was ready for the two of them to start talking again, because goodness knew he didn't want to do it.

As if he was reading Cameron's mind, Adam spoke. "I thought you were going to have a little more neatness and organization now that you've got a woman helping you out," he said. "I thought having a wife was going to be a good thing for you in that way. But maybe I'm not being fair. Maybe she needs a little more time to really make changes around here."

Cameron grunted. He had no desire to talk about Isabelle.

Adam wasn't letting him off the hook, though. He took down one of the brushes that hung on the wall, stepped into a stall, and began to groom one of the horses. "So," he said, his voice just a little too innocent. "How are things going with your new wife?"

"She isn't my wife."

"All right, not yet," Adam allowed. "She will be, though. I haven't gotten a great look at her. I've only seen her from a distance but she seems pretty. What do you think?"

"She's all right, I suppose." That was downplaying things, if Cameron was to be completely honest. Isabelle was very attractive. She was a tiny woman, both very short and very slender, with pale blue eyes that he couldn't help but notice even though he had done his best so far not to look at her much at all. Her hair was dark and though he had only ever seen it tied up in a sensible bun, he could tell how shiny it was. He was interested to see what it would look like if she ever let it down.

He didn't *want* to be interested in that. He very strongly wanted to be able to push it from his mind.

"As long as she isn't unpleasant to look at," Adam said.

"No, she isn't remotely that."

"Then you must be happy to have a wife," Adam suggested.

Cameron scoffed, pulling down a brush and beginning to groom one of the other horses. "She's not my wife now, and she isn't going to be," he clarified. "I'm going to send her back to wherever it is she comes from just as soon as the weather clears and it becomes safe for her to travel."

"You don't really want to do that, do you?" Adam asked, his tone growing quiet. Gentle.

He was hesitating, Cameron knew, because the two of them so rarely talked about this subject. Adam was taking a risk in trying to learn Cameron's true feelings about Isabelle, but Cameron wasn't ready to speak about that. Not to anyone.

So he offered something trivial instead. "I do want to send her away," he said. "Even if I was looking for a wife, which I'm not, she's far from the sort I would be looking for."

"What do you mean? I thought we just agreed that she was good-looking." The brush stilled in Adam's hand and he looked at Cameron over the horse's flank, eyes narrowed.

"There's more to life than just looks," Cameron said evenly, continuing to brush, forcing himself not to allow his gaze to linger for very long on Adam.

"But you can't possibly know much else about her yet," Adam said, clearly mystified. "She's only been here for a couple of days. How can you already want to declare that she isn't right for you?"

"I know enough about her," Cameron said. "For one thing, there's the fact that she's a terrible housekeeper."

"Whereas you yourself are so tidy?"

"That's just it," Cameron said. "If I'm to have a wife, she can't share my flaws, can she? It's all well and good for her to have flaws of her own but if her defects are the same as mine then we'll only make one another worse. I should be married to someone who is going to keep this place nice and clean, not someone who leaves chores undone."

"I think it's hardly fair of you to expect her to be in control of all the household chores," Adam said. "After all, she's only just arrived, hasn't she? She might not have a clear idea of everything that needs to be done to maintain this place yet. You should give her time to learn."

"Being responsible for the housekeeping was her idea, not mine," Cameron retorted. "It was the very first thing she said to me. That she thought I could use a woman's touch around here. If that's really the way she feels, she has to prove to me that she can be that woman. And if she can't do that, I don't really know what she has to offer me."

"You're being much too hard on someone who has just come into your life," Adam said quietly. "Have you even spoken to her about this?"

"Are you going to brush that horse?" Cameron asked. "Or do you need me to come over there and do it for you?"

Adam raised his eyebrows. "Are you dodging my questions?"

Cameron sighed. He stopped brushing and leaned against the horse, suddenly weighed down by everything that had happened in the past couple of days. "It's not possible to speak to her," he said.

"Why on Earth not?"

"Because she always has that baby attached to her hip," Cameron said. "And the baby is always squalling. I just can't believe how much noise comes out of something so small."

"You'll get used to him," Adam said. Then he hesitated. "Or is it her?"

"Her, I think."

"You *think*?" Adam's eyebrows shot up. His lips pressed together.

"Don't judge me," Cameron said. "I don't know anything about that baby."

"Cameron, if you're going to marry that woman, the baby is going to be *your* baby," Adam pointed out, shaking his head. He walked over and hung his brush back on the wall, even though the horse could probably have stood to be groomed a bit more.

On an ordinary day, Cameron would have questioned the choice, but as things stood he wanted nothing more than to get out of here. He was tired of talking to Adam, tired of trying to explain himself. "I told you," he said, "I have no intention of marrying her. It isn't going to happen. That baby isn't going to be mine."

"Cameron, if this is about…"

"Enough," Cameron barked, knowing all too well what Adam had been about to say and wanting nothing more than to avoid hearing it. "I don't want to discuss this further. She isn't staying. They aren't staying."

"Well, I guess that's your choice," Adam said. "But if you'll permit me to say what I think before you storm off, I think you should give it a chance, Cameron. I think you should give *her* a chance. You might be glad you did."

"You've had your say." Cameron tossed his grooming brush in the direction of the hook. He didn't miss Adam's gaze tracking it as it hit the wall and clattered to the ground, and he half expected his foreman to make some comment about how it was obvious Cameron did need a woman looking after him if that was the best he could do when it came to putting things away.

Instead, Adam's voice became very quiet. "This is about Ruth, isn't it? And Philip?"

Anger boiled through Cameron. His muscles grew tense, his hands formed into fists. He turned his back on Adam, sure that if he so much as looked at his friend right now, he would lash out and hit him. "Don't you say those names to me."

"I know you're thinking about them, though," Adam murmured. "A woman with a baby showing up unexpectedly and wanting to marry you... How could you not be thinking about your wife and child?"

"I told you to stop it." His body tensed, blood rushing. Nobody did this. Nobody said those names to him. Nobody reminded him of the family he'd had in the past. Even Eloise knew better, knew the way fury and horror surged up within him when he was forced to think about everything he had lost in that fire.

That incident had taught him the meaning of the word *unbearable*. Before that night, Cameron had genuinely believed that there was nothing in the world a person couldn't live through. He had believed he was strong enough to come out the other side of any trial.

In those days, he had been a man of faith, and he would have said definitively that God was with him during trying times.

But that wasn't true. He knew that now. God would never have allowed a child of his son's age to be taken in such a cruel way. God would never have let violent death come to a woman like Ruth.

God might have chosen to leave me alone in the world. I'm not like them. I deserve this. But they never could.

When he had realized they were gone, he had learned that there were some things a man could not survive. He could go on living, but something inside him had died when his wife and his child had died. Some piece of him was gone now and it would never be resurrected. It would never come back.

Adam was right. He couldn't marry Isabelle, couldn't care for her child, because the part of him that was capable of that had burned up in the fire.

"The reason doesn't matter," he said, turning back to face Adam. "What matters is that I'm not going to do this. Eloise might have thought it was a good idea to try to force my hand, but she was wrong. Even you have to admit I wouldn't make a good father. It's a terrible idea for everyone involved."

"So, what, you're just going to put her on a train back home? Does she even have anything to go back to?" Adam crossed his arms and leaned against the wall. "I'd imagine that most women who become mail-order brides are leaving situations where they weren't happy. She might not have much waiting for her. You might be sending her back to a desperate life. Can you really do that?"

"I don't know anything about the life she left behind," Cameron protested. "That isn't my responsibility."

"I think it is, Cameron. She came here to be with you. Like it or not, you *are* responsible. If you're not going to keep her here with you, you should at least take the time to find her a new situation. Help her find someone who *is* willing to marry her and take responsibility for that baby."

Cameron groaned. "So now I'm responsible for a woman I don't even know? A woman who has nothing to do with me? Just because my sister decided to bring her here without asking me?"

"I guess it's up to you." Adam folded his arms and frowned. "All I know is that I wouldn't be able to send her away unless I knew she was going to be all right, wherever she landed. And I know you well enough to think you won't be able to do that either."

Cameron sighed, closing his eyes briefly so that he wouldn't have to make eye contact with his friend. The truth was that Adam was right. He didn't relish the idea of causing harm to anyone, and he could tell just by looking at this woman and her baby how desperate they were.

I don't think she would have come here if she'd had any other option. This wasn't her first choice.

"All right," he said. "You have a point. I won't send her off until I'm sure she's going somewhere she'll be safe and cared for."

"I knew you wouldn't," Adam said. "You're a good man, you know, Cameron, even when you don't want to believe the best of yourself."

Cameron walked over to the brush he had tossed aside and picked it up. "Let's just finish up with these horses," he said.

"Women who came here looking for marriage aren't the only ones relying on me. I have my horses to tend to, and they were here first."

Adam chuckled. "So they were." He went to the hook and took his own grooming brush back down. "All right. Let's get it done. But I think you should spend some time with her tonight, if you can. Show her that you care about her, even if you only care a little bit."

Chapter Four

Today was the third day in Wintervale, and nothing had gotten better. In fact, things seemed to be growing steadily worse and Isabelle had no idea what to do about it.

Eloise was still nowhere to be seen. Isabelle had looked out every window of the house, trying to locate the other woman's home, knowing that at this point she would be more than willing to walk to it. She saw no sign of any structure other than the barn where she had found the useless goat. The goat that had given them almost no milk.

She'd gone out once more to try to milk it again, with similar results. This time, she had managed to squeeze a bit out of the cold and chapped udders and she had been in a celebratory mood briefly. She'd hurried back to the house but when she had seen the milking bucket on the bare kitchen table next to Abby's bottle, she had been forced to confront just how little milk she really had. What was worse, Abby had stopped screaming.

Isabelle kept her swaddled and tucked up against her own body for warmth and comfort but she couldn't provide nourishment. Without that, Abby no longer had much strength. She shivered against Isabelle's body, her little eyes closed, and made almost no sound.

Isabelle's hands shook as she tried to pour the milk into the bottle. Milk was so hard to come by and Abby was getting thin. She'd never dreamed it would be like this when she got here, that there wouldn't be enough food to care for Abby.

Babies shouldn't be thin. This is wrong.

How could Cameron allow this to happen? Maybe he hadn't expected them. Maybe he didn't want them here. But how could he be so heartless? Tears pricked at her eyes. Mistreating her was one thing, but how could anyone set eyes on Abby and refuse to offer her basic care?

He wasn't here today, either. She had seen him when she had been out looking out of windows, but he'd been far off in the distance. He had been on horseback and she was sure he was doing something important to the running of the ranch—not that she had any idea what it could be. She had never lived on a ranch before. If she had, maybe she would know how to milk a goat. Maybe she would be a little more self-sufficient than she was.

And maybe Cameron should help us. This is his ranch, and he knows full well that there is a hungry baby here. He should be doing something *to help us. It's inexcusable for him to leave us on our own like this all day, to do nothing at all to help.*

Her hands were shaking too badly to get the milk into the bottle, so she set everything down and walked away from the table for the moment, rubbing Abby's back slowly. She was in the habit of trying to soothe her now and it was almost as if she could hear cries that didn't exist. "Shh," she murmured, even though Abby was making no sound.

She thought perhaps the baby would look up at the sound of her voice, but she didn't. She gave no response at all. Concerned, Isabelle looked down.

Abby was slumped against her, eyes closed. Her body was limp.

An ice pick of fear stabbed into Isabelle. "Abby?" She gave the baby a gentle shake. "Abby?"

Abby's eyes fluttered open. She whimpered slightly, snuggled more closely into Isabelle, and closed her eyes again.

Isabelle let out a shuddery breath and fell back into her seat at the kitchen table, one hand cradling Abby's tiny head. The fear was a vise on her heart and for the first time since all this had begun, a thought came into her mind that she had been keeping at bay.

What if she doesn't survive?

She might not. It was winter, and Isabelle was caring for her all alone. The reason she had come to Wintervale had been to keep Abby alive, to gain assistance she didn't have back at home. But no one was helping her here. In fact, things were worse than they had been, because at least back at home she'd had friends to help her. No one she had wanted to depend on in the long term—that was why she had needed a husband—but none of them would have allowed Abby to starve before the winter had come to an end, and Isabelle knew that.

Now, though, the two of them were completely on their own and there was nothing to be done.

She had to speak to Cameron. She would have to wait here in the kitchen for him. He had to come back eventually. When he did, she would tell him how dire things were. She would tell him that she knew he didn't want the two of them here but he also didn't want the baby to die under his care and so he was going to *have* to help. That was all there was to it.

She rose to her feet again and fetched a couple of candles that stood on the shelf nearest the door. She had been eyeing these candles for the past hour, wanting to go and get them, too timid to do so. This wasn't her home and it felt wrong—

intrusive—to touch anything here. It tightened the fear in her chest, for surely Cameron would be angry that she had done this and would hold her and Abby even more at arm's length than he already was.

The light flickered when she lit the candles, and the small, dingy kitchen was a little warmer and a little more like a home. She breathed out and did her best to take heart.

We can get through this. I know we can. God is putting us to the test, but He has a plan, as He always does, and I will put my faith in Him as I always do. I have the strength for that.

She pulled the bucket toward her once more and resumed trying to transfer the contents to the baby's bottle...

Her hand trembled. Suddenly, milk was all over the table. Dripping onto the floor.

The bottle was still empty.

The despair that took Isabelle in that moment was like nothing she had ever experienced in her life. It choked her. She thought she might drown in it.

To burst into tears should have been a relief, an easing of the tension, but it wasn't. She was acutely aware of the fact that her tears couldn't make her feel better. Nothing could help her now. Isabelle's tears increased until she was openly sobbing, crying harder than she had since Vivienne's death. Then, as if to make matters worse, Abby stirred in her arms and began to cry right along with her.

Isabelle's hand went to her neck, to the cross she wore that had once belonged to Vivienne. She knew how Vivienne had treasured it and had considered leaving it so that her friend could be buried with it. In the end, she'd changed her mind. It should go to Abby one day, she had decided. Until then, Isabelle would hold onto it.

It had seemed like such a wise decision at the time but now she was questioning everything she had ever thought was a good idea. Should she have taken the cross?

Should she have taken the baby?

If I hadn't taken her, she would have gone to an orphanage and that surely would have been worse!

Maybe. But as grim as that life would have been, an orphanage would have reliably kept Abby alive. *Oh, God, forgive me. I can't see the way forward. I don't know what I'm doing. I don't know how to make this right.*

Sometimes, when she prayed, she felt a sense of peace, as if God was reaching down to touch her shoulder and tell her that He was watching over her. Today, though, she felt no such thing. There was no answering sensation of comfort. There was only hollow fear and a sense that, in spite of her best intentions, she had done nothing but make mistakes that would doom her and Abby both.

The door opened and Cameron came inside.

Isabelle was so startled by his sudden appearance that for a moment she couldn't even find words. She couldn't manage to greet him, to ask him where he had been, to explain why she was sitting at a table covered with milk. She couldn't even stop crying. Everything was so dismal that her tears didn't embarrass her, the way they might have if she had been a little bit more in control of herself.

Cameron squinted at her. "Are you hurt?"

She shook her head and managed to stop sobbing outright, though she continued to sniffle.

"What's wrong?" he asked.

The tone of his voice was bland, as if her tears hadn't affected him at all. It was as if he wanted the answer as a matter of curiosity, not because he felt genuine care for her. But she couldn't afford to withhold anything from him now. She needed his help too desperately.

So she drew a breath and pivoted in her chair to face him. "It's the baby," she managed. "She's so hungry and she's had nothing to eat. The goat doesn't produce enough milk to feed her, and…" Her voice trembled. "And I've just spilled what little I was able to get."

"You've been out there trying to milk that goat again?" Anger crossed his face like a shadow. "Didn't I tell you not to do that? It's freezing out there."

"I *know* that." His reprimand sparked her anger, which was a relief. It was so much easier to be angry than it was to be sad. Anger warmed her, fueled her, and she sat upright in her seat instead of slumping against the back of it. "I know it's cold. Did you think that had escaped my notice? When I came here, I thought I was coming to a man who wanted me and the baby. I thought there would be food for her here. At the very least, I would have thought you would be the one to go out and milk the goat for us, but you don't. You disappear for hours each day without even trying to speak to me about what we might need. She's starving, Cameron. She loses weight by the day and she's getting weaker. I'm afraid she might…"

She couldn't finish the sentence. She couldn't name the thing she feared most. Not out loud. To say it would be to invite it down upon them.

Isabelle was not a superstitious woman. God didn't do things to people just because people acknowledged those things as possibilities. She knew that. But she was in such a state of grief and fear that it was difficult to let go of an unpleasant thought once it had entered her mind. What if she spoke that awful word aloud and then it did happen? How would she manage her guilt and grief then?

I can't lose Abby. I couldn't stand it if that happened.

"Why don't you just feed her yourself?" Cameron wanted to know. "Why are you giving a baby that young goat's milk in the first place?"

"She isn't mine." Isabelle had forgotten he wouldn't know this. She had spent the whole train ride here under the impression that she was coming to meet someone who had planned to marry Vivienne. She had expected that the man in question would know perfectly well that Vivienne had been expecting a child and that when Isabelle arrived with a baby in her arms, he would make the connection.

But Cameron had never known about Vivienne and it didn't seem as if Eloise had been aware of the baby.

Cameron took a step further into the room, his frown deepening. "What do you mean, she isn't yours? Whose is she?"

"Her mother was my friend, Vivienne, the woman who was originally intended to come here and be your wife," Isabelle explained. "When Vivienne died, we arranged that I should come in her place… that is, Eloise and I arranged it, although I was under the impression that my arrangement was with you."

"Your arrangement was never with me."

"Yes, thank you," Isabelle said, her voice taut and terse. "I'm well aware of that now. But you wanted to know why I couldn't feed the baby myself… that's the reason. I'm not her mother by birth. I have nothing to give her. And now I fear the worst may happen because I'm not equipped to take care of her. You have to help us, even if you don't want us here. You have to help us before it's too late and we lose everything."

He stood and regarded her for a long moment, a moment during which Isabelle found it impossible to breathe. What would he say? Would he finally offer some form of help? Or would he turn on her yet again?

His lips pressed together. "So you haven't been able to feed her. That's why she's crying all the time."

His voice was softer than it had been since she had arrived, and something unknotted in Isabelle's chest. "Yes," she said. "That's right. I'm worried for her. She's starving, and I… I don't know if there's anything I can do. I need help."

He lingered for a moment, his eyes searching hers.

Then, without another word, he turned and walked out of the room.

She hadn't thought his cruelty could surprise her any longer. She had thought herself braced for the worst he could do. But this shocked her, and she couldn't help it—she let out a gasp.

She had told him all that and he was just walking away as if she had said nothing.

What was *wrong* with this man?

Well, she could have confidence in one thing, at least. God had done her a favor by saving her from this marriage. She would have been married to a man who had no care for her, who didn't take an interest in Abby, who seemed to want to do nothing at all to help either one of them. She knew she ought to find that a relief, and in a way, she did. It would be one less thing for her to worry about, that was for certain, and there were plenty of things she *did* need to be worried about right now.

But understanding that God hadn't wanted this for her didn't bring Isabelle any closer to understanding what He *did* want.

And it didn't put food in Abby's belly, either.

Chapter Five

Isabelle was interrupted in her morning cleaning ritual by a knock at the door and her heart leapt. Perhaps this would finally be Eloise! Perhaps she would have realized the predicament she had left Isabelle in by stranding her with her surly brother, and she would have come to help. Isabelle ran to the door, casting the broom aside, and flung it open—

It wasn't Eloise. The woman standing there was older than Eloise, perhaps in her fifties, with slicked-back gray hair. She was as short as Isabelle herself, which was an uncommon occurrence, but she was sturdy and stocky. She struck Isabelle as the sort of woman who was used to doing a lot of chores with very little complaint.

"You're Isabelle, aren't you?" the woman said. "I'm sorry. I don't know your last name."

"Heart," Isabelle said.

"Isabelle Heart?"

Isabelle nodded slowly.

"That's a sweet name." The woman smiled. "My name is Edith Calloway. I'm Pastor Calloway's wife. You won't know my husband, of course, I know you're new in town. My husband, John, is the pastor at our local church, St. Matthew's. I hope we'll be seeing you there once you've gotten a little more settled in. But in the meantime, I wanted to come by and greet you myself. I heard you were having a little trouble with an infant."

"You... you did?" Isabelle was struggling to keep up with the conversation. "I mean... I suppose that's true, yes, though I wouldn't have said... I mean, I'm not *having trouble*..." That was a lie, of course. She was having nothing but trouble. It hurt to speak about Abby as if she was a problem when Isabelle knew that she herself was the one to blame but that didn't change the fact that the two of them were certainly having troubles.

"Perhaps this will help," Edith said. She stepped to one side and pulled something into the doorframe.

For a moment, Isabelle thought it was the same goat she had been trying to milk, but she saw almost at once that it wasn't. This goat was younger and fatter, and Isabelle found herself staring at it as though God himself had reached down and placed it before her. She shook herself and returned her gaze to the pastor's wife, who was smiling at her.

"What do you think?" she asked gently. "Is this something you could use?"

"I..." Isabelle found herself crying again. How much more crying could she possibly have in her?

"Oh, darling." Edith stepped through the door and wrapped her arms around Isabelle. Isabelle suddenly realized how long it had been since she had last been hugged. She sank into the warmth of the embrace, shivering with exhaustion and the strange relief of having someone beside her who actually cared about her.

She might not know me, but even so, she wants the best for me. She wants to help with Abby. This was what she had hoped it would be like when she had arrived here. She had hoped that the man she had come to marry would greet her this way—not with a hug, necessarily, but with *help*.

"Now, why don't you tell me what's the matter?" Edith asked.

"It's the baby. She hasn't had enough to eat. She's starving. I mean, I'm afraid she might *actually* be starving," Isabelle whispered. "I'm trying so hard to care for her. But I'm not her mother by birth and I worry all the time that nothing I can offer her will ever make up for that fact. I know there are plenty of babies who aren't cared for by their birth mothers and her birth mother is gone forever. There's no bringing her back. But I'm failing her at every turn and if I can't get her to eat, I may lose her."

"You've been trying so hard," Edith said gently. "I can see it, Isabelle. Let me help you. Why don't you sit down? Get off your feet for a while."

"I should be doing something to help out around here," Isabelle said. "That's what I told Cameron I would be doing."

"No. Never mind that. You're exhausted. Have you even been sleeping?" Edith squinted and peered at her. "You don't look like you've slept recently. Here." She led Isabelle to the most comfortable armchair in the living room. "You sit here."

"This is Cameron's chair."

"Yes, well, Cameron isn't here." Edith's tone was brisk and offered no room for argument. Isabelle sank into the chair with exhausted relief. Edith went to the blanket on the floor and lifted Abby into her arms. "Oh, you poor thing," she said. "You do seem as if you've struggled for food." She looked back at Isabelle. "What's the baby's name?"

"Abby."

"Abby. Sweet little Abby. Short for Abigail?"

"Yes. Well…" Isabelle frowned. The truth was that Vivienne had only ever said *Abby*. She hadn't had much time following the baby's birth. "Yes," Isabelle decided abruptly. "Yes, it's short for Abigail."

She liked *Abigail*. Vivienne probably would have liked it too. More to the point, it was one of the only times Isabelle had considered herself worthy to make a decision about Abby since Vivienne had died. Before now, she would have agonized over this choice, wondering whether she had any right to choose the baby's name, wondering what Vivienne would have wanted.

But sitting here with Edith, seeing another woman look to her as if she was rightfully Abby's mother, gave her the strength she had struggled to find.

In every way that mattered, Isabelle *was* Abby's mother now. She was the only mother Abby would ever have. That meant she was going to have to be strong enough to stand up and make decisions when they needed to be made. She couldn't be paralyzed by fear that she was doing something Vivienne wouldn't have liked.

"All right," Edith said now, handing Abby to Isabelle. "You two wait right here, all right? I'll be back in just a few minutes."

She was out the door before Isabelle could respond.

Isabelle looked down at the baby in her arms. Abby seemed more peaceful than she had in days. It was almost as if she understood that they were being cared for now, that someone had come to help them. She yawned and stretched, blinking up at Isabelle as if to say, *What next*?

"I don't know," Isabelle answered the unspoken question aloud. "Edith seems kind. I wonder how she knew we needed help."

There seemed to be only two possibilities.

Eloise might have told her. That was unlikely, though. Eloise had been absent for days. Could she possibly have realized Isabelle was having trouble feeding the baby and sent someone over?

As unlikely as that seemed, the only other option was far less likely. It seemed so outside the realm of possibility that Isabelle had to laugh at herself for even conceiving of it. Surely *Cameron* wouldn't have gotten help. He had barely managed to tolerate a conversation with Isabelle. He didn't care about her and he didn't care about Abby. He'd made that abundantly clear.

She was distracted from her thoughts by Edith's return. She had a bucket in her hands and she walked through the living room toward the kitchen. "I tied the goat up in the barn next to that other goat," she called out. "I hope that was all right to do."

"Of course." Isabelle leapt to her feet and hurried after Edith into the kitchen.

When she arrived there, she nearly burst into tears all over again.

The bucket was nearly full of milk. There was so much that it sent a shiver of emotion through her. She couldn't hold back a little whimper of joy and she clutched Abby tightly. "*Oh.*"

"That goat's a good milker," Edith said gently. "You sit down, now. I can manage this." She was already preparing a pot on the stove to boil the milk. "I'm sure that baby can't wait for her lunch. I'll have a bottle in your hands in a matter of minutes."

"I don't know how I can ever thank you enough for this," Isabelle whispered. Her throat was thick with emotion. "I don't know what we would have done."

"You and I are members of the same community, and we help each other," Edith said. "It's that simple."

"How did you make it out here in this terrible weather? It's been snowing every day for the past week."

"I won't pretend it was easy, but in hard times, we do what we must," Edith said. "My wagon is sturdy and I have plenty of warm blankets."

"Well, I think you should stay here until Cameron is able to escort you back to your home," Isabelle said firmly. "I'll feel much better knowing that you aren't alone on the road." *Really, it's the least he could do.*

"That's kind of you," Edith said. "I'm happy to spend time with you and with that adorable baby." She hesitated. "She isn't your child by birth, you said?"

"She was my best friend's daughter. Vivienne," Isabelle said. "We were friends all our lives. She was there for me in childhood, when I believed I was too ugly to ever find a friend."

"Wait a moment," Edith protested. She turned her back on the milk to face Isabelle. "You thought you were too ugly to find a friend? You're very pretty. What do you mean?"

Isabelle bit her lip. She had spoken without thinking. "I have bad scars on my arm and shoulder," she explained. "They're on my face as well, but they've faded there. They were more prominent when I was younger and I know people stared at them." She lifted a hand to her face. The scars were hard to see now if you weren't looking for them, but she still knew just where they were and could feel the impressions in her skin. "Vivienne was never bothered by what my face looked like," she said. "She was just such a loving person. The best friend anyone could ever have asked for. And now she's gone." Grief filled her at the memory, at the unfairness of what she and Abby had both lost.

"What about the baby's father?" Edith asked softly. "Why didn't he take responsibility for her after Vivienne died?"

"I never knew who the father was," Isabelle said. "Vivienne never told me. When she discovered she was pregnant, her family kicked her out and she came to live with me in the apartment above the tailor shop I inherited from my family."

"How tragic." Edith carefully poured the milk into a bottle and squeezed a little bit of it out onto her wrist to check the temperature. Satisfied, she passed the bottle to Isabelle and sat down next to her at the table.

Isabelle shifted Abby in her arms and offered her the bottle. A moment later, Abby took it. Isabelle closed her eyes and felt the soft pull as the baby suckled. *Thank God.*

"So, why did you come here?" Edith asked after several moments had passed.

Isabelle sighed. "Vivienne's father wouldn't allow her to be buried in their family plot," she said. "He wanted to disown her. I couldn't stand such disrespect to my best friend. He had always been jealous of the tailor shop, always had his eye on it. I gave it to him in exchange for allowing Vivienne to be buried with dignity as a part of her family."

"That's terrible."

"It was. He held up his end of the bargain, though, and I'm grateful for that." She shifted Abby carefully to the opposite arm. "Anyway, once I had lost the tailor shop, I had nothing keeping me in the home where I'd grown up. My parents were killed in a robbery. I have no siblings and my best friend in the world had just died."

"Her family didn't want to take the baby?"

"They wanted nothing to do with Abby." Isabelle's jaw tensed with anger. "Not that I would have sat back and allowed them to take her anyway. Not after they were so cold to Vivienne. I know it was difficult for them to accept her circumstances, the fact that she became pregnant even though she was unmarried, but…"

She froze, recalling that she was speaking to a pastor's wife. What if Edith thought Abby was unworthy of her help?

But Edith smiled tenderly. She reached over and took Abby's foot in her hand, shaking it gently. "I see the worry in your eyes," she said. "You don't need to feel that way, Isabelle. I'm not here to judge anyone. Remember, Jesus tells us that our role is simply to love one another as best we can. If He was alive today, He would show kindness and support for your friend. He would invite her to His table. That's what I believe we ought to do as Christians."

The tension left Isabelle's body, and she smiled back at Edith. "That's what I think, too," she said.

"I hope you'll come join us at St. Matthew's on Sunday." Edith sat up a bit straighter. "All the women would love to meet you."

"I can't possibly leave Abby on her own."

"Of course you can't. You must bring her with you. Everyone will be eager to meet her, too," Edith assured her. "You'll think about coming, at least, won't you?"

"Of course," Isabelle said. "I do enjoy church. It will be good to have a church to attend here." *Even if I'm not going to be here for very long.*

"Good," Edith said, sitting back in her seat, obviously satisfied. "I'm so pleased I met you today, Isabelle."

"I am, too." A flicker of warmth came to life within Isabelle and for the first time in a very long time, she felt as if everything might be all right.

She looked down at Abby, who had fallen asleep in her arms.

But that's only if Cameron decides to let us stay, she remembered, the thought extinguishing the warmth within her like a bucket of cold water over a flame. *It doesn't matter how kind the pastor's wife is, how lovely the church is, if we have to leave as soon as the snow melts.*

Chapter Six

The house was silent when Cameron returned from tending to the livestock. Silent, but not dark, and that was different. Standing in the kitchen, having come in the back door, he saw the flicker of light in the hall that meant a fire in the living room fireplace and knew that must be where Isabelle was.

It would have been easy enough to turn away from the living room. He didn't have to see her. On any other day, he probably would have done exactly that.

But she'd been on his mind today. The way he had seen her break down over not being able to feed that baby echoed in his thoughts, unwilling to leave him be. Then there was the realization that the baby wasn't hers, something he genuinely hadn't known when he'd met her. That made a difference to him, somehow. He hadn't judged her for having a child, but to know that she had taken in someone else's baby... that made her a different sort of woman. A special sort. *Kinder than I am.*

He couldn't help it—he thought of Philip. The thought always came like a knife through his heart and he physically staggered at the memory of how it had felt to hold his son in his arms. The minuscule weight of him. The warmth. The knowledge that he was so helpless and relied on Cameron for everything.

What would have happened to Philip if he had been the one to survive the fire and Cameron had died along with his wife?

He was sure someone would have taken Philip in. Adam, if no one else. But whoever had done it would have been a hero. Knowing that Isabelle had been that hero for someone meant that Cameron would never quite see her in the same way as he had at first. He admired her now. He couldn't help it.

As he stepped into the living room, he didn't see her at first. The fire had indeed been lit but the room looked empty. Frowning, he stepped farther in to see what was going on.

Then he spotted her. She was lying on the settee, one arm slung over her face, her eyes closed. It was the most unguarded he had ever seen her, and his heart softened that much further.

On the floor beside the couch was an emptied-out milk crate that had been lined with blankets Cameron didn't recognize. Tiny blankets. Not his. Isabelle must have brought them here with her. The baby lay in the milk crate, also asleep. For the first time since they'd arrived here, she had some color in her cheeks.

She was fed. The plan must have worked.

Isabelle had been right, of course, when she'd insisted that he had a responsibility to her. That he needed to help her take care of the baby. Even though he hadn't signed up for this in any way, this was still his house and they were still his duty as long as they were here. He had known that Edith Calloway would be able to provide a goat that would actually give milk. The pastor and his wife had connections all over Wintervale and the surrounding area. She had no doubt known right away who to call to get the thing donated. Well, Cameron didn't want a donation. He'd arrange for a payment to be made to whoever had given the goat. Or, more likely, he'd pay the church, because it was likely the Calloways had used the church charity fund to get this done.

Cameron was not going to rely on charity and neither was anybody who was under his care. That wasn't an option he was willing to consider.

He would have made all the arrangements with Edith himself, even gone to get the goat himself, but he had known exactly what would happen if he spoke to her directly. The Calloways had never gotten over the fact that Cameron had stopped attending church. Well, of course they hadn't. That made sense, he supposed. John Calloway's responsibility as pastor was to bring people to church and obviously his wife was deeply passionate about that, too.

He didn't want to have that conversation with her again, though, the way he had so many times after his wife and son had died. He didn't want to hear her tell him how missed he was, that everyone wanted him to come back. He didn't want to nod and smile and wonder how quickly he could get out of a conversation that was never going to end the way she wanted it to.

I don't belong there anymore. I can't. I don't believe in it.

But he was glad the Calloways had come through, glad there was a goat now who could actually give a significant amount of milk so that the baby would be able to be fed. Isabelle hadn't said the words, but Cameron had heard what she wasn't saying. She had been worried the baby would die. In all actuality, she was probably right to worry about that in the middle of winter.

It was not possible for Cameron to admit to himself the thought of a baby dying, though. Not in his house. Not under his care.

Not again.

He could articulate the words in his mind but he couldn't allow himself to process the concept as something that could actually happen. It *couldn't* happen.

It would be too painful. Painful on a level that he couldn't survive. Even though he didn't know this baby, even though she wasn't and would never be his, the reminder of his past loss would gut him. It would stab him in an old wound that had never healed properly, leave him bleeding, and he'd never recover.

They are just going to have to go. Even having them here is too big a risk and I can't open myself up to that.

The baby fussed and Cameron went to the makeshift cradle. Before he could stop himself, he bent down and scooped her up, not wanting her to wake Isabelle. Would she cry at being held by an unfamiliar person?

She didn't. She gazed up at him with big dark eyes and he noticed for the first time how little she resembled Isabelle. Isabelle had those sweet blue eyes that looked like the sky on the first day of spring. Isabelle had pale skin, too, and the baby—Abby—was more olive-toned.

Honestly, she looks more like me than she does Isabelle.

The knife in his heart twisted again. She wasn't his baby and he couldn't ever allow himself to forget that.

But the soft coo she made reminded him so viscerally of Philip that the knife in his heart twisted even harder. He wanted to put her down and walk away from this pain.

He also wanted to hold on to her.

He glanced at Isabelle. She hadn't moved and she deserved to get some sleep. He paced back and forth in front of the fire, rocking the baby gently in his arms.

"If things were different, I would let you stay," he whispered to her. "It's not that I don't want you to be safe. It's that… it's that I *do* want you to be safe. Safe and loved. And I'm the wrong person to give you those things. I'm not fit to be anybody's father. Not anymore. You'll move on from here and you'll find someone who *is* a good father. Your mother will find that person for you. She's a good mother, you know. I see how much she cares. You're very lucky to have her. I hope you know that when you get older."

Abby stared at him and waved her tiny fist in the air.

"I can't keep the people I love safe." It was the thought that had haunted him ever since the fire that had stolen his family from him. "I can't protect anyone and you deserve someone who can protect you." The truth was, just having her in his arms like this reminded him of all the ways he had failed. If he had been better, stronger, more alert and aware, his wife and his son would still be alive. That was what he told himself over and over and he was convinced that it was true.

He walked over to his armchair and sat down, cradling Abby against him. She didn't protest that either. She just blinked up at him, soft and wondering, and reached one arm in his direction as if she thought she might be able to touch his face.

He closed his eyes briefly. Philip had done the same thing many times. It was so familiar.

I can't do this. I can't have a baby around. I need to make other arrangements for these two as quickly as I possibly can... and how could Eloise have possibly believed that this would be all right? She knows better than anybody what I've been through. How could she have thought I'd be able to stand this?

Cameron leaned back in his chair, looked up at the ceiling, and let out a heavy sigh.

"Are you all right?"

The voice jolted him forward in his seat and his arms tightened around Abby. She let out a little cry of shock at the sudden movement but she didn't burst into the sobs Cameron had grown used to hearing from her.

Isabelle's eyes were open. She had pushed herself upright on the couch and was blinking at him, trying to wake up. She wrapped her arms around herself and rubbed her shoulders.

"Are you cold?" Cameron asked.

"No," she assured him. "Just stiff."

He rose to his feet anyway, crossed the room, and fetched the quilt that was draped over the rocking chair in the corner. With one hand, he shook it free of its folds and draped it over her shoulders. She took hold of it and wrapped it more securely around herself, smiling gratefully up at him. "Thank you," she said. "That was thoughtful of you."

He sat back down in the chair. "I was surprised to find you sleeping out here."

"I was tired," she said. "Do you want me to take the baby?"

"I..."

"You can hold onto her, if you'd like to," Isabelle said quickly. "I don't mind."

Cameron was overwhelmed with an awkwardness that prickled at his skin, an idea that maybe he should never have picked the baby up in the first place. He rose ever so slightly from his chair. "Does she need anything right now?" he asked. "Can I get anything for the two of you?" He passed Abby back to Isabelle.

"You don't need to do that," Isabelle said. "We're all right." She hesitated. "We're better than all right, actually. Do you know about the goat?"

"I do."

"Did you have the goat brought here?"

"I'm not completely heartless," he said wryly. "I know you must think I am."

"You don't know what I think," she said, her voice soft. "Thank you. Abby finally got enough to eat. I've been so worried about her, and now... now I can actually believe that maybe she's going to be okay."

"I didn't realize that she wasn't yours," Cameron said. "I didn't know you needed help feeding her. If I had known that, I would have done something sooner."

"I realize that. And it's all right. I just... thank you. Thank you for speaking to Mrs. Calloway. It was exactly what we needed. I owe you her life."

It was too much. It was more than Cameron could stand, like alcohol being poured over an open wound to clean it. There was a part of him that sensed it would be good and healing to hold himself in place, to listen to the words she was saying, and yet he couldn't manage to do it.

He rose to his feet. "If you need anything tonight, I'll be up for a few hours. In my study."

"Wait a moment." She stood up too, the baby still in her arms. "You don't have to leave. You should stay here with us. We could get to know one another a little bit better. We've hardly spoken since I've been here. And... I really am grateful to you, Cameron, for what you've done for us. I can't express how grateful I am."

"You don't have to express it," he said. "Stay here. Go back to sleep, if you'd like. I've had a very long and busy day and I would much rather go off on my own. I'll see you tomorrow, perhaps."

He had no intention of seeing her tomorrow. He was trying to get away. That was all there was to it. He didn't want to be anywhere near this woman or her baby, both of whom had made him feel things he wasn't prepared to cope with. He would be better off on his own. And he would be *much* better off once the two of them were out of his life for good.

He fled the room quickly, heat in his face, knowing that he was a coward.

How could he not feel fear, after all he'd been through? How could the idea of facing another loss like the one he had already experienced not terrify him? Anybody would have been afraid.

I can't give my heart to anyone ever again. I can't have a wife. I can't care for a child. I must be on my own, as much as it's possible for me to do that. I can't risk getting hurt the way I've already been hurt once.

His thoughts went to Mrs. Calloway, who he knew would insist that he needed to come back to church if she heard him say these things.

That felt just as hard as allowing himself to care for people again. He had been a man of faith once, he'd put his trust in God. After what had happened… he couldn't help feeling betrayed.

He had learned his lesson, well and truly. A man couldn't put his faith in anything or anyone else in this life. His only option was to take care of himself.

Chapter Seven

"I'd like to go into town today," Isabelle said.

Her hands were fisted in her skirt, as if she was holding on to her courage. She had been here two weeks now, and yet speaking to Cameron was still difficult. He was so intimidating to her. He avoided her at every turn. In fact, she was sure she wouldn't have had the opportunity to speak with him today had she not come out to the barn and found him brushing one of the horses.

He looked up from that chore now, his face pulling into a frown. "What do you want to go into town for?"

"I'd like to see it," she said. "I didn't get a look on the day I arrived, because the train got in late and the sun was already down. I'd also like to visit the mercantile, if we can, so that I can get some fabric for new clothes for Abby. She hasn't had anything new since her mother died and now that she's eating properly I know she's going to start to grow properly." She couldn't stop the smile that spread across her face as she said those words. It was such a joy not to have to worry about Abby shrinking away to nothing, to know that she was going to be strong and healthy thanks to that goat. She wrapped her arms around the baby, who was strapped to her chest as usual. She could perceive the increased weight of Abby's body already. Abby was also more alert than she had been a few days ago. The arrival of the goat had changed everything. Her first week in Wintervale had been marked by fear. The second week, though, had been all relief and joy, Abby's increasing health, watching her waving her hands and kicking her feet, looking all around her, eyes wide at the sight of the horses. She was looking well.

Thanks to Cameron.

"You can't go into town by yourself," he said, hanging the brush up on the wall. "You don't even know the way. I couldn't let you do that."

"You could have your ranch foreman take me," Isabelle suggested. She hadn't met the man, but she had seen him around the ranch, always hard at work. She was sure he would be up to the task.

"No," Cameron said brusquely, dusting his hands off on his trousers. "Adam has chores to get done. I'll take you, if that's what you really want."

Isabelle's eyes widened. "You will?"

"It's not a problem. I could stand to visit the mercantile too, actually. Pick up a few things." He glanced over his shoulder. "That brush is pretty worn out. I could get a new one."

"Well… That would mean a lot to me, Cameron."

"I'll hitch up a horse. Are you ready to go? Need to bring anything with you for the baby?"

"No, she just ate, so she'll be all right for a few hours," Isabelle said, her heart beating faster at the prospect of getting out for a little while. How lucky that the snow had eased up enough for the roads to clear—though she did have to wonder what that meant for her time in Wintervale. Would Cameron have her on the next train out?

If that was his plan, he hadn't said anything about it and Isabelle wouldn't be the first to bring it up. Though she was sure he hadn't forgotten his determination to get rid of her, it felt unsafe to remind him of it. Her position here was so precarious. If she mentioned leaving, it might tip the scales against her and she might find herself gone in a heartbeat.

That wasn't what she wanted. Though she hadn't been sure about coming here in the first place, though things had been difficult when she had first arrived, it was impossible to ignore how much better their lives were. They had a roof over their heads and a steady source of food, both for Isabelle and for Abby. She would be a fool to give that up.

***

The town of Wintervale turned out to be smaller than Isabelle had anticipated. It took about twenty minutes to reach it from the ranch and she spent that time stealing glances at Cameron and trying to think of things to say to break the silence. Trying, but failing. Every time she thought she had come up with something to say to him, she would lose her nerve. It was enough, surely, that he was taking her into town. To expect actual conversation was probably too much right now.

But then they reached town and the words burst out of her, "This is a lovely place."

She meant it, in spite of how small it was. It was really just a single road with stores on either side of it and a few small houses that probably belonged to the shopkeepers. The buildings seemed as if they were mostly new—either that, or they had been well kept up. Most of the store windows were decorated for Christmas, with garlands strung up around them and brightly colored wrapped packages in the displays.

How lucky I am to have come to a new town at this time of year and to get to see the best of it like this!

Cameron parked the wagon. "The store you want is right there," he said, pointing to the largest one. "Why don't you go on in and pick out what you want and I'll be in before it's time for you to pay."

"I wasn't going to ask you to pay for me," she said, a slight squirm of guilt working its way through the pit of her stomach. She didn't have much money of her own, but she had some. The sale of the tailor shop had given her enough for her train ticket and a little more besides.

"You're my guest," Cameron said. "It's the least I can do."

Well, better not to put myself in the poorhouse, if he's willing. "All right," she said. "Thank you, in that case."

She wrapped a protective arm around Abby and hurried over to the mercantile. It was a large and spacious store with shelves around the walls, run by an elderly man who smiled when he saw her and went back to wiping down his countertop. She liked the fact that he didn't seem to feel the need to make conversation. There were precut bits of fabric that would suffice to make clothing for a baby and she selected several of them. Hope bloomed in her chest as she did so. For the first time, a future seemed possible—a future in which Abby would grow and need larger clothes, a future in which it would be important for Isabelle to make plans that incorporated more than just the day they were living in.

Cameron arrived and saw what she was holding. "Is that enough?"

"I think so," she said, handing him what she'd chosen. "Enough to get us started, anyway. I really can give you some money. I don't want to take advantage."

He waved a hand and walked over to the counter, setting them down. "Put these things on my account, Mr. Richards," he told the man there. "And add one of those brushes."

"Right you are." Mr. Richards took a brush down. "Good seeing you, Mercer. It's been a while since you've been in town. You usually send that ranch hand of yours."

Cameron didn't comment on that, which was of no surprise to Isabelle. She'd already noticed he was someone who didn't speak unless he felt it necessary to do so.

"Is the church far from here?" she asked.

She hadn't meant the question for either man specifically, but they both looked at her so sharply that she couldn't help stepping backward. It was clear by the widening of Mr. Richards' eyes and the set of Cameron's jaw that she had said something wrong. She actually found herself replaying her words in her head, wondering what the problem could have been. She'd asked about *church*, hadn't she? Why were they acting as if she had said something inappropriate?

It was Mr. Richards who answered, eventually. "St. Matthew's is at the end of the street," he said. "You can't miss it."

"I'd like to stop by," she told Cameron. "As long as we're here, I mean. I would like to meet the pastor, and to see Mrs. Calloway if she's there and thank her for the goat." She ran her fingers over the top of Abby's head. "And she told me everyone would be eager to meet the baby."

"There won't be too many people there right now," Cameron said gruffly, all but turning his back on her. "It's Saturday."

"No," Mr. Richards countered. "The ladies are there right now for their weekly Bible study. That's always on Saturdays. You'd be able to see Mrs. Calloway, if that's what you're after."

"Would you mind?" Isabelle asked Cameron.

She felt funny asking it, because it was obvious that he did mind. What she didn't understand was *why* he minded. She wasn't asking to linger there all day, and they were already here in town. How much could it matter?

"I'm not going to the church," Cameron said.

"We wouldn't have to stay for long," Isabelle said. "I know you want to get home, and I appreciate you bringing me into town at all. I just want to stop by."

He turned away from her. "No."

"Why not?"

"I don't go there."

"What do you mean, you *don't go* there?" She was perplexed. "You sound as if you're against it or something. You sound like you hate the place."

"I don't hate anything. But it's not a part of my life. You must have noticed we didn't go last Sunday."

"Well, I assumed that was because of the weather," she said. "We haven't gone anywhere since I arrived." Her heart sank. "You're telling me the weather had nothing to do with it? You're saying that you don't go to church… at all?"

"That's right," Cameron said.

She stared at him. What did this mean? Was he telling her he wasn't a Christian?

Does it matter? It would matter if I was going to marry him, but he's made it clear that isn't going to happen.

She squared her shoulders. "Well, you can do what you like," she said. "I'm going to go and see the church and I'm going to thank Mrs. Calloway for her help."

"You do that," Cameron said, his voice cold. He still didn't turn back to face her. Mr. Richards was looking from one of them to the other as if in shock, his eyes still wide. "I suppose I'll just wait for you at the wagon."

Isabelle couldn't help it. Tears pricked at the backs of her eyes. She didn't want to cry in front of either one of these men, though, and she turned and hurried from the store before that could happen.

As she made her way down the street, too upset to take much notice of her surroundings, she wondered whether she ought to go back. Had she embarrassed Cameron by walking away from him, by defying him publicly like that? He had been so kind to her today, kinder than she'd seen him be yet. He had brought her into town just because she had asked for it and he'd bought her the fabric for Abby's new clothes.

But even so, asking her not to go to church was one thing she couldn't go along with. She would have done a lot for this man, in spite of how cold he had been to her, because he had taken them in and because he had saved Abby's life. It meant the world.

But she wouldn't abandon her faith. She wouldn't go that far. Not even for him.

***

The church was small but clean, wooden and whitewashed, and Isabelle smiled at the sight of it. It looked like her church back home. She could tell, even from the outside, what it would be like inside. There would be a single room with benches facing the front. There would be a plain altar. Everything would be plain. She liked that. She didn't enjoy it when a church was too ornate and elaborate. Humility suited her more.

She walked in and was pleased to see that it was just as she'd imagined it. A group of women sat at the front, near the altar, and they all turned when she came in. One of them rose to her feet and after a moment, Isabelle recognized Edith Calloway.

"Isabelle," she said warmly. "You came!"

"I can't stay," Isabelle said. "But I was in town and you had mentioned the church and that the people here might like to get to know me, so I thought I would stop by and say hello. And I wanted to thank you again, too, for the goat. Things have been so much better since you brought her to us."

"And you brought the baby, too!" Edith said. "Everyone, come meet Isabelle and baby Abby, who I was telling you about!"

A moment later, Isabelle found herself surrounded by a press of women, all of them cooing over Abby.

"She's *beautiful*," one of them said enviously. "And so lucky to have had someone like you in her life! Edith told us what happened to her mother. What a terrible tragedy. But you're truly a gift from God, Isabelle."

"Will we be seeing you at the service tomorrow?" another woman asked.

"I don't know," Isabelle was forced to admit. "I would like to be there, of course, but..." She hesitated, unsure of what to say. "I don't know if I'll be able to make it into town," she decided. Since Cameron didn't attend church, it would be awfully hard for her to make it in. There was no chance he would allow her to take a wagon in by herself and after the conversation she'd just had with him, she couldn't imagine asking him to drive her into town again tomorrow so that she could worship. He would surely refuse.

What am I going to do? It was so warm and homey being surrounded by all these women who so clearly liked her already, who cared about her and wanted her in their community. To be in this church, to be close to God, was the best thing that had happened to her since she had come to Wintervale. She needed this to be a part of her life here. But she also needed to give Cameron space, because if she became a nuisance to him, he would surely turn her away. There would be nothing that would remind him more quickly of his desire to be rid of her than if she started to annoy him.

I wonder what happened to him to make him not want to come to church—to make him avoid it with such a passion?

I wonder if it's the same reason he seems to have so many walls up when it comes to meeting new people?

Chapter Eight

The morning after their trip into town, the storm resumed.

Cameron was glad. He had anticipated that Isabelle might ask to be taken to church and he didn't want to do that. He didn't want to risk running into Pastor Calloway, being pressured to rejoin the congregation. He didn't want to explain his reasons for staying home to Isabelle.

The weather was the perfect excuse. It allowed him to hole up in his study without being seen by anyone, without talking to anyone. He didn't even have to explain to Isabelle that going into town wasn't an option today. He was sure she knew it without being told and she wouldn't ask.

He didn't leave the study until late afternoon. This was the messiest room in the house and Cameron liked it that way. Books he had started to read and hadn't finished were piled on every surface. He hadn't dusted in years—had he *ever* dusted?

Cleanliness aside, the room was perfect. It was home to an armchair that had once belonged to Cameron's father and by now the material was so worn and faded, the stuffing so used to the shape of his body, that it was like sitting on a cloud.

When he did get up, it was only to get a glass of water. He had every intention of returning to the study and to the adventure book he'd had in his lap all morning. He hadn't managed to take in a word of it. His thoughts kept flitting to the way Isabelle had looked at him when he had told her that he wouldn't go into the church, to the hurt and anger in her eyes. It bothered him, he realized, to know that he had bothered *her*. It wasn't the same as saying no to Pastor

Calloway. It was easy, he now realized, to say no to the pastor. Irritating, but not painful.

Isabelle was different. He couldn't help thinking that he had disappointed her again and again from the moment she had arrived here. He'd failed to anticipate the baby's needs. That was the first thing. Then, there was the fact that she had come expecting a marriage, a life, and he was refusing to give her that.

She had all these expectations about who I was going to be and I'm not any of it.

The least he could do, he thought, was take her to church. Except that he couldn't. He couldn't offer any more of himself to God. He had been faithful. He had prayed. He had given as much as he could. And he had lost *everything*.

How could he sit in a church now, knowing all that? How could he give up everything again?

I won't let Him take anything more from me. Not even an hour of my time on a Sunday morning.

As he walked to the kitchen, he heard a high-pitched voice coming from the living room and he recognized it as the voice Isabelle adopted when she spoke to the baby. Before he could stop himself, he was peering in to see what was going on.

She was sitting on the couch before the fire, her back to him. Looking over her shoulder, he could see that she had a bottle in her hand and that she was feeding Abby. Her head was tilted to one side. He couldn't see her face, but he was sure she was smiling.

Was that because he had seen her with a smile often enough to know what would put that expression there?

Or was he thinking of something else?

Someone else?

Ruth.

He backed out of the doorway quickly and quietly, before she could realize that he was there, and hurried toward the steps that led to his home's tiny attic. He climbed up quickly and pulled the door shut behind him, breathing heavily, shaking as if pursued by a ghost.

How long had it been since he had let Ruth come into his mind in that way?

Thinking of Philip was painful. Thinking of Ruth was a different kind of pain. Philip had been full of possibility, but Ruth... she was a person. Someone he had *known*. Someone he had loved deeply.

He pressed a hand to his chest, wondering if it was possible for his heart to leave him.

It had been Ruth that he had thought of just now, seeing Isabelle on the couch. He had recalled her sitting there holding Philip in her arms, her head cocked to the side in just the same way. Though Ruth had looked nothing like Isabelle—she had been tall, blonde, plump, and ruddy-cheeked—there had been such a similarity in the way the two women held themselves that Cameron had thought he might choke on his grief.

This was the reason he couldn't have Isabelle and Abby in the house.

It was going to break him.

He leaned backward, trying to recover his breath, and ran into something. A box. There, in Adam's untidy handwriting, were the words, *baby things*.

Cameron's heart stopped completely.

He had never bothered to ask what had become of all the baby things after his son's death. He hadn't wanted to know. He had assumed Adam must have done something with anything that hadn't been taken by the fire but he had never so much as mentioned his son's name to his ranch foreman. Asking this question would have been far too much.

Hands trembling, he reached out and opened the box.

On the very top, piled in as though as an afterthought, was a hand-carved mobile. Suddenly, Cameron was tumbling into the past.

"He isn't going to recognize any of those shapes, you know," Ruth said fondly, putting a warm hand on Cameron's shoulder. *"He'll never know how hard you worked."*

"Sure he will," Cameron objected. *"Someday he'll grow up and have a child of his own, and he'll hang this mobile over his baby's cradle, and he'll know then. He'll say to his wife, 'Look how hard my father worked to make this mobile for me when I was a baby. Look how loved I was.'"*

They glanced down at baby Philip, who was waving his fists in the air. Cameron knew enough to know that a baby of that age probably couldn't even discern what he was looking at.

Ruth was right. Philip didn't know that Cameron had painstakingly carved and painted six different animal shapes to hang over his cradle. Philip wouldn't know, even if he could see the animals, what they were. He certainly wouldn't connect them with the fact that his father loved him.

Not today. But someday, he would understand all of those things.

Ruth turned in Cameron's arms and embraced him. "You're a good father," she said quietly. "You're the best father in the world."

Cameron knew he wasn't the best father in the world. But he did think he was a good one. He loved his son and was determined that Philip was going to have the best of everything in life. And it would start here, with a hand-carved mobile.

"You don't mind it?" he asked Ruth. "Even if you think it's silly, you'll let me hang it up, won't you?"

She laughed. "I don't think it's silly at all," she assured him. "I'm only teasing you a little, Cameron. I love it. I love that you made it for him. And I absolutely want us to hang it up. Not right now, but once he's awake, we can do it."

Cameron beamed. "I always dreamed of this," he confessed. "Making something like this for my child."

"You'll have to make new ones for each child we have," she said. "So they'll all have one to keep once they're grown up. I hope you don't mind that."

"I don't mind at all." He pulled back and squinted at her. "Are you saying you're ready to have another?"

She laughed. "Are you ready for that? He's still keeping us very busy! And no, I don't think the time has come for that just yet. But soon enough, I should think. I don't want them to be too far apart in age."

Cameron nodded his agreement. He pictured what it would be like to have a young child on his shoulders and a baby in his arms. It was beyond anything he could imagine right now, but life was long and full of potential. Full of possibility. And as he held his beloved wife in his arms and looked down on their infant son, he knew that the adventures that lay ahead for them were far greater than anything he would be able to imagine from his vantage point here and now.

The creak of a floorboard jerked Cameron from his reverie.

Isabelle.

Not Ruth. Isabelle. She was walking around downstairs. He closed the box and shoved it away from him, wishing he had never found it, knowing how difficult it was going to be for him to forget that it was here now that he had. He would be aware of it over his head like a storm cloud about to break.

How odd that he'd found this *now*, when Isabelle and Abby had come into his life and stirred up all these old emotions. Had he come up to the attic *because* they were here? Was he deliberately looking for these haunting things from the past, trying to cause himself distress?

Ridiculous. Why would I do such a thing?

He had to put it all out of his mind or he would fall into despair, and he couldn't let that happen. He shoved the box deep under the eave, where he would have to go looking for it if he wanted to find it again, and descended from the attic to see what was going on below.

He found Isabelle in the kitchen taking out pans and arranging them on the stove. "What are you doing?" he demanded.

She turned to face him, eyebrows lifting in surprise. "Making supper," she said.

"It's late for that. You should have started an hour ago." He *was* hungry, he realized, though he certainly hadn't been until just this moment. "What were you waiting for?"

"I thought..." she trembled slightly. "I thought it was best that Abby eat first. And I stand by that decision. It's my responsibility to take care of her."

"It's also your responsibility to tend to things around this house," he said. "That was what you offered when you arrived here."

"You're not going to let me stay," she said, lifting her chin slightly. "You can't scold me for not being a good enough housekeeper if you aren't planning on keeping me around anyway."

"I haven't said anything about whether you'll be able to stay."

"Well, are you going to let me?" she asked him. "I'm tired of the guessing games, Cameron. I want an answer. If you mean to keep me here, then you can be angry with me for starting supper late, and for not having the place clean enough, and anything else you want to scold me for. But if you're not letting me and Abby stay here, you can't be upset about those things, because then it *isn't* my job to take care of your house. Because then we're just guests and we don't have to live up to your standards. So which is it? Am I here to keep house for you and to go on doing that permanently? Or am I only here until the weather breaks and you find something else to do with me?"

Cameron opened his mouth to answer, but before he could, he heard a wail coming from down the hall.

Isabelle sighed. "Great," she said. "That's wonderful, Cameron. Now Isabelle's awake."

He shook his head. "You can't hold me responsible for that," he said. "You're the one who started shouting."

That much was true. He had been out of line when he'd reprimanded her for being late with supper and he knew it, but he hadn't raised his voice. She was the one who'd woken the baby.

She wiped her hands on her apron, her lips pressed tightly together. "Well," she said, "now supper is going to be even later, because I have to tend to her. And whether you like it or not, Cameron, a baby is more important than you are. She can't wait to be taken care of. You can. So you are going to have to find a way to be patient."

So saying, she hurried from the room, brushing past him, coming so close that Cameron almost thought she was trying to clip him with her shoulder as she went by.

He turned and looked after her.

A part of him wanted to pursue her, to tell her that he was sorry, that he hadn't meant what he'd said. It was true. He hadn't meant to react that way, and he knew he was in the wrong. It was that box full of baby things that had him in such a tempestuous mood. He had *needed* to take his temper out on someone or something, otherwise he would have been upset all night. And he could admit that it had worked. The tension he had felt up in the attic was gone now and Ruth and Philip felt as far away from him as they ever did.

It was Isabelle who took up space in his thoughts now.

It was Isabelle who made him wonder what he should do, how he should manage himself. He couldn't go on treating her the way he had been. She was right about that. She deserved to know what her future held. She deserved to be told that she wasn't going to be able to stay, that he intended to make another plan for her. He should give her a timeline for that, let her know what steps he was going to take and when she could expect to be put on a train.

He wasn't sure why he hadn't been able to be honest with her about all those things.

I don't want her to go, he thought suddenly.

But he *did* want her to go. He didn't want a woman and a baby in his house, in his life. It was their presence that had stirred up all the pain he was currently going through.

But maybe feeling something—even pain—is better than being numb.

Letting out a gruff sigh, he claimed the glass of water he had come to get in the first place. His thoughts were nowhere near resolved, and by the looks of things, neither was his supper.

Chapter Nine

The knock on the door startled Isabelle. Nobody ever knocked on the door to this house. Either Cameron walked right in—and, usually, right past her—without speaking, or else the place was silent apart from her movements and Abby's.

She put down the plate she had been washing and looked over at the baby, who was lying in her milk crate in the center of the dining table and making soft, happy noises. *You have no idea the predicament we're in.*

She turned toward the door.

Did she dare answer it? She wasn't sure. It might be anyone at all, and the thought of letting a stranger in unsettled her. She couldn't help thinking of her parents, who'd made the mistake of opening the door one day and had lost their lives for it when bandits had been on the other side.

Best not to take the risk. She moved quietly to the table and lifted Abby into her arms, backing out of the kitchen as slowly as she could. If she could get to the front door on the opposite side of the house, she could slip out. She could go and hide in the barn until whoever it was went away. Her heart pounded madly as she thought of the responsibility she had to protect Abby. If anything happened to her, the baby would be on her own. God knew Cameron couldn't be relied upon to take care of her.

She'd almost reached the hallway when a voice rang out. "Isabelle! We know you're in there. It's cold, for heaven's sake—let us in!"

She recognized the voice but couldn't place it—and then, suddenly, she did. *Eloise!*

Hurrying forward, clutching Abby to her chest, she unlocked the door and flung it open.

Sure enough, Eloise was standing there, her sandy brown hair covered by a scarf and just a few strands of it poking out from beneath. She held a bag in her arms

Edith stood behind her, also holding a bag. "We brought you some things," Edith said. "For the baby. Clothes, mostly, a few toys, some spare bottles. Things like that."

"You did?" Isabelle was touched. A warmth spread in her chest, and she stood back to let them into the house.

"All the women at the church chipped in," Eloise explained, depositing her bag on the kitchen table. "My goodness. I don't think I've ever seen this place look so clean, Isabelle. I hope my brother appreciates what he has in you."

Isabelle's mind was elsewhere. "You said the women at the church did this?" she asked. "Do you attend church, Eloise?"

"Oh, yes," Eloise was taking baby clothes out of her bag and arranging them on the table. "I go every week. Well, I should say that I go *most* weeks. These past few, I haven't even been able to get out my front door because the snow was piled too high. The wind always blows it in drifts in front of my house."

"Wouldn't Cameron dig you out?" Edith had also begun to empty her bag. She took several baby bottles over to the sink, laid a towel out on the counter, and began to wash them.

"He would," Eloise said. "He used to do it every winter. But the snow would just come back. So now we make sure I have enough provisions in my house to last me a few weeks, and then he doesn't bother with digging me out unless I ask him to. He'll come to my window and talk to me, see if I need anything, but other than that, I'm content to wait." She glanced at Isabelle. "I'm sure you must have been wondering why I haven't been by to see you."

"I was," Isabelle admitted. "Especially when the snow stopped. I thought I would see you then."

"I had to wait for it to melt a bit. And to tell the truth, I was staying away deliberately, because I wanted to give you and Cameron a chance to get to know one another," Eloise said. "I owe you an apology. I owe him one too, I suppose, but I owe you a bigger one, because my brother *does* need a wife. He needs to remember how to open himself up to people. But you... I shouldn't have brought you here without telling you the truth about what was going on."

She finished unpacking the baby clothes and took a seat at the table.

Isabelle sat down next to her. "Your brother is difficult to get along with," she confided. "I try my hardest, and I can see that he isn't a cruel man, but he's so gruff. So reserved. He doesn't seem to want to talk to me at all, and he hasn't shown the slightest interest in Abby. I can understand how someone wouldn't want to spend his time with me, but how could anybody not be enchanted by her?"

"I agree with that part," Edith put in, coming over from the sink to join them. She wiggled her fingers at Abby and gave her a broad grin.

Abby giggled and waved her fist up and down, and Edith laughed. "Who could possibly not adore her?" She, too, sat down. She picked up one of the baby outfits and started a new pile. After a moment, Isabelle saw that she was sorting them according to size. She was grateful. She turned the baby in her arms so that Abby could take in the two women who had come to help her—the only real friends she had here, it seemed.

"Can I hold her?" Eloise asked.

"Of course!" It warmed Isabelle to have someone other than herself care for Abby. She gratefully passed her over, recalling how she'd worried when these two women had arrived. How she had thought that, if they were bandits, no one would care for Abby.

Eloise would. If something happened to me, Eloise would make sure Abby was provided for.

Isabelle sat back in her chair, a great weight lifting from her shoulders, and closed her eyes briefly. Only now was she fully aware of just how alone she had been since Vivienne had died.

Abby must have sensed how badly she'd needed this. Or perhaps it was just that she had taken a liking to Eloise. Either way, she didn't fuss at being in the arms of a near stranger. Isabelle heard a little coo and looked over to see the baby kicking her feet happily in the air.

"I owe you an explanation," Eloise said. "Since you mentioned how difficult my brother can be. You're right. And you deserve to understand why that is."

"All right," Isabelle said. "I thought it was just his character."

"It is, but it wasn't always," Eloise said with a heavy sigh. Her gaze drifted to the window for a moment, and she seemed focused on something far away. "He used to be a very caring, kindhearted man. When we were growing up, he was someone I could always turn to, even though he's younger than I am. If he ever saw that I was sad, he would try to find out what had happened. He would do things to cheer me up. Pick wildflowers for me, make me my favorite meal. And when we got older, he looked out for me in different ways. He built my house with his own two hands. I'm not surprised he got that goat for you. He cares for people. It's just that he struggles with letting them see it."

"But why?" Isabelle asked, her curiosity piqued. She glanced over at Edith. The older woman was still sorting through the baby clothes, her head down, and Isabelle had the impression she was trying to stay out of the conversation.

Eloise took a deep breath. "The truth is," she said, locking eyes with Isabelle, "my brother was married before. And he had a child."

The words were like a gale-force wind, sucking the breath from Isabelle's lungs. She would never have guessed this. "What—what happened?"

"There was a fire," Eloise said quietly. "It was years ago. He was a blacksmith in those days. We lived in town, both of us. We hadn't bought the ranch. One day, while Cameron was working, a fire swept through town."

"That's why all the buildings look new," Isabelle realized. It was a punch to the gut. She had sat beside him marveling at a beautiful town that was a reminder of the pain he carried.

Eloise nodded. "That's right," she said. "Lots of things had to be rebuilt."

"I wish I had known all this sooner," Isabelle murmured. "I feel terrible. I've been judging him for his coldness to me, but it must have been so painful for him when an unexpected woman arrived with a baby."

"I expect so," Eloise said. "Had I known about the baby, I probably wouldn't have brought you here at all."

"I thought you did know." Guilt stabbed at Isabelle. "I wasn't trying to keep it a secret. I assumed that Vivienne had told you she was a mother from the start."

"It isn't your fault," Eloise said. "A lot of her communication was with Sheriff Grayson, not with me. I'm guessing she did say something to him, and it just didn't get communicated. I'm not accusing your friend of lying."

Isabelle's eyes filled with tears. She couldn't help it.

Eloise's hand flew to her mouth. "Oh no," she said. "Did I say the wrong thing? I didn't mean to."

"No," Isabelle assured as Edith reached out and put a comforting hand on top of hers. "You didn't say anything wrong. In fact, it's nice to hear kind words about Vivienne. Her parents were so angry with her at the end. It's been so long since anyone has said anything remotely decent about her. And I just miss her so much."

The tears spilled over and began to stream down her face.

"She would be so grateful for you," Edith murmured, patting her hand. "I may not know her, but I know that much. Taking care of her child after she could no longer do it herself. You're a blessing to that woman, and to that baby. And we very much want to see you in church next Sunday. Both of you."

"Well, I don't think I have a way of getting there," Isabelle said slowly. "I'd like to attend, but I don't know if it's going to be possible."

"I'll take you," Eloise said briskly, as if she had already thought about it. "Now that I'm no longer trapped in my house, I'll be going. You're right that Cameron isn't likely to take you to church, but I'll be going, and you'll come with me. Simple as that."

"Thank you," Isabelle whispered, surprised at how moved she was by such a simple offer. To be able to get to church, to know that she would be with her new community in the house of the Lord, meant the world. It was everything she had been longing for since she had arrived in Wintervale, and now she finally felt as if she might be able to make this place a home.

Poor Cameron, though. I had no idea he'd lost a wife and a child in such a brutal way. No wonder he isn't at ease with our presence here!

Well, she was just going to have to be patient with him. She would find a way to warm him up, to break through that closed heart of his.

No one was ever so damaged that they couldn't let love back into their life.

Isabelle believed that with all her heart.

Chapter Ten

Cameron walked through the kitchen door and shut it forcefully behind him. He stamped his feet a few times to shake the snow off his boots, then bent down to remove them. He took off his coat and hung it on the peg by the door. It was only once he had turned back around that he realized the kitchen table was covered.

His first reaction was mild annoyance. *How many times do Isabelle and I need to discuss this? She told me she was going to take responsibility for the cleaning and tidying around here.* He took a closer look at the items on the table and they hit him like a punch to the gut.

It was an array of baby things.

Donated things. Leftover things from other babies. He could see that at once by the wear on the clothing. The realization was sickening.

Every family in the community did this, of course. There had been an influx of donations after Philip's birth. When he had begun to grow, Cameron and Ruth had taken the newborn clothes they no longer needed to the church so they could be given to someone else.

Those clothes won't be here. Abby is too big for the clothes Philip had.

But she wasn't, really. The time she had gone without enough food to eat had taken an obvious toll. Cameron didn't know how old she was, but she was small. What would he do if he saw an item of clothing that he'd seen before? Something he had seen on his own son?

The idea of it sent a shudder through him, and a ripple of anger chased it. He shouldn't have to cope with this.

He turned away and walked into the living room, letting out a slow breath to try to restore his calm. There was no reason to be upset with Isabelle for this. She didn't know about Philip. She couldn't possibly realize how he would have felt upon seeing those things. Abby *did* need clothes. He couldn't expect Isabelle to go on making fresh ones while the baby continued to grow. *No wonder the house isn't getting cleaned as quickly as I'd like it to. She does have an awful lot on her plate.*

He stepped into the doorway that led to the living room and stopped short, staring.

The room was full of boxes. They covered so much of the floor that he wasn't sure he would be able to walk in without tripping. Isabelle knelt at the center of the boxes, her back to him.

Cameron hesitated, then deliberately stepped on the creaky floorboard to announce his presence.

She turned. "Oh," she said in a hushed voice. "You're back early today. I meant to have everything cleared away before you got in. I just got Abby to sleep about an hour ago, so I haven't been able to do as much as I would have liked."

"What is all this?"

"I went up to the attic," she said. "I know you wanted me to organize the house, and I thought that would be a good place to start. I can see that most of these boxes will need to go right back into storage, but there were a few things that seemed like they'd benefit from being unpacked. Like those boots, for instance. They're barely used. They're not doing anyone any good packed away."

She pointed to a pair of black work boots. Cameron received a jolt. He'd forgotten all about them. He had purchased them just a few weeks before the fire and in the aftermath he hadn't thought about them at all. Seeing them again now threw him painfully back into the past.

And yet... *She's right. They aren't doing anyone any good sitting in a box, and they might be more use to me now than they would have before. I do go through plenty of boots working on the ranch.*

He nodded. "That's a good find," he admitted. "I'm grateful to you."

She beamed.

The smile lit up her whole face. He had never seen her like this, had never gotten to know this side of her. This must be the real Isabelle. This was the woman her friends and loved ones got to see. Radiant. Happy. It was like the sun had come into his house. And it had been dark in here for so long...

She cleared her throat. "I wouldn't have guessed you had a Bible," she said.

"I don't." He was mystified.

She pointed. "Right there. It was in one of the boxes."

He turned.

The sight of the book—the familiar worn, brown leather cover—choked him. It was out of place on the end table beside the settee that Ruth had never seen, the one the town had donated to him when he had moved into this place.

That Bible belonged in her hands.

He could see her now, turning the pages, reading out a favorite verse. *We know that in all things God works for the good of those who love Him,* she would say, smiling at him fondly. She had so loved the book of Romans. Though Cameron had never been as passionate about his faith as Ruth had, he had liked that one, too. He had liked how clear it was, how it had spoken about the way a person ought to live day to day. Those were the matters he thought about. He could believe in a God who was interested in shepherding people from one day to the next, helping them with the trial that was living a life.

At least, he had believed in that once.

"Why would you take that out?" he asked, turning back to Isabelle, fighting to keep emotion out of his voice.

"I thought you must have forgotten about it," she said, clearly oblivious to his distress. She was still beaming. "We could read it together. We could share our favorite passages. I know you don't like to go to church, but that wouldn't be church. It would just be sharing our faith. I was so pleased when I saw that you owned a Bible."

Cameron couldn't speak. He didn't know where to begin.

Having her in the house was painful enough, but to see her take out Ruth's old Bible and offer to read it with him... *no.* He turned and walked out of the room, toward his study, meaning to put a solid wooden door between the two of them. He couldn't break in front of her. He couldn't let her in.

She caught him in the hallway and put a hand on his arm. "Cameron," she murmured.

It was the first time she had spoken his name, and it froze him where he stood.

It was also the first time she had touched him. Her hand was small and warm and soft, and Cameron was reminded forcibly of the first time he had seen her and the tension that had flowed between the two of them.

He hadn't experienced anything like this since Ruth had died. He hadn't believed he would ever know this kind of heat and tension again.

He hadn't *wanted* to. These thoughts and sensations should have died when his family had died.

He shouldn't be able to care for someone like this. To be drawn to her. To want in the core of his body to bring her closer even as he pushed her away.

It certainly shouldn't be happening when he was *angry* with her.

But her touch was a knife that had cut right through the anger, a hot blade melting away the cold he felt.

"I'm sorry," she said softly. "I should have guessed. That Bible belonged to your wife, didn't it?"

He turned and looked at her. The words caught in his throat.

"Eloise told me what happened." Isabelle's blue eyes were soft and warm, and her hand lingered on his arm. "I should have known there was a reason you were so opposed to having us here. I'm sorry."

He inclined his head, acknowledging her apology, and turned his face away from her. The memories crashed over him hard and fast. Ruth reading late into the night by candlelight. Her warm smile. Her laugh. The way she would share a favorite verse and then pass the book to him and insist he choose his own. The way she would gently coax him toward finding one, even though Cameron had no favorite Bible verses.

"I'll put the Bible away. It was wrong of me to suggest that you and I read it together," Isabelle said. She hesitated. "Did you read it with her? I saw how it hurt you when I suggested you do that with me."

He was stunned that she'd guessed so much. His whole face felt hot, every muscle in his body tight and uncomfortable. He wanted to run away. He wanted not to be having this conversation. Pain burned through him like the sensation right after a shot of whiskey, his whole body rebelling against what was happening. But unlike whiskey, the pain wasn't followed with a pleasant warmth that made the initial discomfort worth it. The agony just kept right on coming.

He squeezed his eyes closed. This was what he had feared when she had arrived here. This moment. It was torment. He couldn't bear it. He needed her to leave him alone...

She didn't, though.

Her hand slid slowly down his arm and came to rest on top of his. Cameron wondered if Isabelle was going to try to take his hand and wondered if he'd mind if she did. Yesterday, he would have said he would hate that. Now, though, in the moment, he almost wanted it to happen.

What's going on with me? How can I want that? She was still all but a stranger to him. He was upset with her for going through his things, for taking out that Bible. The fact that she knew about his past made it worse. Her knowing was a breach he hadn't been prepared for. She'd slipped past his defenses.

And yet…

She didn't take his hand, but she did keep her hand resting over his. "Look at me," she said softly. A request, not a command.

He opened his eyes.

The compassion on her face—wide eyes, soft lips—was like nothing he had seen since Ruth had died. It wasn't that he had been alone. Eloise cared for him, but she had always been tough in the way she showed her love. Not like this. Isabelle was so tender.

How can she care about me? I haven't been warm to her.

"I'll put it away," she said. "Back where I found it, and we won't speak of it again, all right? I'm sorry this happened. It's entirely my fault. Forgive me."

Slowly, he nodded. "Thank you," he managed. His anger hadn't dissipated, but he could see that she was making an effort.

She removed her hand from his. It was a relief to have some distance from her, and he breathed more easily. "Of course," she said quietly. "I'll go take care of it right now. You won't have to see it again."

She turned away.

A thought occurred to him. "Isabelle?"

She turned back, eyebrows lifted.

"Make sure you put it... somewhere safe." His heart skipped a beat. He hadn't known until today that the Bible had survived the fire. He assumed it had been lost, along with most of his possessions. "Put it somewhere you'll be able to find it again. Just in case."

She smiled at him. "Of course I will," she said, and then she was gone.

Cameron let out a long, slow breath, willing his heart rate to return to normal. He went into his study and pulled the door closed behind him. She wouldn't bother him in here.

Though I'm not sure I could call it a bother.

He was so grateful to know that the Bible had been saved. It was as if Ruth had reached out to him from the past and laid it in his hands—or at least, within his reach. That was why he needed to make sure it was packed up somewhere he would be able to find it again. Someday. When he was ready.

It's not that I want a Bible. I could get one of those from the church if I wanted it. It's just that it meant so much to Ruth. It's the most important thing of hers I have left.

Was it possible she *had* meant him to find it? Maybe this was some sort of message. Maybe he was supposed to see that book and understand that Ruth didn't want him to abandon his faith.

She wouldn't have wanted that, of course. He didn't need a Bible to tell him that. A guilty weight settled in the pit of his stomach. Faith had meant everything to Ruth. She wouldn't want to see him closing himself off from God.

But I can't. I can't let myself get hurt like that. Not again.

Instead, to his surprise, his thoughts turned back to Isabelle—another strong-willed woman who had come into his life with her heart on her sleeve.

What am I going to do about her?

What am I going to do about the way I'm beginning to yearn for her?

They were questions for which he had no answers.

Chapter Eleven

Something was wrong with the goat.

It was stamping its feet and bleating before Isabelle could even sit down on the stool. Frowning, she arranged Abby in her milk crate and covered her with blankets. The storm had gotten worse again and she didn't relish having to be out here with the baby, but there was no avoiding the milking.

As soon as she sat down, Isabelle saw the problem. The goat's udders were red and inflamed. It was clearly some sort of infection. Her heart sank. Of course the animal wouldn't want to be touched under the circumstances, and who knew whether it would even be possible to get any milk? This was going to be difficult.

She steadied herself. There was no choice. She would have to do her best, and that was all there was to it.

She reached out and gripped an udder.

The goat let out a maddened yell and kicked out with its back feet. Isabelle had to throw herself to the ground to avoid being hit. She cried out, startled and upset, and across the barn, Abby also gave a yell.

Isabelle scrambled to her feet. "You're going to have to let me do this," she told the goat.

Determined, she knelt beside the animal, foregoing the stool in the interest of expedience. She grabbed the udder again and managed to give it a squeeze.

Nothing came out.

It wasn't a lack of technique this time. She was confident that she was doing it properly. The issue lay with the goat, who was now screaming and bucking in sheer agony. She lashed out with another kick, this time connecting with Isabelle's shoulder.

Isabelle let out a cry of shock and pain as she sprawled on the ground. The strike of the goat's hoof radiated through her shoulder down her arm, numbness chased by sharp pain. She managed to scramble away, gasping, and struggled back to her feet.

Isabelle didn't want to give up, but if the goat wasn't going to give milk, there was no sense in keeping Abby out in the cold. She scooped the baby up in her uninjured arm, grabbed the crate, and ran back toward the house as fast as she could.

By the time she had let herself into the kitchen and pulled the door closed behind her, Abby was shrieking. Isabelle's heart twisted. She was hungry, of course, and she had probably also been frightened by all the yelling while they were out in the barn. Isabelle doubted the cold had done any good, either. She set the crate in the center of the kitchen table and put Abby down in it, even though it only heightened her guilt to do so. A good mother would hold her crying child, not put her down, even if she had just been kicked by a goat.

Isabelle probed the wound carefully with her fingers. Nothing seemed broken. She rotated her shoulder. It hurt, but she was able to move it normally. She would have a bad bruise, she suspected, but that would be as far as it went.

Now that the excitement was over, her heart began to calm, which only made the pain worse. Her shoulder throbbed terribly. She held it with the opposite hand and sank into a seat at the table, biting her lip hard to keep from crying.

"What's the matter with you?"

Cameron had come into the room from the direction of his study. She sat up straighter at once. "I didn't know you were in the house."

"I was doing the finances," he said. "Are you all right?"

His head was cocked to the side, his gaze focused on her shoulder, which she was still cradling with her free hand.

"It's the goat," she said, dabbing at her eyes. "Something's the matter with her. She won't give milk, and she kicked me when I tried to get it. And now there isn't anything to give to Abby, and she's hungry… It's the same awful mess all over again."

"The goat kicked you?" Cameron came farther into the room. "Are you hurt?"

"I'm all right." She touched her shoulder gingerly.

Cameron narrowed his eyes. "Let me see you move it."

She showed him, rotating her arm backward and then forward. "I really am fine. It hurt, but I'll be all right. Just a bruise."

"Show me." He sat down next to her.

She removed her hand slowly, though she flinched at exposing the injury to the possibility of being touched by someone else.

He frowned and leaned close, raising a hand to the collar of her dress.

She stiffened.

Slowly, with exceeding gentleness, he hooked his thumb under the collar and pulled it away from her shoulder, down to the top of her arm.

Isabelle's heart skipped a beat, her injury all but forgotten. To have Cameron look at her in such an intimate way sent fire coursing through her veins. His fingers grazed over the injury and her breath caught.

"Did that hurt?"

He had misunderstood, thankfully. "A little." It *had* hurt a little, but that wasn't what had made her gasp.

"Someone should look at it. You're going to have quite a bruise." He huffed out a sigh. "I've told you not to go out there on your own."

She ignored his scowl. "I'm all right." At least, her shoulder was all right. Whatever else was going on inside her right now would be beyond the skills of any physician to heal, she was sure. The way her heart galloped like a wild stallion—could that be healthy? She should pull away from him. She knew she should.

"Are you sure? We could…" He broke off mid-sentence, glancing at the window, and Isabelle knew why. They couldn't do anything. What would he do, take her to a doctor? Not in this weather. It was all right, she didn't need to see a doctor, but she could tell he was frustrated by finding himself unable to do anything.

She could relate to that. It was the same way she felt when Abby cried.

"I shouldn't have adopted her," she said, her voice breaking with grief.

Cameron looked back at her. "What do you mean?"

"I took Abby in because her mother asked me to," Isabelle said, a shiver of shame coursing through her. Tears pricked at her eyes. "And because I couldn't bear the thought of her being raised by someone who didn't love her as much as I do. But I wasn't prepared to be a mother. She deserves to be raised by someone who knows what they're doing, not by someone who can't even milk a goat without it turning into a disaster."

"What's the matter with the goat?" Cameron asked, his voice calm and even.

"I don't know," Isabelle sniffled. "She has some kind of infection, I think. I couldn't get any milk from her, even before she kicked me."

"Well, it's probably mastitis," Cameron said. "Common enough in milking stock. I can take care of it."

"You can?" Her eyes widened, her spirits buoyed by sudden hope. Could it be this simple? Was this a problem that could be fixed?

"Wait here." He strode across the room and out the door, not giving her the chance to say anything else.

Isabelle didn't even want to believe. It would be too painful if she let herself think this was going to work only to have him come back with nothing. She picked Abby up and sat back in her chair, cradling the baby to her breast, wishing once more that she had milk of her own to give.

Abby was still whimpering softly, less grating on the ear than her cries out in the stable, but no less heartrending. Isabelle got to her feet and began to pace around the room, bouncing the baby gently as she did so and trying to comfort her.

I have to at least consider giving her up.

The thought was like poison. It landed violently in her gut and she wanted to vomit to rid herself of it. She and Abby were all each other had left of Vivienne. If they were separated, it would be like killing Vivienne all over again.

Besides, I don't want to let go of her. I love her. She's my baby now. Even if I'm not her birth mother, I love her as if I was.

It crushed her heart to know that love wasn't enough.

Babies needed more than just love. They needed to eat. Isabelle had failed too many times at the task of providing food. A birth mother would never have had this struggle, but Isabelle would never escape it.

She had believed that having the goat would be enough to put an end to it. But the goat was an imperfect solution. It wouldn't last. Something would always, inevitably, go wrong. Maybe the animal wouldn't survive the winter. Maybe it would get sick. Maybe this infection it was currently suffering would worsen. She only knew that she couldn't stake Abby's life on the well-being of a goat.

Vivienne wanted us to be together but she wouldn't have wanted that. She'd have wanted the security of knowing that Abby was well fed. There must be someone who can take her that would do a better job providing for her than I will. Maybe if I speak to Edith about it, she'll know someone. Someone from the church, maybe...

Tears streamed down Isabelle's face at the thought and she held Abby closer. "I'm sorry," she breathed. "I'm so sorry."

Her parents were gone. Vivienne was gone. Abby was the last person she had, the last person she loved. For the sake of that love, she ought to give her up. Even if it would destroy her to do it.

That was what was on her mind when the door opened and Cameron came back in, shaking his head to rid himself of the snow that had accumulated in his hair. He held a bucket in one hand.

"Got some," he said. "Not as much as usual, I'm afraid, but it should be enough for tonight, and I'll try again in the morning. I gave the goat something for the infection, too, so that should subside. I'm sure we'll do better tomorrow than we did tonight."

Isabelle drew a deep breath, pressing Abby tightly against her body, and stepped closer to the bucket. She hardly dared to look. Her nerves twanged.

He was right. It wasn't as much as they had been able to get in the past.

But it was enough.

She moved to put Abby back in the crate, but Cameron held out his arms. "I can hold her while you prepare it," he said. "If you'd like me to, I mean."

Isabelle only hesitated a moment. Then, she settled Abby in his arms.

It was clear to her at once that this man had indeed had a child of his own. She would have been able to tell by the way he held Abby even if she hadn't been told. He knew to cradle her head carefully, to rock her gently and keep her always in slight motion. He was relaxed with her, not stiff or awkward the way Isabelle had seen some people be when they held babies for the first time. He had done this before.

She turned away. Even though Abby was her baby—for the moment, anyway—this seemed too intimate to watch. This must have weighed heavy on him. She focused her attention instead on preparing the milk; she boiled it and poured it carefully into the bottle. By the time she returned to the table, Cameron's expression was steady. If he'd had an emotional reaction, there was no sign of it.

"Would you feed her?" she asked, holding out the bottle. "I don't want to disturb her. She looks pretty settled there."

Cameron nodded and accepted the bottle. "I've never done this before," he admitted.

Because Cameron's baby was fed by his mother, not from a bottle. It was as close as either of them had come to acknowledging what she was now sure they were both thinking. "She knows what to do," she told Cameron. "Just hold it for her, and she'll do the rest."

Cameron nodded and positioned the bottle. A moment later, the reassuring sounds of Abby suckling filled the kitchen.

Isabelle slumped in her chair. Relief filled her at the sight of Abby eating, but it wasn't the cool release she would have expected. There was bitter dread around the edges. Cameron had saved them today, and her gratitude was like a song—but it kept hitting a sour note when she remembered that she had relied on someone else. He wouldn't be in Abby's life forever. When winter ended, they would have to move on, and she wouldn't be able to rely on Cameron. "I don't know if I can keep doing this," she murmured.

She had been talking to herself, for the most part, but of course Cameron heard her, and he responded. "Doing what?"

"I keep letting her down," Isabelle explained. "I don't know anymore if I did the right thing by taking her in. I question it all the time. I didn't want her to go to an orphanage, and her mother wanted her with me. I love Abby. But I can't even *feed* her." Her eyes filled with tears. "What kind of mother can't feed her child?"

"Anyone can see how much you love her, Isabelle," Cameron said gruffly.

Isabelle dropped her head. "But what good is that to her?" she asked. "She can't live on my love. She needs food. And she isn't getting it. Over and over, I let her down." She focused on Abby, who was warm and settled in Cameron's arms. Her eyes had drifted closed. She was more content than she had been all day. "It isn't me she needs. She needs milk. I can't give her that."

"The goat was unwell, Isabelle. That isn't your fault." Cameron's voice grew more firm. "It could have happened to anyone. It *has* happened to me, many times. That's how I knew what to do about it."

"But when it happens to other people, their babies don't go hungry," Isabelle protested. She sighed and listened to Abby suckling, trying to let the sound reassure her.

"Not every baby out there is being raised by the mother that gave birth to it," Cameron reminded her, fixing her with a steady gaze. "Nothing you can do will bring her mother back. It's not your fault Abby's mother is gone, and it's not your fault she can't come back."

His words were firm and direct, and yet Isabelle's throat swelled shut with emotion. No one had said these things to her. She wanted so badly to believe them. It was a balm to the incurable ache in her soul.

"Thank you," she said. "It's so difficult sometimes."

"Because you want her to have the best," Cameron said.

He knows this feeling. She nodded. "And I know I can't give it to her," she said. "No matter how good a caretaker I am…"

"You can call yourself a mother. You're the mother she has."

Isabelle swallowed hard. "No matter how good a *mother* I am, I'm not the mother she should have had. I'll never be the mother she deserved. It will always be a tragedy that she ended up with me."

"That's not true," Cameron murmured. "That she lost her mother is a tragedy. But having you… that's a good thing."

"How can it be a good thing and a bad thing?" Isabelle asked.

"Because life is complicated." He shifted the baby to his other arm. She didn't fuss at the momentary separation from her bottle as he changed hands, and soon enough she was eating happily once more.

Cameron went on. "We can't make sense of it most of the time. But when I see the way you look at this baby, when I see how you worry over her…" He hesitated, a new tightness in his voice. When he spoke again, his voice cracked slightly. "I know she's loved. And that can't be anything but good."

Isabelle let out a long sigh.

Maybe he was right.

Maybe losing one more person who loved her would be the worst thing that could happen to Abby now.

Chapter Twelve

"I don't know what's the matter with that horse," Adam admitted. "There's definitely something wrong. He hasn't eaten in days."

Cameron sighed, handing his friend a shovel. "I can't afford a new horse right now." He leaned on the split-rail fence overlooking the paddock. It was still too cold for the animals to be out for very long at a time, and Cameron didn't like to leave them unsupervised during those periods, so he and Adam had bundled up in warm coats and were watching the horses trudge through the snow as they worked on clearing a path along the front of the paddock.

The ill one in question was clearly eager to get back to the stable. He'd stood unmoving near the door since he'd been let out, not even attempting to walk around with the others. The point of all this was for the horses to get some exercise, but this one wasn't interested.

"I wonder if it's just the weather," Adam speculated, taking the shovel and driving it into the snow in front of him. "It's been snowing for so long. That could be affecting the animals."

"I thought of that when the goat got sick," Cameron agreed. "She's doing better now, at least."

"Well, maybe we should have a veterinarian come out and look at the horse."

"I can't afford that, either," Cameron said. Looking through the books yesterday had confirmed his worst fears. His payments on the ranch were long overdue, and he knew the bank wasn't going to tolerate it much longer. "If I'm not careful, I'm going to lose this place altogether."

"Did someone from the bank come by again?" Adam asked.

"No one has been here. But they will," Cameron said. He began to dig himself, tossing the snow off to the side. "You know they're not going to let my debt stand." He sighed, gazing out over the horse paddock. "I really thought I'd have this place paid off by now. I thought I would have gotten on my feet by now."

"Cut my pay if it will help," Adam suggested.

"I can't do that. I barely pay you as it is." Taking advantage of their friendship was a constant worry for Cameron. He was deeply grateful to Adam for coming to work as his foreman after the fire, and for doing it at such a low rate. Adam had always insisted that Cameron was the one doing him a favor, that he was going to need a new place to live and work since his own home had been taken in the fire, too. But Cameron knew perfectly well that Adam could have resumed work at the town's butcher shop, where he'd worked the counter. It hadn't paid a tremendous amount, but it had paid more than what he was getting from Cameron these days. Adam had come out here out of friendship, not necessity, and Cameron was determined to reward that with decent pay… just as soon as he was able.

The two men dug without speaking for a while, easing their way forward along the path they were creating. The strain to Cameron's muscles was satisfying after so much time stuck in the house.

"You know, I ran into Russell Duvall in town yesterday," Adam said. "Speaking of money."

Cameron groaned and drove his shovel into the newly cleared ground, turning to face his friend. "What did he want?"

"You can guess, I'm sure. He wants to know when you're going to sell."

"I'm not selling." Cameron kicked one of the fence posts. "I hope you told him that."

"I don't know what good me telling him is going to do. He's been told half a dozen times. You know he won't give up. He's convinced there's more gold here." Adam tested a frozen mound of snow with his shovel, as if there might be gold in the powder.

"Just because a few nuggets were found down in the river before I even bought the place." Cameron knew about that, of course. It had been in the surveyor's report when he had purchased the land. "There is absolutely no reason to believe there's any more than what's already been found. A man like Duvall will tear this land apart looking for something that isn't there. I'm never going to let him get his hands on my ranch."

"Well, look, I know you don't want to," Adam agreed. "I only bring it up because, with the bank on your case about the debts, if you *had* to sell…"

"Oh, not you, too!" Cameron turned his back.

Adam put a hand on his shoulder. "I'm not saying you should. All I'm saying is that if you decided to consider it, Duvall might be a good buyer, because he believes there's gold here. You might get him to buy for a good price."

"You know perfectly well I wouldn't." Cameron started moving forward again, scooping up even bigger piles of snow.

"You know he won't give me what he thinks it's worth, no matter how much he wants it. He's the most greedy man I've ever met in my life."

"I do know. But if he thinks there's gold here, he might give you more than what the ranch is *really* worth, even if he gives you less than he *believes* it's worth."

Cameron stopped and turned a slow circle. "Adam, look at this place."

Adam mimicked his posture, looking out over the paddock.

"It's worth so much more than gold," Cameron said. His voice was hushed. "Russell Duvall's pockets aren't deep enough to pay me what this ranch is worth. Even if he was fair-minded, he never could. I won't turn this place over to him. Not ever."

"All right," Adam agreed. "I just wanted to discuss it as an option. You should consider everything."

"Well, I don't need to consider that one," Cameron said firmly. "And I don't want to discuss it any further. If you see Russell Duvall again, just ignore him. If he forces a conversation and a simple *no* isn't good enough, tell him he has to talk to me directly. He's not getting my ranch."

"All right," Adam said. "Can we talk about another option, then?"

"Please." Cameron hoped this would be an idea for raising money for their bills. He didn't relish the idea, but if they could sell a couple of the horses, that might help. Maybe Adam had an idea as to how they could get by around here with a smaller number.

"Isabelle," Adam said, leaning up against the fence rail.

Cameron frowned, looking over at his friend. He gripped his shovel in both hands, unable to make sense of what he was being asked. "What about her?"

"I think you should consider marrying her." Adam turned to face Cameron head-on and fixed him with a steady gaze.

"Oh, you're really full of ideas today!" Cameron rolled his eyes. He turned and began to move snow vigorously, almost aggressively.

"How is it going between you?" Adam asked, trailing behind him. "Is she settling in better? Are you getting used to having her here?"

"She's good company." He was surprised to hear himself admit it, and he didn't want to share too many details. He didn't want to let his friend know that he'd had a wonderful conversation with Isabelle just yesterday. He couldn't tell Adam how he'd held baby Abby in his arms, fed her, and been so forcibly reminded of his own son that once he'd left the kitchen he'd fled to the study and locked himself in so she wouldn't see the emotion on his face. He couldn't tell Adam how it had choked him and made him wonder if he had forgotten how to breathe.

He focused on Isabelle instead. "She's a good woman," he said gruffly. "A good worker. Now that the baby is a bit more settled, things are going well."

"So you're going to let her stay?"

Cameron hesitated.

The answer to the question was yes. He had already made up his mind. But how to justify it? Was there a way to do that without confessing to Adam that he was beginning to feel things he'd never expected or wanted to feel again?

"I'm thinking about it," he said. "She's good around the house."

"And beautiful," Adam said.

Cameron grunted, unable to voice disagreement with that but not willing to admit that he had noticed it, either.

"You can say it," Adam said. "She's very pretty. And she's sweet, from what I've seen of her. You know, you really couldn't do better for a wife. I know you're still hurting from what happened with Ruth and Philip…"

"Don't." Cameron turned his back on his friend, his shoulders tensing. Adam must know how painful it was to hear those names.

"All I'm saying is that she might be the right choice to help you move forward. You can't go into hiding for the rest of your life, you know," Adam said. "You need to start to move on. You owe yourself that. And she might be the right choice to do it with."

"Moving on is one thing," Cameron said. "But I'm not interested in marriage. You know that."

"You might have to think about it, if you really are going to keep her here," Adam said.

"I don't see why I would."

"Because she's an unmarried woman with a baby, that's why," Adam said. "And she's living in your house. Do you know what that looks like?"

"Have you ever known me to care what anything looks like?" Cameron jammed his shovel into the snow.

"I know. Of course you don't care. But I'm not talking about how it looks for *you*," Adam said. "I'm talking about her. She's going to go out into town more and more the longer she's here. She's going to start attending church. And then what happens?"

"She's already met Edith Calloway. They're getting along just great."

"Edith Calloway is a saint in human form," Adam said dryly. "She's not the one you have to worry about, and you know it. What about the other women at that church? You don't think there'll be gossip when people see her with a baby? When they find out she's living here with you, and that she isn't married? I know you don't want a wife, Cameron, but if you're going to have her here, this is something you should think about. You could give her dignity by marrying her." Adam's voice softened. He took a step closer to Cameron. "She deserves that, doesn't she? You said she was a good woman."

The wind howled, as if in agreement that Cameron was letting Isabelle down.

Cameron gritted his teeth. "I can't marry her for that reason," he said.

"I don't see why not."

"Drop it." He scowled, and Adam stepped back and inclined his head, obviously sensing that he'd pushed this as far as he could. He began to dig again, and Cameron refocused his energy on the snow.

The two men worked in silence for a moment. Cameron corralled his anger at Adam's overreach—his friend had only been trying to help—and cast about for a new topic. "Did I tell you Sheriff Grayson was out here this morning?"

"You didn't, but I saw him while I was checking on the chickens," Adam said. "I would have come over to say hello, but he would have been gone by the time I made it through the snow. What did he want?"

"He offered me a loan to help fend off the bank."

"Well, tell me you took it." Adam raised his eyebrows hopefully. "You need that right about now."

"No," Cameron said. "I'm not going to take his money. I can't."

"You're too proud. You know, he probably heard Duvall was sniffing around," Adam said. He started back in the direction of the stables, forcing Cameron to walk alongside him in order to keep up the conversation. "He's probably trying to help make sure the ranch doesn't fall into his hands. No one likes that man. He's a foul creep."

"Well, be that as it may, if I can't afford to keep my own ranch then I can't afford to own it," Cameron said. "I'm not going to let Sheriff Grayson bail me out on this one."

Adam sighed and stopped digging. "You should learn to accept people's help. You know how much he admired both you and Ruth. And he helped Eloise make the arrangements for you to have a new wife."

"Did he?" Cameron froze halfway through digging, a pile of snow on the end of his shovel. He hadn't known that. He glanced at Adam and saw no trace of deception in his friend's face. "Why would he do that?"

"He wants to help you. Everyone wants to help you. You should try accepting it."

"I accept your help, don't I?" Cameron countered, lifting an eyebrow. He gestured to the long path they had just dug out. It was now possible to walk the length of the paddock without getting snow in one's boots.

"Barely. You don't accept my advice, that's for sure." A smile quirked Adam's lips.

"I take some of it. When I think you're right, I do." He handed his shovel to his friend. "Let's get these horses inside before they freeze. That's enough exercise for today. Honestly, I think we're at risk of freezing ourselves if we hang around out here for too much longer."

He vaulted over the fence and walked toward the horses before his friend could protest, meaning to shepherd them back toward the stable. They needed no encouragement. The moment they saw him coming, they began to move in the appropriate direction, clearly aware of what they were being asked to do and all too eager to comply with it.

Adam had gone to the stable and opened the door to put the shovels away. The horses, who would ordinarily have required a lot of herding and coaxing to bring inside, huddled by the door to get as close as possible to the relative warmth. Adam and Cameron went to them one by one and led them to their stalls.

"Are we grooming them?" Adam asked once the last horse had been put away.

"Just enough to get the worst of the snow off, so they won't be too cold," Cameron responded. "Honestly, I can take care of it. You can go on in. You're a lot farther from your house than I am, and I don't want you to get too cold or have to go back after dark."

Adam stayed, of course. He worked side by side with Cameron and didn't take his eyes off of him the whole time.

He thinks I'm going to say something else about Isabelle. Cameron couldn't have explained how he was so sure of that, but he was. Somehow, he just knew. That was what Adam was really interested in. Though the subject seemed to be closed for now, he had known Adam long enough to know his friend would bring it up again, and that it would continue to come up until Adam heard an answer he liked.

Best of luck to him. I may like Isabelle now—I may like her a little too much—but I can't see how it's a good idea to marry her just for the sake of public appearances. It would give her too much hope for what our relationship might grow to be. And I don't want to deceive her.

I'll never be able to offer her a marriage. I'll never be able to give that to anyone again. I might be able to give her a home, but truly, that is the only thing this can ever be.

He turned his back to Adam and forced himself to focus on his work.

No matter what anyone thought—Adam, Eloise, anyone in town—he was determined not to give in.

Chapter Thirteen

It's only three weeks until Christmas.

The realization shocked Isabelle. She had been so busy, so preoccupied since coming to Wintervale that the last three weeks had flown by. She couldn't believe that was how much time it had been since she'd stepped off that train and onto the platform… and into this new life.

Things were going well. Better, in fact, than she would have anticipated. It was still so surprising to be able to think that, but it was the truth. Cameron regularly milked the goat for her now, and there was always food for Abby. Sometimes he even sat with her and gave her a bottle. It had begun to seem like a good decision to come here, in spite of Isabelle's initial reservations.

She had also kept up her end of the bargain, and she knew it. The house was in better shape than it had been in years, according to Eloise. Isabelle picked something new to tidy every morning and she had established a routine of sweeping, dusting, and organizing that kept everything in good order.

But now Christmas was getting close, and in all the upheaval, she had forgotten all about it.

It hollowed her to think of that. Christmas had always been her favorite time of year. It had meant extra work at the tailor shop, but she'd relished the long hours. She recalled sitting by candlelight, tending to the orders of her customers, usually with Vivienne beside her, looking out the storefront window at the snow as it started to accumulate on the street outside and thinking about the coming holiday.

Church had always been the biggest part of the day for her. Sitting with her fellow congregants on Christmas morning, the feeling of awe and gratitude a service always gave her would be more overpowering than it was on any other day of the year. It would take root in her heart and blossom outward, giving her optimism for the year ahead, refreshing and strengthening her faith.

But she also enjoyed the trappings of the holiday. She loved to choose gifts for her loved ones. She relished decorating. It was a pang to her heart that she wouldn't be picking out a present to give to Vivienne this year, that she wouldn't be hanging the garlands in the tailor shop. Everything had changed so much.

Well, that doesn't mean I can't hold on to my traditions. I can still get into the Christmas spirit this year. In fact, maybe I have more responsibility than ever to do just that. After all, this is Abby's first Christmas.

Bolstered by that thought, she made a decision—she would decorate the house for Christmas. Cameron had let her know early in the morning that he would be in town for hours. He needed to speak with the sheriff, he told her, and couldn't take her with him this time. She hadn't minded being left to her own devices. With the snow still coming down, the house had begun to feel cozy. It wrapped around her, insulating her like a warm hug from the hostile weather outside.

Now there was an additional benefit to Cameron's absence, because it would allow her the opportunity she needed to get the decorating done. She would have felt shy about starting to do it right in front of him, but once he saw it he would love it.

The attic would be the right place to begin. When she had gone through the boxes she'd found up there, she had left many of them untouched—the ones that were shoved far under the eaves, and would therefore be the most difficult to get out. But those were the ones that would contain whatever holiday decorations Cameron had. He'd have packed them away after last year.

She climbed into the attic. The ceiling was low here. She could only stand upright in the very center of the space, and she doubted Cameron would be able to stand upright anywhere at all. She had to hunch over and walk in an undignified squat to reach the boxes she wanted. She dragged a few of them into the center of the room and paused to listen for Abby, afraid she might have woken her from her nap.

There was no sound.

Isabelle sat down on the floorboards and opened the first box, hoping to get lucky right away so that she wouldn't have to stay up here too long.

For a moment, she wasn't sure what she was looking at. She reached in and took it out. It dangled from her hand. Her eyes focused on a carved wooden duck.

A mobile. For a baby.

For his baby.

It was handmade. That was immediately obvious by the way the duck had been carved. She turned it in her hands and admired the other animals. There was a horse, and a dog, and a pig... they were imperfect, but they were beautiful, shaped by the loving hands of a father.

He made this for his son.

She set the mobile aside reverently, her heart racing. Her breath was coming unevenly now. Cameron would not want her to be looking at these things. But she hadn't done it on purpose, and now that she had found this box, there was little point in turning back. She reached in and pulled out a silver rattle, the sort no baby could ever actually play with but that a parent might keep as a memento of a child's birth. She turned it in her hand, guessing at what she might find, and was rewarded by an engraving:

Philip Allen Mercer

Tears filled her eyes. What a tragic loss. She had never guessed that Cameron might still have all these things. She pulled out a tiny set of booties and held them up, heart aching at the realization that they were smaller than the ones Abby wore. Had his baby been that young?

With a sigh, she put the booties back and looked around the attic. There were too many boxes here, and who was to say which ones might contain memories like this? This was private. She shouldn't be looking at these things without Cameron present. He probably wouldn't want her looking at them at all.

She wouldn't abandon her idea of decorating the house. Christmas needed to be celebrated. But she would leave the boxes in the attic alone.

Getting to her feet, she dusted off her skirts. A resolve filled her. Abby would be napping for at least another hour. In that time, there was plenty a person could do...

***

Forty-five minutes later, a surge of satisfaction filled Isabelle as she stood back and admired her work.

It hadn't taken very long out in the cold to collect what she needed. She had loaded her arms with fallen evergreen branches and filled a basket with pinecones. Once inside, she had woven it all into garlands and wreaths. Her stomach had knotted as she'd worked, recalling this time last year and how she had sat doing this very thing with Vivienne, neither of them knowing that it was Vivienne's last Christmas.

Not that I would have wanted to know that. How could we have enjoyed our time together if I had?

It was certainly festive in here now. The familiar smell of pine filled the room. A garland was draped over the mantle, and wreaths hung on every wall. It was impossible to stand in this room and ignore the fact that Christmas was coming. Isabelle's heart radiated with joy at the thought. Her first Christmas with Abby... that was something to be excited about.

The kitchen door banged shut, and Isabelle's heart beat faster. Cameron was home. "Come in here," she called out to him, not raising her voice too loudly for fear of waking Abby.

His footsteps moved in her direction, and she had time to marvel at the fact that she had called him to her knowing that he would come. If someone had told her that was the way things would be between the two of them when she had first arrived here, she wouldn't have been able to believe it. Everything had changed for the better.

He stepped into the room and she turned to face him, beaming. "What do you think?" she asked. "I've been decorating for Christmas. It looks festive, doesn't it?"

Cameron didn't answer. He turned in a slow circle, taking in the room.

Isabelle grew nervous. She had imagined that he would break into a smile upon seeing this, but instead he was frowning slightly. Was it possible he didn't approve of her makeshift decorations?

"I didn't know whether you had anything you usually put up for Christmas," she said, aware that her words were coming much more quickly than was normal, but unable to slow herself down. She was tumbling downhill. "If you have your own decorations we can add them in, of course. I just wanted to do something, since the season is upon us..."

He turned to face her. His jaw was tight, his eyes narrowed. "No," he said. "I don't have Christmas decorations."

"Oh. Well... do you like what I did?"

"I want you to take all this down." His words were clipped. "Put it all outside, where it belongs."

She didn't understand. "You mean you want me to decorate the outside of the house? And not the inside?" That was discouraging, to say the least. If all the decorations were outside, they wouldn't see them.

"I don't want Christmas things all over my house," Cameron said sharply. "Take them down."

"But... surely we both want things to be festive leading up to the day itself," she protested. "Or do you have different traditions? What do you do for Christmas?"

"I don't do anything," he said. "I don't celebrate."

"You don't celebrate *Christmas*?" He couldn't have shocked her—hurt her—any more if he had slapped her across the face.

He sighed. "Isabelle, you know I don't attend church. We've discussed it."

"I know," she said, hating the way her voice shook and betrayed her emotion. "But... not even Christmas? I knew you wouldn't want to attend the church service, but I was sure we'd have a celebration here."

"I don't see the point of it," Cameron said tightly. He turned away from her and started for the door.

Anger spiked through Isabelle. She had been so much more than patient with Cameron. She had been so understanding. When he had told her he didn't want her here, when he had told her he wouldn't take her to church, when he'd gotten angry with her for going through the things in the attic... she had been kind. She had understood. He was grieving.

But this was too much. Yes, he had suffered, but he couldn't ask her to give up Christmas.

He especially couldn't ask her to give up Abby's first Christmas.

"Cameron, I know that... faith isn't part of your life." She stepped closer to him to discourage him from walking away. It still pained her to acknowledge that. This man was the closest person to her, apart from Abby. He was helping her, in many ways, to raise Abby. There were days when the gratitude she felt for his presence in her life overwhelmed her. But there were also days when she wondered how she'd come to feel so attached to someone so different from herself.

"You're right," Cameron said. "Faith isn't a part of my life."

"But Christmas... it's about joy. Togetherness." She almost said the word *family*, but she caught herself just in time, heat rising to her cheeks at the near slip. Of course the idea of celebrating family wasn't going to convince him of anything. "Surely you believe in those things?" she pressed on past her near-blunder. "Even if God isn't a part of your life, don't you want to celebrate the season with the people who mean something to you?"

"It's a day I could be working," he said. "I don't see it as anything more than that, and I don't see a reason to take the time away from more important things."

His jaw clenched briefly as he spoke, and he wouldn't meet her eyes.

"*Working*?" She repeated in disbelief. "Cameron—look at me."

A beat. He turned to face her, but he didn't meet her eyes.

"You're choosing work over Christmas?"

"I don't care about Christmas." It was nearly a bark.

"But *I do*. This means something to me, Cameron! It's the most beautiful, sacred time of year to me, and you *can't* take it away from me just because you're not interested!" Heat rose to her face. Standing up to him like this was like stepping outside without a coat—his coldness penetrated to her bones.

He looked up at her, his eyes as hard as diamonds. "This is my house," he growled. "I've taken you in. I've cared for you, and for the baby. I've given you a place to sleep and food to eat. You ought to be grateful."

Guilt welled within her, sickening and disorienting, but not enough to quell the anger. "I *am* grateful," she insisted. "I've expressed that. I haven't taken it for granted. I shouldn't have to give up Christmas because you've already shown me kindness."

"This is my house. We do not celebrate Christmas in my house." He turned his back on her again.

"But—"

"No. That's final."

A sick grief filled her. She understood that she wasn't going to win this argument. "I'll take everything down," she said, her voice soft and sad, only a trace of the bitterness she still felt leaking through.

He inclined his head briefly. "Good."

There was a hesitation, a pregnant pause during which Isabelle was sure one of them would say something more. But neither of them did.

Finally, Cameron gave a nod, as if to signal that he had gotten what he wanted from their exchange, and moved toward the door. She watched him go, heart aching with sadness. This had gone so much differently than she'd hoped it would.

How could they not celebrate Christmas? The day that meant more to her than any other in the year, and now it was just going to be erased as if it had never existed. Treated like just another day.

I can still mark the day. It's not as if he's insisting that I ignore Christmas altogether—and even if he was, I don't think I would do it. Christmas can be special to me. I can read from the Gospel. I can give a gift to Abby. Maybe I can put one of these wreaths up in our room, where Cameron won't have to see it. It doesn't have to pass unremarked.

And it wouldn't. Even so, the thought of a Christmas spent in her room, reading from her Bible, with no one to so much as wish her a good holiday... it was hollow. It wouldn't be what she had always thought of when she pictured Christmas, that was for sure.

It would be lonely and sad, and that wasn't what Christmas was supposed to be.

She had been looking forward to it. To sharing this holiday with the new person in her life. The new *people* in her life, because this was Abby's first Christmas, too.

I have to make sure I create traditions for her. Even in this household, where Christmas is ignored, I need to find a way to bring the joy of the holiday to Abby. If ever I did anything for her, I need to do that. Abby has to know the joy of Christmas.

Chapter Fourteen

"Isabelle! You made it!"

Isabelle's heart lifted as Edith came hurrying over to greet her and Eloise. After yesterday's disagreement with Cameron, she'd had mixed feelings about coming to church today. It had seemed a little like rubbing his nose in the fact that she was going to embrace her faith after he had made it so abundantly clear that was not a part of his own life. Almost as if she was doing it to spite him.

But she wasn't going to abandon her faith. Not for anyone.

Being a part of the community at St. Matthew's was important to her. This would be her first time attending a Sunday service since she had come to Wintervale. The weather had cleared enough to allow her to make the journey with Eloise, and who knew whether that would be true next Sunday? She wasn't going to miss out on the opportunity that had been set before her.

Eloise had offered to hold Abby, and Isabelle had gratefully taken her up on it. Having her hands free left her able to engage with her surroundings. She had been able to admire the massive wreath someone had hung on the heavy oak door of the church, to look closely at the way the branches were woven together. Whoever had done it had used the same technique Isabelle herself would have used, but they were clearly even more experienced than she was at the craft. She resolved to find out who was responsible. If she couldn't decorate her own home, perhaps she could contribute some decorations to the church.

When they stepped inside, though, she saw that wasn't needed. The small room was overflowing with seasonal decorations. Garlands adorned the walls. Holly had been tied to the ends of the pews. A nativity had been set up at the front of the room, one of the largest and most ornate Isabelle had ever seen, and she'd stood admiring it until a voice from behind had cut into her thoughts.

"Do you like it?"

"It's beautiful," she said, turning to find herself face to face with a man who wore a pastor's robes. He was clean-shaven and his silver hair was neatly trimmed, and the smile on his face spoke of welcome. "You must be Edith's husband."

"Pastor John," he said. "Welcome to St. Matthew's. Edith has told me all about you, Miss Heart. We're so glad to see you here this week. It's a gift to have you join the congregation." He looked out over the assembled group—women talking in small clusters with broad smiles on their faces, young children running around with fathers and mothers in pursuit. Everyone was smiling. Everyone was *happy*.

This is the most welcoming environment I've seen in a long time.

"I'm grateful to be here," Isabelle agreed. "The nativity is beautiful."

"It was carved by my father, actually," Pastor John told her.

"I wouldn't have guessed it was so old. It's in remarkably good shape," she said.

"We take good care of it. It means a lot. As you can see, we don't have many fancy things here at St. Matthew's. But what we do have, we treat with great care." He looked over her shoulder. "Ah—this must be the baby I've heard so much about."

Eloise had come up behind her, breaking off from a conversation with a few other women. Isabelle turned, smiling, and put a hand on Abby's back. "This is Abby," she agreed.

"What a beautiful baby," Pastor John admired. He held out a hand. "May I?"

Eloise looked to Isabelle for permission.

Isabelle smiled. "Of course."

The pastor laid a hand on Abby's head and murmured a soft blessing, then tapped her nose gently. Abby laughed, and the sound was a shot of joy to Isabelle's heart.

Pastor John turned back to Isabelle. "You took her in after her mother died?"

"That's right," Isabelle said.

"Well, she's blessed to have you," Pastor John said, smiling at both of them. "I look forward to getting to know you both a little better in the days to come." He turned and moved toward another group of parishioners to welcome them.

"You didn't want to let me ride with you, Eloise?" A new voice spoke up. It was Adam, striding over to join them, a broad smile on his face. He glanced down as a boy of about ten barreled into his legs, looked up in only mild surprise, then turned and continued running. Adam came to a halt beside their group.

"I didn't know you were going to come," Eloise told Adam. "You don't always."

"When I don't come to church, it's because your brother needs me on the ranch," Adam said. "He doesn't really need me today, though he would probably say that he does. The truth is that I think he's better served by being on his own today. He's in a bit of a temper."

"That's my fault." Guilt rose in Isabelle like a tide as she recalled the argument she and Cameron had been through.

"Of course it isn't," Eloise said. "You aren't responsible for my brother's moods, Isabelle. You ought to know that. He was like this before you ever arrived in Wintervale. Something might send him into a spiral of unhappiness at any moment. And it was always something innocuous."

"I agree completely," Adam said. "In fact, he seems more like his old self since Isabelle arrived. Wouldn't you say so, Eloise?"

"I'd say he ought to just marry her as we planned from the start," Eloise said. "When I arranged for a mail-order bride, I knew it was going to be a gamble, but she's lovely. I don't know how we could have done any better."

"Yes, you did get lucky," Adam agreed.

"And I recall you telling me that we shouldn't even try," Eloise said. There was a teasing note to her voice, and Isabelle could tell that this was a conversation that had been had many times before. "You said that he wouldn't be able to accept anyone new into his life and that he would be angry with us for even making the effort. That it wouldn't be worth it."

"Well, I wasn't wrong," Adam defended himself. "He was angry with us."

The two of them were smiling at one another. There was affection between them, Isabelle realized. She had never seen them together before today. She hadn't realized that they were fond of one another in this way. Now, she found herself wondering just how serious things were between them. This looked as though it went beyond mere camaraderie. The way they were smiling at each other, the way their bodies oriented toward one another even as they stood in a group…

There's love here. I don't know if they've admitted it to one another, but I can see it.

It made her heart ache. How beautiful it would be to find love! Even when she had believed that she was coming to Wintervale for marriage, though, she had never imagined that love would be a part of it. No one could look at her in that way. Every time she looked in the mirror while she was getting dressed, all she could see were the scars that still marked her body. Any man who ever looked at her would see the same thing.

And even if a man could accept me with these scars, I know he would never see me as beautiful. He would never be able to look at me and just see me. *He would see an unfortunate, scarred woman. I might have his pity, but I wouldn't have his love.*

She didn't want that. She'd made that decision a long time ago.

Adam turned to her, obviously unaware of any of the thoughts that had been roiling within her. "How are things back at the ranch?" he asked. "It seems to me that you've been settling in well."

"Things are good." She hesitated. "I wasn't expecting to learn that Cameron doesn't celebrate Christmas, though. I'm so glad to see the decorations here at the church, because I thought I wasn't going to be able to have any signs of the holiday this year."

"There will be a Christmas service, of course," Eloise assured her. "I know Cameron won't be here, but I hope you will."

"I wouldn't miss it," she said. "It might be the only celebration I get to have."

Adam's mouth twisted sympathetically. "Cameron hasn't celebrated a Christmas in four years," he murmured. "Not since Ruth died."

Grief settled in Isabelle's heart, weighty and immobile. "I thought it might be something like that," she said. "He must have really loved her."

"Well, he did. But more than that, I think he's living out of fear now," Adam said softly. "I think he's too afraid to allow himself to be happy, in case it gets ripped away from him again. He used to love Christmas. It was such a joyful time of year for him. He'd be out chopping down a tree to decorate the moment the first snow fell. But nowadays, all he wants to do is lose himself in work. He dislikes Christmas more than any other time because it reminds him of the pain he's been through."

Isabelle nodded. It made sense. It also spurred the guilt she had been trying to suppress. She really shouldn't have tried to surprise him with decorations the way she had. Of course it had affected him. *How would I have felt if someone had done something that reminded me of Vivienne and sprung it on me as a surprise?*

But on the other hand, she was reminded of Vivienne every day. Every time she looked at Abby it was a reminder. She didn't *want* to forget about her friend. One of the most appealing things about the holiday had been the opportunity to reminisce about what it had been like to celebrate with the loved ones she'd lost. She couldn't believe Cameron didn't want that.

The group filed slowly over to the pews to take their seats for the service. Eloise and Adam were still side by side, and when they sat down, Adam was immediately to Eloise's right. The two of them bent their heads together, still talking about something, though it was impossible to make out their words.

How nice it must be to love someone.

With her scars, Isabelle could never take that kind of risk. She could never open up to someone. No one would ever see her as an object of romance in that way, so it was better—safer—not to have any expectations.

She sat on Eloise's other side and went through the soothing, familiar ritual of the church service, but her mind was in such a tangle that she didn't retain any of what was said. She couldn't recall, as they walked out afterward, what the sermon had been about. Nothing had stayed with her.

"Did you have a nice time?" Eloise asked her.

"I did," Isabelle said, and it was true. "It was good to meet the pastor. Are we going to offer Adam a ride home?"

"He has to go back on the horse he brought to town," Eloise pointed out.

"Well, I wouldn't mind if he rode with us next time. Just for the record," Isabelle said with a smile. "I didn't realize the two of you were that close."

Eloise blushed. "We've known each other for a long time."

"I'm sure you have." Isabelle couldn't keep the smile off her face as they climbed into the wagon to begin the journey home.

As the wheels started to turn and she looked over her shoulder at the church behind them, she was gripped with a tight, crushing sadness she hadn't expected.

It was all too much. The grief over the fact that she would never find love was something she had almost learned to live with, but sometimes, like today, she came face to face with something that made her remember it in a visceral way. She wasn't an unattractive person, and she knew that she was kind. If it hadn't been for that one moment, that accident when the hot oil had spilled on her body and left her scarred, she would have been free to dream of a future in which someone might see her and fall in love. But in the space of a single moment, when the oil had spilled, that dream had been destroyed. Crushed before she had even been old enough to understand what dreaming was.

And now the man I thought was going to marry me, to at least give me the shape of a happy life, even though I wouldn't have the soul of it… he doesn't want me either. He could have seen past the way I look, because we were never going to have that kind of marriage. But he can't see past his own scars, and I can't fault him for that.

She was stuck here—stuck with a man who could never give her the life she had dreamed of, stuck with a man who couldn't celebrate Christmas because the potential for joy had been sucked out of him by the tragedy of loss.

All these losses. All this grief.

It's too much. I don't know how we're supposed to carry these things around.

In that moment, without effort or conscious thought, a familiar passage sprang into her mind.

So do not fear, for I am with you; do not be dismayed, for I am your God.

The book of Isaiah, chapter 61, verse 3. It was one that had always stuck in her mind, although she hadn't read Isaiah that many times. It was God himself reaching off the page to speak to her directly, to remind her in her darkest moments that he was always with her.

That was still true now. Even though it was difficult to be here, even though everything seemed to be going wrong, God was here. God was watching, and He had a plan.

Isabelle would just have to have faith.

Chapter Fifteen

The living room had been returned to its undecorated state. Isabelle hadn't wasted a moment.

I ought to be happy about that.

Instead, Cameron couldn't help the knot of guilt that had tied itself around his stomach, robbing him of his appetite and making it difficult to even look at Isabelle as he sat on the settee, staring into the fire, only occasionally glancing over in her direction.

She hadn't done anything wrong. She hadn't known how seeing those things would affect him. He had walked into the room, smelled the pine, and been thrown into the past, as if he could hear Ruth's laughter in the air, as if she might walk into the room at any moment. It had been unbearable… but there was no way she would have known that.

She sat in a chair on the far side of the room, a handkerchief in her hand. She was embroidering the edge. He had seen one she'd done earlier—she had tucked it into his pocket, where he'd found it while he was working out in the stable. He couldn't even be angry at the forwardness of the gesture, because the work was so beautiful. Lavender thread formed the shape of delicate flowers around the border of the cloth. Seeing it had reminded him of the fact that she had come from a tailor shop. No wonder she was so talented with a needle and thread.

Abby lay on a folded blanket at Isabelle's feet, her hands waving in the air, legs kicking. Cameron was transfixed by her.

Though he didn't know exactly how old she was, she was certainly young enough that this would be her first Christmas.

And I'm ruining it, because I can't get over my past.

He loathed himself for that. It was selfish.

He looked at the way the candlelight flickered on her face, making her lashes look even longer than they ordinarily did, highlighting her prominent cheekbones and the pink color there. She was so beautiful, and so kind. It made him wish he wasn't so hardened, that he could lower his guard enough to let her in.

Adam is right. She's the sort of woman I could have married, if I was open to having those feelings again for anybody. In another set of circumstances, we might have been close.

He found himself yearning for that. For a world in which she looked over at him and smiled, or even sat beside him while she worked. A world in which they could be fond of one another instead of grating on each other.

Maybe there's something I can do about it.

He cleared his throat.

She looked up. "Is everything all right?"

"I've been thinking," he said. "About those garlands and things of yours."

She tensed visibly.

She's afraid I'm going to be angry. The thought made his gut twist. That he had presented himself to her as someone to fear was a terrible feeling. He didn't want her to be frightened of him, or of his responses.

So he hurried onward. "I was thinking that, if it really means that much to you, you can put them back up," he said, avoiding eye contact. She couldn't be allowed to see his guilt at his initial reaction to what she had done, or she would turn this offer down. She was too selfless for her own good.

"I... are you sure?" Isabelle asked, biting her lip. "I don't want us to have another argument about this. Christmas means the world to me, but if you're just going to change your mind..."

He shook his head, raking a hand through his hair. He was going to have to tell her everything or she wouldn't trust him. "My last time celebrating Christmas was with my wife and son." Every word pulled at his heart, making him ache, but he needed to say it. He needed to confide in her, because she deserved to understand this. "Philip was only a few weeks old at the time, and everything felt so magical. So full of possibility. The next Christmas..." He paused, unable to name what had happened in the interval.

But he didn't need to. Isabelle nodded her understanding. "Of course it would be impossible for you to celebrate that year."

"Not impossible," he countered. "You lost your friend. Abby's mother. And you're ready to celebrate Christmas."

"It's different," she told him softly. She rose slowly to her feet, crossed the room, and sat down beside him, leaving about a foot of space between them. "I know it's different, Cameron. I didn't lose my child." She glanced at Abby. "I can't even imagine what you went through. How painful it must have been for you."

He drew a deep breath. "Ruth loved Christmas," he said, needing to continue now that he had finally taken the lid off the box containing this agony. "It was her favorite day of the year. She prepared a big meal for us that day. We didn't do much in the way of gifts, and I remember the snow was too deep for us to get out of the house for church. But I'd carved a mobile for Philip, and we hung it over his bed. We planned for our future. For his future. I had no way of knowing that in just a few weeks, everything would be gone. And now, every time I think of Christmas, I think about what came after. The way everything was stolen away from me in the blink of an eye. It's too much."

"Then we shouldn't put the decorations back up." She reached out and rested her hand gently on top of his. "Not if it's going to bring up all those painful memories for you, Cameron."

He shook his head. "You don't heal if you leave the bullet in the wound," he pointed out. "Maybe I need to be around all those things, if only to prove to myself that I can do it. Maybe I need to see that Christmas can be celebrated without anything being lost. I need to stop being afraid of the scent of pine. And I can't ruin your holiday, Isabelle… or Abby's. She deserves to have Christmas in her life too. It's for her that I'm telling you to go ahead."

Isabelle nodded. "For her sake, I'll accept," she said. "Because you're right. She does deserve that. I want to give her that. That's one of the reasons it meant so much to me to decorate the house the way I did. I want to show Abby the joy of the holiday. Even though I know she's too young to remember, I feel as if these things do leave an impression on children. I think some part of her will register the way we celebrate and record it, and it will feel familiar to her next year, even if she doesn't have any clear memories of it."

On the floor, Abby cooed happily as if she understood what they were discussing.

"She really doesn't look anything like you," Cameron said, watching as Abby brought a hand to her mouth and sucked her finger.

"No, I know she doesn't," Isabelle agreed. "She's the image of her mother. I think sometimes about what it will be like when she's grown up. I'm sure it'll be like having Vivienne back here with me. She'll go on looking just like her."

"What was she like?" Cameron asked, turning back to face Isabelle. "Vivienne, I mean."

"She was lovely." Isabelle's voice was soft and far away. Her head cocked to the side and her hands knitted together. "She was the best friend I ever had. The best friend anyone ever could have wanted. After my parents died, I would have been alone in the world if not for her, but she stayed by my side and became my family. In every way that matters, she was a sister to me."

"She sounds wonderful," Cameron said. *I should have asked her these questions sooner. I thought she wouldn't want to talk about someone she had lost. But she isn't like me. She wants to remember.*

"Her family didn't think so," Isabelle said bitterly, her eyes refocusing. Her knuckles whitened with tension. "When they learned she was pregnant, they wanted nothing more than to erase her from their lives because she was unmarried. They were ashamed of her. They disowned her and turned her out into the world on her own."

"And you took her in?" Cameron leaned slightly closer to her.

"Of course I did. Any friend would have done the same. She would have done it for me," Isabelle said, eyebrows furrowing.

"Don't sell yourself short. You might believe anyone would have done what you did, but that doesn't change the impact it had for her," Cameron said. "If it hadn't been for your kindness, Isabelle, she would have been alone in the world."

"If it hadn't been for her kindness, *I* would have been alone in the world." Isabelle's voice broke. Her head dropped.

Cameron wanted to take her in his arms. The desire shocked him to his core. He fisted his hands to restrain himself. That was a line he couldn't afford to cross. "It sounds like the two of you were the friends each other needed," he said.

"I think we were," Isabelle whispered, looking up through her long lashes. "I hope I was."

"You took her in," Cameron said. "And then you took her child in. You upended your life to look after that baby."

"How could I have done anything else?" Isabelle looked up at him. The way tears gathered in her blue eyes reminded him of spring rain. "Her family would never have taken the baby. Abby had nowhere else to go. And she's as good as family to me. She always has been."

"Of course. All I mean to say is that it was incredibly brave of you," Cameron told her. "You let something like that divert your whole life when you didn't have to. You had no plan for raising a baby. You couldn't have known what would happen."

"Even now, I don't know what will happen." Isabelle's tears spilled over and traced their way down her cheeks. "You know how I worry. Every day I worry about being enough for her. About whether I'm going to be a good mother, and whether I'll be able to provide everything she needs. I don't have the answers to those questions."

"I don't think any parent does," Cameron said softly. He moved closer to her on the settee. He had intended to keep his hands to himself, but something about her tears undid him. He lifted a hand to cup her cheek and brushed one of them away, wondering if she would shake him off.

She didn't. She leaned into his touch and closed her eyes, taking comfort from him.

A thrill of excitement shot through Cameron. To be this close to her, to be touching her like this, was terrifying, and yet he couldn't bring himself to stop.

"You're the bravest woman I've ever known," he told her, and it was the truth. "I couldn't have done what you did. And the fear you face in raising Abby is the same thing I felt whenever I looked at my son." His heart wrenched at the words, but for the first time in his life, he could talk about this. She needed to hear it, and he had the power to share it with her.

She looked up at him. "You were afraid you wouldn't be enough?"

"He deserved the whole world," Cameron said quietly, sick with grief. "He deserved everything. I could never have given him that. I could have been a perfect father, and it wouldn't be enough for what I felt like my son deserved. And I know that's how you feel about Abby. You want her to have everything, and you can't be everything. But Isabelle… you don't have to be. Being *you* is enough. I promise you that."

She looked up, meeting his eyes.

Cameron's breath caught.

She was so beautiful.

Her features were exquisite—her full lips, lightly parted; her soft, flawless skin, the depth in her blue eyes. But it was more than that. The way she allowed herself to be vulnerable with him displayed a kind of strength he could only aspire to. He was in awe of her.

And somehow, she had gotten much too close.

He wanted to taste those lips. He wanted to feel her skin against his, the softness of her cheek, her long lashes fluttering against his face. He wanted to know the scent of her.

I can't want those things. I can't.

But the allure she held for him was too powerful to be ignored, and he was leaning in. In spite of his good sense, he was going to give in to this temptation, and he would just let it lead wherever it led…

Then Abby started to cry.

Isabelle jerked back. It was as if they had been doused with cold water, breaking the spell that had held them entranced.

She got to her feet, turning her back to him, and hurried over to pick up the baby. Cameron was left wondering what, if anything, she had been aware of between the two of them. Had the moment he'd just experienced been shared? Had she felt the pull toward him that he had felt toward her?

Or had it all been in his imagination?

I would have sworn it was a shared moment. But now that she's not right in front of me, I don't know anymore. How could I know?

That had been a mistake. He shouldn't have allowed it to happen. He had no intention of going down that road with Isabelle, so he couldn't put even one foot on the path. That would be incredibly dangerous for both of them.

He got to his feet as well. "I should leave you in peace," he said.

She didn't answer. She didn't even look at him. Had she heard his words? He hadn't spoken very loudly. Maybe she was too preoccupied with the baby.

Maybe she just doesn't want to speak to me right now.

He didn't know the answer, and he couldn't bring himself to speak again. That sliver of doubt, that hope that maybe she just hadn't heard him, was keeping him afloat.

He turned and fled to his study, closing the door firmly behind him.

How had this happened? He paced back and forth, raking a hand through his hair. He had *liked* Isabelle for quite a while. She was kind and loving, easy to get along with, stubborn only when she was fighting for something she believed in. Those were all qualities he appreciated and enjoyed about her. But there was a vast difference between enjoying her as a person and wanting to *kiss* her.

It was that story she told. The way she was there for her friend, even when it hurt her to do it. She's so brave. I could never be brave like that, and I wish I had been. I wish I could be. She's someone I'll always admire now.

That admiration had lit a spark within him. It wasn't enough anymore to look at her, to observe from a distance how lovely she was. He wouldn't be able to be around her anymore without thinking of what had just happened between them.

And it can't ever happen again.

Chapter Sixteen

"Has the goat given you anything today?"

The voice came from the doorway to the barn and Isabelle glanced over her shoulder to see Adam standing there, watching her as she milked the newly healed goat.

"Do you mind company?" he asked, and when she shook her head, he crossed the threshold and found a second milking stool in the corner. He pulled it up alongside the one she was on. "Want me to take over?" he asked, gesturing.

"It's all right," Isabelle said. "I'd like to keep going for myself, actually. I think I'm finally getting the hang of this. See? The bucket is nearly full."

"So it is," Adam observed, squinting at the bucket. "Well done. I have to admit, when you first got here you seemed so out of your depth and helpless that if you had told me you were going to learn how to milk a goat, I wouldn't have believed you."

"I wasn't helpless!" Isabelle protested, laughing.

"No, you weren't," Adam laughed. "I'm sorry. I said that carelessly. I suppose what I mean is that it was clear you didn't know anything about life on a ranch. In that respect, you *were* pretty helpless."

"Well, that much is true," Isabelle agreed. "I'd never spent any time on a ranch before coming here. I knew the man I was coming to meet was a rancher, but I had no idea what that was going to be like."

"And now look at you. Milking the goat!" He nodded approval as she successfully squeezed a steady stream of milk from the udder.

"It's surprising what a person can learn to do when they have someone depending on them," Isabelle said. "I wouldn't have thought myself capable of this either, but Abby doesn't eat unless I get the milking done."

"That's not strictly true, though." Adam shifted to a more serious tone. "You know Cameron would do it for you if it turned out you couldn't manage."

Isabelle said nothing. She bent down, pretending to struggle with her task so that she could avoid answering Adam.

The truth was, he was right. Of course he was. Cameron had demonstrated time and again that, in spite of his gruff exterior, he did care. He did want her to be happy, and he wanted Abby to be fed. If she'd struggled with the milking, he would have done it for her.

That wasn't the reason she couldn't bring herself to look at Adam right now.

Thoughts of the last conversation she'd had with Cameron had haunted her since it had happened yesterday. She had lain awake in her bed listening to Abby's even breathing and thinking about what it had been like to have his rough fingertips against her face. Remembering the strength of his hand as she'd leaned into his touch. Then, there had been that moment when the two of them had come so close together that the wild, wonderful thought of kissing him had occurred to her.

I would have done it. If Abby hadn't woken when she did and driven us apart, I would have forgotten all sense and reason.

It was madness. She had never even wanted to kiss a man before. Not a specific man, anyway. Certainly not a man to whom she wasn't married, a man who was giving her shelter through the winter but whose home she would be leaving behind as soon as the weather cleared.

She'd daydreamed about what it would be like. Even in her daydreams, she always quashed it quickly. There was no point in allowing herself to fantasize about something she could never have, and with her scars, no man would ever want to kiss her. If one did, it would be out of pity.

I won't allow myself to be pitied.

And yet, she had been so sure that there was something between them in that moment. If she hadn't known better, she would have sworn that he was thinking the same thing she was.

He couldn't have been. Even if he wasn't thinking about my scars at first, the moment he touched my face, he would have noticed them. They may not be very visible, but you can tell when you touch my face. She held herself back from reaching up and running a hand along her cheek then and there, something she often did when insecurities nipped at her. She didn't want to draw attention to the marks on her face in front of Adam.

"Do you need a hand with that?" he asked, seeing her pretense at struggling with the milking.

"It's all right." She sat upright and collected herself. "I've got it now. I was only struggling for a moment."

She resumed the milking. There was no point in getting caught up in thoughts about what might be possible between

Cameron and herself. Even if it hadn't been for the scars on her face, he was still grieving his first wife. She couldn't ask for the love of a man who was walking around with that much heartache.

She needed a change of subject. "I spoke with Cameron yesterday, and he said I could put up the Christmas decorations after all." Not very much of a change, but allowing herself to talk about him was like water on a burn. Too much would be painful, but just a little bit made the pain subside.

Adam raised his eyebrows and sat back on his stool. "Did he really? I didn't see that coming."

"Do you think he didn't mean it?" Anxiety pricked at her.

"No, if he said it, I think he meant it," Adam said. "I wouldn't have expected it of him. He's been so inflexible about this for the past four years."

"I haven't done anything yet," Isabelle said. "I wanted to wait, in case he changed his mind."

"I'd say you're safe from that happening," Adam told her. "If you want my opinion, I say you should go right ahead. I'll even do it with you. Wait until Eloise hears about this. Christmas coming to the ranch again!"

"And I'm sure you're excited to tell Eloise," Isabelle teased him, and was pleased to see him blush.

"He didn't say we would do anything for Christmas," Isabelle went on quickly. "I think he only meant to let me have a little festive cheer."

"Even that's more than we've had in a long time." Adam rose to his feet. "I hope you never underestimate what a difference you've made to this place, Isabelle. And to him. I don't know if he tells you. I don't know if he sees it himself. But since you arrived, he's changed a great deal. Eloise has noticed it, too."

Heat rose to Isabelle's cheeks. She wanted to believe that what Adam was saying was true. She didn't think he was trying to deceive. But what if he was just believing what he wanted to believe? Of course he and Eloise would like to think that Isabelle's presence here had been beneficial to Cameron. They loved him and wanted good things to come to him. That didn't make it true.

The milk bucket was full, so she got to her feet. "I should get inside," she said. "Abby was napping, but I don't like to leave her for very long. Cameron has gotten closer with her, but I don't know how she would react if she woke up crying and he was the one who came to her. It should be me."

Adam nodded, stepping back from the door to let her pass. "We should talk to one another more often, Isabelle," he said. "I'd like to get to know you better."

"I'd like that, too." Isabelle smiled at him, feeling warm inside. The longer she spent here, the more she found the structure of a life. She had the church now, and Adam was a friend. Even though she wasn't going to be married the way she'd originally expected, there was plenty for her in Wintervale.

She trudged through the snow back up to the house, her heart light. Thoughts of Cameron and what had almost happened between them still whirled in her head, refusing to let her mind settle, but those thoughts were invigorating, even though they shouldn't have been. *What harm is there in a little more daydreaming, though? I'm not lying to myself. I know it can never be. But every woman is entitled to dream.*

She opened the door to the house.

For a moment, the box on the kitchen table didn't register as anything more significant than clutter. She was struck with a pang of impatience—*does he have to leave his things lying around after all the fuss he made about wanting me to clean?*

Then she looked closer.

On top of the contents of the box was the Bible she had found—the one that had impacted him so powerfully, the one he had demanded that she pack away.

Underneath it, there were Christmas decorations. Wreaths and garlands. Even a nativity, much smaller than the one at the church had been, but present, nonetheless. She unpacked it reverently and set it on the table, knowing she would need to find the perfect place to put it.

In front of the box, she recognized the baby mobile she had found in the attic. She picked it up once more, struck by its beauty and the care that had been put into it.

Beneath it was a folded piece of paper with her name scrawled on the top in messy handwriting. She opened it.

Isabelle -

Please use these things to decorate the house any way you'd like. I don't want you to have to go outside and collect new decorations to replace the ones you got rid of when I asked you to.

The mobile is for Abby. I carved it for Philip, years ago, but it was always my dream that he would pass it along to someone else one day. For years, I couldn't bear the idea that that wasn't going to happen. Now I understand that life is what I make of it, and if I want this mobile to brighten a child's day, I have the power to make that happen. I think Ruth would have wanted it that way.

The Bible is for you, and I am sure she would have wanted that. I know you have your own, of course, but I hope you will accept this one, too.

Faith was the most important thing in the world to Ruth. I know she would grieve that I've lost mine, and that hurts me. But she wouldn't want you to suffer the same fate. She would find your faith beautiful, and she would want to do everything in her power to help you keep it. The idea of you having the Bible that was hers is meaningful to me. In a way, you would be keeping her alive. So I very much hope you will accept this gift.

Below the message, he had scribbled something barely legible that she realized after squinting at it for a moment was his name.

Isabelle looked around. Cameron hadn't been outside with Adam, and she'd expected to find him in the house, but he wasn't here. He must be in the study now. He hadn't wanted to be here when she found these things. She longed to go knock on the door and thank him right away, but decided against it. Better to respect his implied wish to be alone.

She picked up the Bible and leafed through. She hadn't done this on the day she had found it. That had seemed too personal. Someone's Bible was an intimate possession, and she'd never opened another person's without permission. But if he was giving it to her, that meant she was allowed to look inside.

Ruth had marked passages on many of the pages—perhaps the ones she liked best. Tears came to Isabelle's eyes. It was something she did herself. *I feel as if I know her. How heartbreaking that she died so young—just like Vivienne—without getting the chance to see her child grow up. She was just at the beginning of her journey. It's all so awful.*

She looked down at the book in her hands.

Without meaning to—without thinking about it—she had stopped turning pages, and it lay open to the book of Psalms. And there was a single passage marked on this page.

The righteous cry out, and the Lord hears them; he delivers them from all their troubles.

Psalm 34:17-18. Isabelle's favorite. The one she had turned to for comfort so many times in her life. The one that was marked in her own Bible.

Ruth loved it too.

She closed the Bible and clutched it to her chest. The warmth that spread through her felt as if it was coming from somewhere else, some source outside her own body. As if something had reached out and touched her. Something... or *someone*.

Thank you, Ruth. Thank you for this gift. Seeing that Psalm, having the Bible fall open to that page and knowing that was the line that had been marked, made her sure that Cameron was right, that Ruth would have wanted her to have this Bible.

And that means she would also want me to be here—here with Cameron. I promise you, Ruth, I'll do all I can to help him. I want to believe what Adam does, that he's benefitted from having me here. I'll try my best to make that true.

She put the Bible down and picked up the note once more, scanning his words.

For him to have given her these things must have cost him a great deal. If it hadn't been painful, he would have simply handed them to her, or told her to fetch them from the attic and left it at that. He had gone to all the trouble to write a note, in all likelihood, because he hadn't been able to say these things to her face. Because it would have hurt him too much.

It made the gifts that much more meaningful. He wasn't simply a stubborn man refusing to let her have the things that would make her happy. This was much more complicated than that. He had chosen her happiness over his own comfort.

I shouldn't let him. I shouldn't let him suffer so I can have Christmas.

But he had made a choice. That choice had been his gift to her. She had enough respect for his dignity to honor that fact.

There was no longer any doubt as to whether she should decorate. She couldn't refuse this generosity. Carefully, reverently, she began to unpack the box, laying the items out on the table. She'd find homes for everything and have the place looking bright and jolly by the time he came out of his study.

Chapter Seventeen

The house was festively adorned. A wreath hung on every door. Garlands hung on the mantle and along the doorframes. Green and red ribbons had been tied around the backs of the kitchen chairs. Ornaments had been artfully arranged on every surface.

We ought to have a tree for those ornaments, really, Cameron thought, looking at them. If Isabelle had thought the same thing, she didn't show it. She had decorated herself and Abby for the occasion too, both of them in newly sewn clothes—white, with holly and ivy patterns on the fabric. Isabelle had let most of her dark hair fall around her shoulders for once, tying just the crown back with a red ribbon.

She held Abby in her arms, spinning in slow circles in the living room and softly singing *Joy to the World*. There was no doubt that joy was exactly what she was feeling. Her eyes crinkled with it, and her smile was so wide that Cameron doubted she could have suppressed it if she had tried.

He stood in the doorway, leaning against the frame and watching her. *She's so beautiful.* He'd always found her pretty, but there was something more today, something magical. Seeing her this happy, her positivity radiating outward to fill up the room, attracted him so powerfully that he clung to the doorframe to prevent himself from walking toward her.

It had been the right thing, letting her put these decorations up. Even if it did remind him of the past—even if he did occasionally feel as if Ruth had just stepped into the next room, and the hollow place she had left in his chest had begun to ache. Seeing Isabelle so happy filled that hollow in a way nothing had since.

He shook his head. He couldn't stand here watching her all day. She hadn't noticed him yet, and he feared it would be awkward when she did.

So he backed out of the room quickly, turned, and hurried out of the house. There was plenty of work to be done today and that would serve to keep his mind off the woman who had brought Christmas back to his home.

***

"Oh, my word," Adam breathed, freezing in shock.

On first glance, it appeared as though the horses were gone. None of their heads poked above the doors of their stalls. None of them had snuffled for a carrot when Adam and Cameron had walked in. Cameron's heart had stilled in his chest at the absence as he'd tried to piece together what was going on.

All too quickly, it had become clear. They were lying down, some of them on their sides, others on their bellies. Heads hung low. Eyes were closed and ears and tails didn't move to flick away the flies that were buzzing around.

Are they dead? His gut clenched and he hurried forward.

No. They were breathing. But the sickness that had afflicted the first horse must have spread. "I should have quarantined that one," he groaned, jerking his head toward it. "I suppose I thought it would pass…"

"No," Adam said darkly, kneeling beside a stallion and lifting its lip to expose bluish gums. "I don't think this is that kind of illness. Look. Fatigue, irregular breathing, gums like this… this is something else."

"What do you mean?" Cameron came forward and dropped to his knees beside his friend. He rested both hands, palms down, on the horse's body and felt the short inhale and exhale of breath. "What else could it be?"

Adam looked over at him, eyes narrowed. "Poison."

Cameron breathed in sharply.

Now that the word had been spoken, he could see that Adam was right. These weren't the symptoms of any standard illness. And for it to hit the whole herd like this, all at once…

"I don't understand," he managed, numbness creeping over him. "How could it be poison?"

"I don't know," Adam said, rising slowly to his feet and looking around as though he expected to see a clue somewhere in the stable. Cameron stood too and brushed the dust off the knees of his trousers. "I don't know *how* it could have happened. But I'd put every cent in my pocket on knowing *who* is responsible. It's got to be Russell Duvall."

Cameron's muscles tightened with anger. "That man needs to get it through his head. I'm not going to sell to him. No matter what he does, he isn't getting his hands on my ranch."

"Well, be that as it may, if we don't find the source of the poison, we're going to lose these horses," Adam said. "It has to be the water—the river at the back of the paddock. They drink there sometimes. It would be easy for an outsider to poison it. Much easier than slipping something into the feed. I think if we go look down by the riverbanks, we'll see dead rabbits, and that will confirm it."

"So we have to stop the horses from drinking at the river, and hope they haven't already ingested enough to do lasting harm." Cameron couldn't keep the scowl off his face. Finances were such a problem already, and if he lost his horses, the ranch would simply never recover.

"Oh, no! What's going on in here?"

Both Adam and Cameron spun toward the door of the stable. If Cameron's mood had been dark before, it turned positively thunderous at the sight of the short, stocky, wiry-haired man standing in the doorway. *Duvall.* He took a step forward, ready to bring the encounter to blows.

Another, slighter man—this one with dark hair and a pointed chin—stepped out from behind the first, a gun dangling from his hand.

Adam caught Cameron by the arm and held him back. "Duvall," he said. Then he turned his gaze on the gunslinger. "And I don't know you," he added, narrowing his eyes.

The gunslinger didn't respond. He tapped his finger idly against the grip of his gun, his gaze leveled on Cameron.

Cameron shook Adam off and straightened up. "What are you doing here, Duvall?"

Russell Duvall smirked. "I happened to be passing by," he said smoothly. "Heard you two talking."

"You didn't hear us talking from all the way up on the road." It was a ridiculous lie, one Cameron knew he wasn't meant to believe. Duvall could only be trying to unsettle him, and the maddening thing was that it was working.

"Well, maybe I didn't," Duvall agreed. "But I *was* passing this way." His smirk broadened. "My friend here wanted to meet you. This is Cyrus Pike. New in town. Looking to make some new acquaintances."

"So he wandered into my barn with his gun out?" Cameron growled. He took a step forward. He couldn't let this Cyrus Pike get the impression that waving a pistol around was going to intimidate him. "What are you really doing here?"

"It looks like you've got some sick horses," Duvall commented, pursing his lip in mock-sympathy. "I've seen this sort of thing before. Maybe I can help." He started forward.

Cameron moved to block him. "We don't need any help from you. Get off my property," he growled, his lip curling.

Duvall stepped back, making a show of raising his hands innocently. "There's no need to get angry," he said. "These things happen on ranches. It might be best for you to sell the place and start over. If you lose all the horses…"

It was all Cameron could do to keep from hitting him. He dug his nails into his palms. If it had just been Duvall here, that would have been one thing, but the fact that he was flanked by Pike and his pistol changed the equation. Neither Cameron nor Adam were carrying guns at the moment. Cameron hadn't thought he'd need one to come out and tend to his horses.

I won't make that mistake again, that's for sure. I'll have a pistol on my hip every time I leave the house from now on, until I'm sure Duvall has given this up for good.

"I'm not selling," Cameron said. "I've told you that a dozen times. Did you do this to my horses?"

"I don't know what you mean." Duvall pressed a hand to his chest and widened his eyes, the very picture of innocence. "How could I have made your horses sick?" He sighed and shook his head. "You know, at times of great tragedy, it makes sense to look for someone to blame. But most of the time, things aren't that simple. I'm offering you a solution. I'm trying to help."

"Well, no one here is interested." Cameron turned his back, even though it was unwise to take his eyes off a man who was armed. If he had to look at that smug smirk on Duvall's face for even a second longer, he was going to snap. Hot rage sparked through his veins, and it took all his self-control to keep from kicking something. He didn't want Duvall to see how much all this was affecting him. Duvall would enjoy that too much.

When he spoke next, Duvall's voice had darkened considerably, the laughing tone altogether gone. "I'd consider carefully," he said. "You might want to be stubborn and ride this place into the ground, but what about that pretty young thing you've got living with you these days? Is she also content to have her life ruined by your stubborn pride?"

Isabelle.

The implied threat to her well-being was more than Cameron could stand. With a roar of rage, he spun around and closed the distance between himself and Duvall, grabbing the shorter man by the collar of his shirt.

Duvall choked a little, but he laughed up at Cameron all the same. "Touchy about her, are we?"

Cameron was vaguely aware of the gun pointed at him, but that was a secondary concern. He wanted this man out of his sight immediately. He dragged Duvall to the door of the stable and flung him out into the snow.

Duvall staggered back a few steps and was unable to catch himself. He landed flat on his back in the snow. The mirth on his face disappeared. With a snarl, he scrambled to his feet. "Don't you disrespect me."

"You're on my land," Cameron said coolly. "No matter how much you wish otherwise, this is still my land. And if you come around here again, I'll go to the sheriff and let him know you've been poisoning my horses."

"You can't prove anything," Duvall hissed, his fists clenching and his lip curling.

"Is that a risk you want to take?" He looked at Pike, who still held the gun leveled at him. "I'd put that down, son," he growled. "We might not be able to prove anything about the horses, but if I end up shot here, the sheriff *is* going to figure out what happened."

After a moment's hesitation, Pike slowly lowered the gun, his face twisted into a surly scowl.

"Get off my property," Cameron barked. "Both of you. And the next time I see you, trust me, the law will be getting involved."

With one last menacing look over his shoulder, Duvall strode away, Pike in his wake.

The tension remained in Cameron's body even as they disappeared from sight. He turned and faced Adam, who was watching him with wide eyes.

"I think we have a problem," he said, his voice as heavy as his heart.

Chapter Eighteen

"Abby, these candles are the perfect finishing touch," Isabelle announced, arranging three fat candles on the mantle behind the garland that she had already positioned there. "I think we're really ready for Christmas now." She turned to the baby, who was lying on her back on a blanket spread on the floor. "Are you ready?"

Abby gurgled and waved a hand at the mobile that dangled over her head. Isabelle had tied the string to a stick and had wedged the end of the stick into a crack in the floorboards, where it sat snugly. The wooden animals hung over Abby, and every time she walked by, Isabelle would give them a nudge so they seemed to dance.

She'd made several new dresses for herself. The one she currently wore was a deep forest green, and she had created a matching outfit for Abby to wear. She smoothed her hands over the skirt, then carefully tucked a lock of hair behind her ear. This was all so wonderful, and she was sure that Cameron was going to love what she had done when he came home. She couldn't wait to thank him for allowing her to decorate—for everything he had given her.

Inhaling deeply, she smelled the spices of the pumpkin pie she'd been working on. It was meant to be a surprise for Cameron. She was sure he would never have told her himself, but Eloise had mentioned that pumpkin pie was his favorite—that he'd had it at every holiday meal back before their lives had changed when Ruth and Philip had died. She would make it again on Christmas Day, but for now, they had reason to celebrate. The fact that Christmas had come back to the house after so many years was more than enough of a reason to celebrate with something special.

"I think that pie is just about ready," she said, walking over and picking Abby up. Her shoulder gave a slight twinge where the goat had kicked her, but it wasn't nearly as bad as it had been in the first few days after the incident.

She went into the kitchen, where the smell was even more potent. Closing her eyes, she breathed in the familiar scent of the season. For a moment, she was transported to Christmases past, surrounded by family or laughing with Vivienne. Those days were gone now, but that didn't mean all the happiness had gone with them. The days ahead seemed sunny and bright.

She settled Abby into the new highchair that had been donated by the church, brought to the house just yesterday by Edith and Pastor John. Then she turned to the oven to remove the pie. The crust was a perfect golden brown, she noted with satisfaction. It was going to be delicious.

The slam of the door made her jump, and in her shock she nearly dropped the pie. Securing her grip on it, she turned around, her heart racing with sudden alertness.

Cameron was standing in the doorway, snow accumulated on his hat and gloves. The deep scowl on his face and the furrow of his brow told her that she hadn't imagined the slamming of the door. Though she didn't know why, it was apparent that he was in a bad mood.

She put the pie slowly on the counter, nervous to point out its existence to him while he was clearly so angry. Moving over to stand behind Abby, she put her hand on the baby's head gently and waited to see what Cameron would do next.

He took off his hat and beat it once against his leg, knocking the snow to the floor. He peeled off his gloves. Then he turned to the gun that always hung beside the door, took it down and began to examine it.

Isabelle cleared her throat. The tension created by the silence was like a cord about to snap. "I made a pumpkin pie," she forced herself to say. "A special treat for dinner tonight."

He grunted.

"Eloise told me you liked pumpkin pie?"

No response.

All right then. She summoned her courage. "I wanted to thank you," she said. "For giving me permission to decorate the house. That was thoughtful."

Another grunt.

What's the matter with him? Even when she had first arrived in Wintervale, he hadn't been like this. Cold and distant, yes, but not angry. Nothing, as far as she knew, had happened to make him angry. It couldn't be about the Christmas decorations this time. He'd told her she should put them up! But he hadn't even commented on them. If he'd noticed them at all, she certainly couldn't tell.

Isabelle tried one more time. "You know, Abby really loves that mobile," she said, her voice wavering slightly now as she tried to suppress her nerves. "She's been laughing up at it all afternoon. It's something to see. It was so kind of you to pass it on to her."

Cameron put the gun back on the wall, and for a moment Isabelle was sure he would finally turn to face her. He would acknowledge her now that he was finished with whatever he had been doing.

He didn't. He pressed a hand to the wall, and she watched his shoulders rise and fall, his back expand and contract, as he took a deep breath.

Something was really wrong. Something was *hurting* him. An ache took root in her chest at the realization. He was being volatile and it distressed her, but the idea of him in pain was even worse.

"Cameron," she said quietly, coming around Abby's chair, closing the distance between them. Her heart pounded, but she wasn't afraid. Tentatively, not wanting to startle him, she reached out and put a hand on his shoulder.

He allowed that for a moment, and her hopes rose. Maybe he was going to let her in. They *had* been more open with one another recently. "What happened?" she asked, keeping her voice gentle. "Whatever it is, we can figure it out together."

He froze under her hand. Though he hadn't been moving to begin with, she felt the way his muscles grew hard and tense. "Nothing happened."

"I know something did. I can tell." She took a small step closer. "You know you can talk to me, whatever it is."

She'd never been this close to him. She could see the fine hairs on the back of his neck, could smell the scent of him, musky and manly. Her racing heart broke into a gallop.

He could have been my husband.

He wasn't. She had to remember that. She had to keep her distance. And yet, the world in which things had gone another way, in which she had arrived here and he had seen her and wanted her and the two of them had embarked on a journey *together* instead of merely side by side, had never seemed more real.

Then he shrugged her off and spun around, facing her directly for the first time since coming into the house.

His expression shocked her, and she took a quick step backward, her hand flying to her mouth. His eyes blazed with anger. His jaw was set, and his fists were clenched at his sides.

"Leave me be," he growled. "There's nothing to talk about."

Isabelle didn't have time to respond. He turned around and strode toward the door and by the time she had registered what had happened, he was already gone.

Her heart sank. This wasn't what was supposed to happen. She had been so sure they'd finally reached a turning point. The gifts he had given her and Abby had been so special. So meaningful. Now, he was mad at her all over again. *Why? What could I possibly have done?*

Abby let out a soft whimper of distress. Isabelle went to her side and picked her up, grateful to have something to do. Abby gave her purpose when things were hardest.

And speaking of purpose...

Something hardened in the pit of her stomach. She didn't have to sit here and wallow in her sadness, hoping that things would improve. She could do something to improve her situation... and maybe, if she was lucky, even find a way to help Cameron.

She grabbed a shawl that hung by the door and wrapped it around herself and Abby. Her boots were by the door, the laces loose from the last time she'd taken them off, making them easy to step into. She didn't bother with lacing them up. She wouldn't need to do that just to step out onto the porch.

The moment she opened the door, the cold wind sucked the breath from her lungs and stung her cheeks. She pulled the shawl up over Abby's head, feeling the baby snuggle into her body for warmth. The tiny movements melted her heart. *She really is my baby. No matter how the two of us came together, we're together now and she is mine.* The thought was like cool water on a burn.

Cameron stood at the far end of the porch, leaning on the railing and staring out over the yard. She didn't close the distance between the two of them, but walked to the rail herself, one arm wrapped securely around Abby's back. If the baby started to tremble with the cold, Isabelle would take her inside. For now, she seemed to be all right.

She thought maybe Cameron hadn't noticed her—he didn't turn to face her—but then he spoke. "What are you doing out here?"

"I want to talk to you, Cameron," she said, raising her voice over the whistle of the wind. "Something is obviously wrong."

"It's none of your concern." His shoulders tensed.

"I think it is," she retorted. "When you come back after a day's work and don't even talk to me? When you pull that gun off the wall and look at it like you mean to use it on someone? Don't I have a right to know what's got you so upset?"

"No," he growled. "Go back inside, Isabelle. It's cold out here. You're going to freeze."

She wasn't going to freeze. Her blood had run hot at those words and she stood her ground. "You can't tell me what to do," she snapped.

He turned slowly, his eyes narrowed, and for a moment she second-guessed herself—but no. She wasn't going to be pushed around.

"I can't tell you what to do?" he repeated. "This is my house. Did you forget?"

"Of course I didn't forget. How could I forget? You never let me forget that. Any time I try to do something, you remind me that I can't so much as breathe without your permission."

"You're being dramatic," he grunted.

She planted her free hand on her hip. "No," she said. "I'm not. I try to milk the goat—which I *have* to do in order to keep Abby fed—and you scold me for going out of the house on my own. I work as hard as I can to bring cleanliness and order to a house that hasn't been tended to in years, and you complain that I'm not doing it quickly enough for your liking. I put up holiday decorations to bring a bit of cheer to the place, and you get angry and force me to take them down."

"I let you put them back up, didn't I?" He threw up his hands.

"Yes, and then the moment you came into the house and saw them, you acted as if you couldn't bear it. You wouldn't even speak to me. I had dared to let the thought enter my mind that you might actually tell me I'd done a good job, that the place looked nice! But of course you wouldn't. I don't know what possessed me to think it." Her throat swelled up, and she had to swallow hard before continuing to speak. "I don't know what's going on, Cameron, but whatever it is, I can help. I can listen to you. I have good ideas." It was a plea, but she didn't allow her voice to soften in the slightest. He had to know how serious she was. He had to be made to understand. "I *want* to help you. But you can't treat me like this. You can't shut me out, get angry with me, and not even tell me why!"

Cameron's arms dropped to his sides. He stared at her, eyes wide, jaw working slightly.

She had been speaking very quickly, she realized. Her breath fogged the air in front of her. Abby stirred against her as though agitated by the pitch and volume of her voice.

She forced herself to settle down before speaking again, and when she opened her mouth, her tone was considerably more calm. "I care about you, Cameron," she said, her gut wrenching with the words. They were difficult to admit, but it was the truth, and maybe he needed to hear it said. "I want to help you. I want to be someone you can turn to when things are difficult. I want you to confide in me."

She hesitated, then took a step closer, wondering how he would respond.

He turned his back to her.

Her heart hardened. Every time she tried to open up to him, it went like this, and she couldn't keep doing it. It was torment.

"All right," she said. "I'm not going to try to force your hand. If you don't want my help, you won't have it. But just know I'm not going to let you take your anger out on me. Not anymore. If you can't be kind to me, you can stay away from me, whether it's your house or not. I've done nothing to deserve harshness from you. I've done nothing but try to care, try to show you I can be good to you... and you don't want any of it."

He didn't react, didn't turn back to her or speak, but his shoulders hunched around his ears and she knew that her words had affected him.

Isabelle turned to go inside but paused as she reached the door.

She unwound the shawl from around herself and Abby and hung it on the hook there.

When he turned, he would see it, and he wouldn't be able to ignore that she had tried.

Chapter Nineteen

Isabelle woke to the sun shining through her window, having deliberately left the curtains open the night before. Rising early was the only reliable way to get a few moments to herself. Abby tended to sleep through the early mornings, and while Cameron was an early riser, he would use his morning to get ranch chores done, meaning that he wouldn't be in the house.

She dressed as quietly as she could, walking on her toes. She lingered over one of the new dresses she had made, running her fingers along the bright red fabric, but she couldn't bear to put it on. Even though she was still determined to celebrate Christmas, yesterday's argument with Cameron had soured her mood. She dressed in plain brown instead and let herself out of her bedroom, creeping down the hall and into the kitchen to prepare a simple breakfast before Abby woke up.

As she reached the kitchen doorway, her breath caught in her throat.

Cameron was there.

He was sitting at the table, a piece of paper clutched in his hand. His grip on it was so hard that it had crumpled slightly. He leaned on the table with both elbows, his head hanging low.

All her anger fled from her mind.

It didn't matter that they had argued. It didn't matter that she had been unbearably frustrated with him. To see him like this made her want nothing more than to ease his pain, whatever had caused it.

She crossed the room slowly and sank into the chair opposite his. "Cameron?" she murmured, restraining herself from reaching across the table to rest a hand on his arm. "Are you all right?"

He looked up at her and she received another shock, one that made her stomach clench. There were dark circles under his eyes, which were bloodshot with obvious exhaustion. He looked as if he hadn't slept all night.

"This arrived late yesterday evening," he said, holding up the paper. "It's from the bank."

Isabelle couldn't believe he was actually responding to her, much less showing her anything that was going on in his life, but she recovered quickly from that surprise. She wasn't about to waste this opportunity to find out what was causing him such grief.

"The bank?" She frowned, unsure how to process that. If she'd had to guess what was happening, she would have assumed it was something far more personal. That maybe he had found an old letter from Ruth. Clearly, she had been wrong—but how could a bank letter have upset him this much? "What does it say?"

"They're foreclosing on my loan," he told her.

She wasn't sure exactly what that meant, but it didn't sound good. "What's going to happen?"

He let out the deepest sigh she'd ever heard, dropped the paper, and pressed his hands flat to the tabletop. "If I can't come up with the money—and I don't think I can—I'm going to lose the ranch. They'll repossess it from me so that they can sell it and recover the money from the loan I took out when I bought this place."

"What?" Isabelle gasped. "They'll just take your ranch from you? They can do that?"

"Technically, it isn't even my ranch until I pay off the loan," he said gloomily. "So, yes, they can certainly take it and sell it out from under me." He sighed again and wrapped his hands around the back of his neck, threading his fingers together and gripping tightly. "It was never mine. It was always a—" A muscle worked in his cheek. "Always a dream. I thought I'd be able to make it happen until the horses got sick."

"Wait a moment." Isabelle's mind raced to catch up with everything she was learning. "The horses got sick? When did this happen? Why didn't I know about it?"

"I only discovered it yesterday," Cameron said.

The pieces fell into place. "That's why you were so upset when you came home. Why didn't you tell me?"

He shook his head. "Didn't want to talk about it," he said gruffly.

She leaned forward across the table. "But you can cure them," she said. "Can't you? You were able to heal the goat so quickly. You're wonderful with animals, Cameron. You'll help the horses, and the ranch will be fine. Everything will be all right."

"I don't know," he murmured. "It's not some ordinary sickness they've got." He hesitated. "They've been poisoned."

The word hit her like a brick, and she gasped and pulled back. "Poisoned? But who would poison the horses?"

"Russell Duvall," he spat the name as if it was also poison.

"Who is that?" She cast her mind back, trying to remember if she had ever heard that name before. She was sure she hadn't been introduced to a Russell Duvall at church.

"He's a miner and a prospector. Wants to buy the ranch." Cameron grabbed the bank letter and balled it up aggressively, then tossed it back down on the table. "He thinks there's gold here."

Isabelle frowned. "Is there?"

"It doesn't matter. I'd never sell to that cowardly snake."

"But if there's gold, couldn't you get it and use it to pay the bank?" She couldn't be the first one to have thought of this. It was the obvious solution.

Cameron shook his head. "There isn't any gold," he said. "Years ago, a few nuggets were found, that's all. Duvall developed an obsession with the place. He's sure there's more. But we would have found it by now, with all the work we do around here. He's just got the idea stuck in his teeth and won't let it go. He wants to buy the ranch so he can get the gold, and I won't sell it to him."

"So you think he poisoned the horses?"

"I'm sure he did. The river water is full of poison. The shore is lined with dead animals to prove it. And now he's letting the bank know I'm in trouble so they'll yank the place out from under me and he can buy it from them." He sighed. "I hate the man, but unfortunately, this is probably going to work. I'm going to lose everything, and he's going to get it."

The words were a low growl. Isabelle didn't think she had ever seen him so distraught, and her heart ached. She could no longer resist the urge to reach across the table and touch him.

As she rested her hand on his arm, he looked up at her. His eyes were pained, desperate. It was the closest she had ever seen him come to asking for help.

She couldn't help. She knew it. They both knew it. This was a problem she could do nothing to solve.

Say something. There has to be something you can offer him. Some words of comfort, if nothing else. But Isabelle couldn't think what those words might be, and the lack of them gutted her.

They were interrupted by the sound of a cry from the direction of the bedroom. Both of them started, and Isabelle pulled her hand back quickly. "That's Abby."

Cameron was already on his feet. "I'll go get her."

"No, you—" She meant to tell him he didn't need to go, that she would handle it, but he was already on his feet. He hurried toward the back of the house and the room Isabelle shared with Abby.

Isabelle buried her face in her hands. There was truly nothing she could do to help Cameron with this problem. It was too big for her. The bank taking his ranch away from him, some miner poisoning his horses to make that possible… even Cameron couldn't solve this, so what could Isabelle do? She could offer to be there for him. She *would* do that. But that wouldn't make the problems go away. The bank would still take the ranch from him.

Cameron came back into the room with Abby cradled in his arms and Isabelle's heart clenched. He held her so naturally, so easily. It was obvious that he'd had a child before. No man was born knowing how to hold a child so tenderly.

Her affection for him grew, warming her like a sun until she was sure that beams of it must be shining from her eyes.

Whatever was happening now, surely there was a way to get through it. It would be tragic to lose the ranch, of course. She knew it would break Cameron's heart. But whatever came next, she *would* be by his side. He had given her so much help with Abby since she had arrived here, and God knew that had been difficult and painful for him. It was only right that she return that favor now.

"Good morning, Abby," Cameron murmured, and as he looked down at her, his face softened. He smiled, though it didn't reach his eyes. "You're looking beautiful today, darling."

Abby burst into a merry laugh.

Cameron barked out a short laugh of his own in response and Isabelle's heart melted.

How bad could things be? When they all had each other, could brighten one another's days like this, surely they could make it through anything.

Cameron rose to his feet once more and held Abby out to Isabelle. "You should take her," he grumbled, the smile fading from his face. "She'll be wanting her breakfast."

"She doesn't usually eat right away when she wakes up," Isabelle said, but she held out her arms to accept the baby. "She should eat in about an hour, I think, but until then we're all right. You can take her back if you want to. She seemed happy for you to hold her. I don't remember the last time I heard her laugh like that."

He looked at her, his face impossible to read. She hoped he would take Abby back. She wanted to see him cheered up, and it seemed the best way to make that happen.

He shook his head. "I think we need to look to the future here, Isabelle," he said gravely.

"The future?" *What does that mean?*

"If I'm going to lose the ranch…" He trailed off, not meeting her eyes. He shoved his hands in his pockets and looked down. "It's time we talked about finding a new arrangement for you and the baby."

"Wait a moment," she protested. "You're going to throw us out?" Her blood ran cold.

"Of course I'm not going to throw you out." He sank back into his chair, and now he did look at her. "I would never do that. To either of you. You can't think that I would."

She nodded slowly, but her heart was racing. He was right—she couldn't believe that he would throw her out of the house. It didn't sound like him at all. At his very worst, he had never been the sort of man to resort to cruelty. But what did he mean by *a new arrangement*? "Where are we supposed to go?"

"This was always a temporary situation." Cameron's voice was heavy, as if the words he was saying pained him. "We always knew that you would be moving on eventually. The snow *has* cleared enough. Trains are leaving the station."

"Are you going to send us back to where we came from?" She shivered at the thought. Hearthstone had been home for a very long time, but everyone she'd been close to there was gone now. How could she be expected to go back?

"If you want to go back there, it's an option," Cameron said, meeting her eyes. "But I know you left for a reason. I'm sure we can find someone else who would take you in. I've always known you would make a good wife to someone, Isabelle."

That was a compliment. She knew it was. But it was a dagger to her heart all the same. He knew she would be a good wife, but he hadn't wanted her to be *his* wife.

It's because his heart still belongs to Ruth. I know that.

That didn't make it hurt any less.

She *wanted* him to want her as his wife. She hadn't realized that until this very moment. She wanted to stay with him, to love him and care for him. And he was going to send her away.

She ached to say something. She needed to find the words that would change his mind.

But no matter how she tried, they wouldn't come.

"I'll speak to Pastor John," Cameron said, his tone becoming businesslike. "He'll be able to help us put the word out and find you a new home."

He rose to his feet and left the room, but as he turned away, Isabelle could have sworn by the crinkle of his eyes and the press of his lips that she saw a shadow of grief cross his face.

Chapter Twenty

God has a plan for us. I know He does. No matter what has happened in the past, no matter what has gone wrong, God has always had a plan, and His plan has always kept me moving forward. I have always been all right in the end. I'll be all right this time, too.

The thought repeated over and over in Isabelle's head as she went about the rest of the day. It ran through her mind as she lay in bed that night, trying unsuccessfully to fall asleep. It was still with her the following morning as she got up and began to go about her day, though a numbness had spread through her at the realization that she would soon be leaving the ranch behind.

God had a plan. She believed that. She knew that the right thing to do was to put her faith in whatever God had planned. It would work out for the best.

Sometimes, it was very hard when her own plans and God's didn't line up with one another. She had been building something here. She had been getting close to Cameron, in spite of his resistance to letting anybody in. *And now it seems as if it was all for nothing.*

She stood in the kitchen, heating up Abby's milk, glad for an easy task. She was having trouble focusing on what was going on around her and anything more complicated might have been too taxing.

Cameron had left a note on the table: *Tending to the horses. Back in a few hours.* She read it three times, as if it might reveal some additional information, and then tucked it into her pocket, heat rising to her cheeks at the realization that she was going to save it. How foolish, treating something like this as if it was a personal letter. But she would put it between the pages of her favorite novel, just as she had done with the letter he'd written her when he had given her the Bible. It might just be a note about ranch chores, but it was more than he would have bothered to give her during her first days here. At least this note showed that he cared about her a little bit, that he had been thinking about how she would react to finding herself in an empty house.

How pathetic that she was left to cling to such a meager sign of his affection for her. It shamed her, and she knew she could never let him find out that she'd cared enough to keep this note. But she also knew that she wouldn't let it go for a long time—if she ever did.

A knock at the door interrupted her thoughts, and she sucked in a breath, wrapping her arms tightly around her stomach. Would this be the pastor already? She had no idea what kind of timeline she ought to expect. What if there was already a new situation waiting for her? What if she was about to be told to pack and leave tomorrow morning?

I'm not ready.

Hands shaking, she crossed the room and pulled open the door.

The man who stood there was unfamiliar to her, but she understood right away that he was the sheriff by his brown uniform and the star-shaped badge on his chest. He offered her a smile. "Good morning, ma'am," he said. "May I come in?"

Isabelle hesitated, unaccountably nervous at the sight of a lawman. "Is something wrong?"

"Not at all," he assured her. "Just here for a chat with Mr. Mercer."

She looked him up and down, trying to make a decision. Letting a stranger into the house was an uncomfortable prospect. On the other hand, it wasn't as if she didn't know who he was. And he was a friendly-looking man. He was a few years older than Cameron, with hair that was beginning to turn grey around his temples. The lines on his face around his eyes spoke of a habit of smiling frequently. He was a tall, lanky man—not as tall as Cameron, but tall enough that Isabelle had to crane her neck to look him in the eye.

"Cameron is out taking care of the horses," Isabelle said. "But… come in. You're welcome to wait here until he returns."

"Much obliged." The sheriff stepped through the door and removed his hat. "You and I haven't been introduced. I'm Sheriff Grayson."

"It's nice to meet you," she said. "I'm Isabelle Heart."

"Yes, I hear good things about you from the pastor and his wife," Sheriff Grayson said with a nod.

Isabelle beamed, then turned to the table. "Would you like to sit down? I'm working on the baby's breakfast, but I'd be happy to prepare a pot of coffee while we wait for Cameron to come back."

"If it isn't too much trouble." He ambled over to the table and took the seat next to Abby. "I've heard a fair bit about this baby, too. Seems like a real sweetheart."

"She is," Isabelle said, deciding she liked the sheriff. "Cameron isn't in any trouble, is he?"

"No, no, not at all. I heard about the horses, and the bank foreclosing on the ranch, and I wanted to come and see if there was anything I could do to be of help."

"Cameron thinks he knows who's behind it," Isabelle said. Then she bit her lip. Maybe Cameron wouldn't have wanted her to reveal that part.

But the sheriff seemed unsurprised. "We all know who's behind it," he said. "Russell Duvall has been itching to get his hands on this ranch for a long time."

"Well… if you know, can you stop him?' Isabelle asked, anxiety and hope trading blows in the pit of her stomach. "There must be something you can do about it, right? If he poisoned the horses, that's a crime."

"That is a crime, but as far as I'm aware, we don't have any proof of what happened," the sheriff said, spinning his hat between his hands. He leaned back in his chair and met Isabelle's eyes. "Without proof, I can't act against him."

"If he really did it, there must be evidence." Isabelle leaned forward across the table. "You're the sheriff. You can find out what happened, can't you? You can investigate. You can *get* the proof."

"Well, I'd like to think so," Grayson sighed. "I'm certainly going to try. If it's out there, I'll find it. But a man like that… who knows how well he might have covered his tracks?"

Isabelle fumed. It was so unfair. That someone could do something like this to Cameron and even stand a chance at getting away with it… How could that be? Fists clenched at her sides, she went over to finish preparing the coffee. She poured some for herself and some for Grayson, placed both cups on the table, and picked Abby up. Settling back into her chair, she began to feed the baby. At least this was something she could do.

Grayson adjusted his hat in his hands again, then shook his head. "I tell you," he said, "if it's not one thing, it's another. First Melody Strasser took ill, and we had to cancel the Christmas fair. And that always means so much to everyone in town. People are so disappointed."

"Christmas fair?" Isabelle repeated. "I didn't know there was such a thing."

"I suppose no one would have brought it up under the circumstances," Grayson agreed. "It's usually the event of the season. People from all the local businesses get together and sell things, as well as women who've produced crafts in their spare time. It's a real treat for everyone in town. But Melody organizes it every year, and she's been too unwell to take the reins this season the way she usually would. It's such a disappointment."

The thought turned over in Isabelle's mind. A Christmas fair... Grayson was right. That would have been something truly special, something to brighten the season and bring the community together. Maybe it would have given Cameron the burst of cheer he so obviously needed right now. But since it had been canceled, it was no use dreaming about it. Just one more thing she couldn't count on. One more thing that wasn't going to come to her rescue.

The door opened, and Cameron walked in. He came to a stop, his eyebrows shooting up. "Oh," he said. "Sheriff Grayson. I see you've met Isabelle."

"And she's a charming woman," Grayson said with a smile. "You're lucky to have her here, Mercer." He rose to his feet. "But it's you I'm here to see."

"Of course." Cameron took off his coat and hung it on the peg by the door. With a quick glance at Isabelle, he unstrapped the gun at his side and hung that up, too. "We'll go into my study," he said.

Grayson tipped his hat to Isabelle as they walked out. "A pleasure to have met you," he said.

She nodded. "The same to you."

Once the men had left the room, she turned her attention back to Abby. The baby had stopped eating, perhaps in response to the distractions, but now she opened and closed her mouth, searching for the bottle. Isabelle gave it to her, leaned back in the chair, and closed her eyes.

A Christmas fair. That would have been just the thing to brighten up this season. What a disappointment that it had to be cancelled...

An idea began to grow in her mind.

At first it seemed foolish. Only a fantasy, not something to be taken seriously. But the more she allowed the thought to stir within her, the more sense it seemed to make, until by the time the sheriff and Cameron emerged from the study, she had begun to take it seriously.

"I'll check on things down by the river before I go," Grayson said. "You never know what might make itself apparent. I'll let you know if I find anything helpful."

"Thank you," Cameron said, stuffing his hands into his pockets. "I know this is a long shot."

"Well, sometimes long shots pay off," Grayson said. He turned to Isabelle. "Thanks for the coffee, Miss Heart."

"Thank you for your help," Isabelle said.

"Just doing my job, ma'am." He tipped his hat once more and let himself out of the house.

Cameron dropped into a chair and let out the heaviest sigh Isabelle had ever heard. "He's optimistic," he said. "But I don't know. I'm fighting a war on all fronts right now. If it was just Duvall, I might be able to handle things, but with the bank coming for the ranch too..."

"I had an idea about that," Isabelle said eagerly, shifting Abby in her arms so that she could lean closer to him across the table.

Cameron looked up at her, eyebrows lifting. "Oh?"

"The Christmas fair."

"How do you know about that?" He frowned, brow furrowing. "I never mentioned it. I haven't even attended in years."

That was no surprise. "I heard it was cancelled this year. Sheriff Grayson told me. And he told me everyone in town was so disappointed, and I thought... what if we had it here?"

"Here?" He shook his head. "We couldn't do that, Isabelle. We're about to lose the ranch."

"That's my point! If we offered to host a cherished town event, the bank would almost *have* to delay the foreclosure.

They wouldn't want to snatch the place out from under us right before the Christmas fair, especially since everyone in town has already faced the disappointment of missing out on it. If they all got their hopes up again, the next person to disappoint them would lose a lot of favor. The bank doesn't want that." She was so excited that she nearly rose out of her chair. "I know it wouldn't stop them from reclaiming the place in the long term, of course. But it would buy you some time to find some money, to come up with a plan… something."

As she'd spoken, Cameron's eyes had grown wider and wider. "You know," he murmured, "that isn't a half-bad idea."

"Really? You think it might actually work?"

"It would definitely work. You're right that the bank won't want to go through with a foreclosure if the fair is being held here. They'll put it off. And I *could* use the extra time… and, of course, that means we don't have to rush you and Abby out of here either." A grin spread across his face. "We can take our time about it and find the place that's really *right* for the two of you. I have to admit, I've been worried about that." His smile flagged slightly. "I know I was hard on you these past couple of days, especially right after I found out about the poisoning."

"It's all right," Isabelle said quickly, heat rising to her cheeks.

"It isn't," he countered. "I was upset, yes, and under a lot of pressure, but you still deserve to be treated well, Isabelle. I'm sorry I took it out on you."

Isabelle's heart was in her throat.

The fact that he'd come to that realization and gone to the trouble to articulate it to her—it meant the world. It meant that he was actually thinking of her, considering her feelings. It was something she had come to see more and more of from him lately, but their most recent argument had left her wondering whether it had all been her imagination. The fact that he was able to turn things around and take accountability so quickly made her sure it hadn't been. He really did care.

But he doesn't love you.

You love him. He doesn't love you. If he did, he wouldn't be sending you away. He would find a way to stay together, regardless of anything else that was going on.

This isn't love.

To think of Cameron using that word was new, and it was so shocking that she was terrified he must be able to read it on her face. If he could, though, he said nothing.

Of course he wouldn't say anything. It's never even occurred to him that he and I might have that sort of relationship—and that's smart, because we won't. He doesn't love me, and I shouldn't allow myself to love him.

Unfortunately, though, Isabelle was beginning to realize it was far too late. She had fallen for him, and there was nothing she could do about it.

Chapter Twenty-One

"We know it's short notice," Isabelle said. "But we think it's worth making the effort."

Two days had passed since the sheriff's visit to the ranch and the conversation in which she and Cameron had decided to host the Christmas fair. Those two days had been an absolute whirlwind of activity.

Adam and Cameron had taken the lead on preparing the ranch itself for the event. That meant clearing ground with a vengeance. Fortunately, the snow had stopped, so when they got rid of what had accumulated, there were bare patches of ground behind. Those places wouldn't be snowed over again by the day of the fair. Isabelle was confident about that. The men had also set about building booths and setting them up to make it easy for people to display their wares.

That was what Isabelle and Eloise were suggesting to Mr. Grimes, the stout, blond baker, today.

"Your pies look magnificent," Isabelle said, looking at the display case. It was true. They were marvelously decorated. Pieces of pie crust had been cut into long, swooping arcs, tiny berries, and leaf shapes. They had been arranged in intricate patterns to mimic Christmas garlands and holly. The whole place smelled of sweet fruits and savory spices. It was enough to make Isabelle want to set aside her reason for coming here in the first place, order herself a piece of pie, and settle in to enjoy it.

But she couldn't do that, and she knew it. This was too important.

She had left Abby with the pastor and his wife for the day. Both John and Edith agreed that their intent to save the Christmas fair would mean a great deal to the community and they'd offered to do all they could to help. Isabelle was extremely grateful. It left her free to focus on the task at hand.

"His pies are the best in town," Eloise said. She turned to the baker. "And you always sell them at the fair, Mr. Grimes. That's where everyone who can't bake gets their pies for Christmas dinner. You don't want to let people down, do you?"

"Oh, well, of course I don't." Mr. Grimes brushed some of the flour off the countertop. "But you're right, Miss Heart. One week? You've given me almost no time to plan. To say nothing of the fact that it will take time to bake pies! How can I be ready in a week?"

"I really do understand," Isabelle assured him. "But it has to be a week, because it's only two weeks until Christmas. We'll have the fair next Friday, and that will ensure that everyone has time to attend before things get too busy."

"I suppose that makes sense," Mr. Grimes agreed. "And I wouldn't want to miss out on the fair, you're right about that. It's always the highlight of the season. I *was* disappointed that it wasn't going to take place this year…"

"So you'll do it?" Eloise asked eagerly.

"Oh, I can't say no to two such lovely faces." Mr. Grimes' own face broke into a broad smile. "Very well, ladies, you win. I'll sell my pies at the fair."

"Thank you!" Isabelle said, delight and satisfaction swelling within her. "We'll see you at the ranch!"

She and Eloise left the bakery and stepped back out into the chill December air. "Where to now?" Eloise asked, drawing her shawl tightly around herself to keep out the wind.

"Cameron agreed to let me join him for the meeting with the bank," Isabelle said. She still couldn't quite believe he'd said yes to that. "I think he thought it might go better if there were two of us there—and if I was able to describe my plans for the Christmas fair. He says I do a better job explaining it than he can."

"Do you want me to come with you?" Eloise asked.

"No, why don't you go to the bookshop?" Isabelle suggested. "It would be wonderful if there were some holiday books available for patrons to buy at the fair."

"That's a great idea," Eloise agreed with a warm smile. "I'll meet you outside the bank, then?"

"Perfect."

The women went their separate ways. Isabelle hurried toward the bank. It was a medium-sized stone building and, as such, was one of the oldest in town, having been spared damage from the fire that had taken so much else. She hurried up the steps to where Cameron was waiting for her.

"We got the baker," she gasped, slightly out of breath from the combination of cold and exertion. "He's going to sell his pies."

"Perfect." Cameron nodded, smiling. "And you're just in time for this meeting." He held out his arm for her to take.

She stared, then looked up at him.

"Best to present a united front," he said quickly.

Did that mean making it look as if there was something between the two of them that wasn't there? She gritted her teeth. It would be difficult—painful, even—to play happy family with the man she had fallen in love with, the man who would never and *could* never return her affection.

But he was right. By going along with this, she was establishing herself as a part of the community, and that would help to make the kind of impression they needed.

She took his arm and allowed him to lead her into the bank.

***

"Well, that went as well as could be expected," Isabelle said half an hour later as the two of them emerged from their meeting.

"As well as could be expected?" Cameron repeated incredulously. He picked her up and spun her around right in front of the bank steps, and Isabelle was so shocked that she let out a laugh. "You were *wonderful*. You didn't even give him a chance to argue! Thanks to your plan, we have the ranch until the new year!"

His eyes met hers, and he seemed to realize just how close the two of them were to one another. Hurriedly, he set her down, but he lingered a moment to make sure she had her footing. Isabelle's heart beat a rapid staccato as his hands rested just above her hips. He was so close to her, his eyes locked on hers.

Was he about to kiss her?

Would he really do such a thing right here in *public*?

Her heart slammed against her ribs. It was *so* inappropriate. *Shockingly* inappropriate. They weren't married. For him to kiss her at all would be daring. To do it on the steps of the bank, where anyone might see them, would be bordering on scandal.

But if he tried it right now… Isabelle knew she wouldn't resist. Even as she knew it wasn't the right thing to do, a part of her was already succumbing to delicious yearning, wondering what his lips might feel like against hers.

No. No, this isn't anything. He's excited about the fair and the bank agreeing to back off. That's all. This isn't a sign of the way he feels about me. I have to keep my head and my heart far apart.

"What a beautiful couple the two of you make!"

Isabelle turned and found herself face to face with a man barely taller than herself. He was muscular in a thickset way and his hair was bristly enough to make her wonder if she could use it to scrub the dinner plates. He looked her up and down with a smirk that made her skin crawl.

"What are you doing here, Duvall?" Cameron barked, his arms flexing and his hands curling into fists.

So this was Russell Duvall. Isabelle sucked in a breath. This was the wretched man who had set out to ruin Cameron's life. She wanted to hurl accusations at him. She wanted to tell him all about the fair, to tell him that he was going to lose this little game he had started. The words bubbled up inside her, but she forced them down. She would do Cameron no favors by starting a fight with this man.

Duvall grinned insouciantly at Cameron. "What do you mean 'What am I doing here?' I live here."

Cameron folded his arms across his chest. "You live at the bank?"

"Don't be an imbecile. But I do *use* the bank, as a citizen of the town of Wintervale," Duvall said. "In fact, I have an appointment beginning in just a few minutes."

"I'm sure you do," Cameron growled. "But it might not go as well as you're hoping."

"I wouldn't worry about me if I were you," Duvall said. "I know you have troubles enough of your own." His voice became cloyingly sweet as he continued. "How are your horses, by the way? They were so ill when I stopped by the other day. But I suppose some men aren't meant to be ranchers."

The anger that rippled through Cameron at that was visible. His lips pulled back from his teeth and his eyes narrowed, making him look downright animalistic.

He's going to hit Duvall.

Without thinking about what she was doing, Isabelle reached out and grabbed Cameron's hand.

He can't get into a brawl. We need the bank to be convinced that siding with us is going to garner the goodwill of the community, and that won't happen if there's a fistfight in the middle of town.

She stepped forward slightly, keeping her grip on Cameron's hand, but positioning herself between him and Duvall. "You'd better leave us alone now," she said quietly. "You've made your point, but we have other things to do today than listen to you."

She started past him, pulling Cameron along with her.

"Don't you turn your back on me, girl," Duvall growled, the sweetness gone from his demeanor.

A trickle of fear ran down Isabelle's spine, but she knew she couldn't show it to him. She schooled her expression carefully and turned around to face him once more.

"I want you to know," she said quietly, "that I believe God will forgive what you've done."

At once, she felt the incredulous stares of both men on her. "I beg your pardon?" Duvall demanded.

"God forgives everyone," Isabelle said. "Even people who have done awful things. Nobody is beyond redemption. It's never too late to make amends." She took a step forward, wondering if it was possible that her message might reach him. "I know you've done some things, Mr. Duvall. I know you might have some regrets. And I just want you to know that you can still begin again. You can have forgiveness for your sins. All you have to do is ask for it."

Cameron's hand gripped hers tightly, but she didn't dare look at him to see how he was responding or what expression was on his face. She kept her eyes firmly on Duvall.

His eyes narrowed, his expression growing dark. "I don't know what you think you're talking about," he growled. "Whatever you think you know… you know nothing."

She shook her head. "I'm not going to try to explain it to you. We both know the things you did, and we both know you're going to pretend otherwise. If I'm wrong about that, then go ahead and admit it. But I'm not wrong, am I?"

He started toward her.

Cameron yanked her back, thrusting her behind his body, and raised his fists. "Stand down, Duvall," he warned. "You don't want a fight here. The sheriff is on my side in this. He's looking for a reason to arrest you."

"If you hit me, you'll have started it," Duvall sneered.

"Not if I hit you defending a woman. And everyone will believe us when we tell them you came at her. Like it or not, people know you around here, and that's exactly the kind of thing you're known for." His voice was low and ominous.

Isabelle shivered. The way the two of them were facing off was like a storm about to break—powerful and potentially dangerous.

For a moment, Duvall stood still, clearly making up his mind about what he wanted to do next—whether he wanted to force the issue.

Good sense seemed to take over at last. His lip curled. "This isn't the end of it," he snarled. "I'll settle this with you yet, Mercer. And that ranch *will* be mine."

He pushed past Cameron and stormed into the bank.

Cameron watched him go. "His meeting isn't going to go well if he stomps in there looking like he's about to rob the place," he said darkly. "Especially since the bank manager just dealt with you, Isabelle. Anyone would look like an animal after that, but…" He shook his head and turned back to Isabelle. "We should be on our way. I don't want to be here when he comes back out."

"Neither do I," Isabelle agreed heartily.

They started off down the street. She longed for him to take her hand again, or her arm, but he didn't. Her heart sank. That had only been for show. She'd known it, but it still hurt to have it confirmed.

He glanced over at her as they walked along. "What did you mean by telling him that God will forgive him?"

She cocked her head to one side. "It's what I believe."

"The things he's done… they aren't mistakes. He's been deliberately horrendous. He'll continue to be that way. He's not the kind of man who deserves forgiveness, Isabelle."

His voice was tense, but he didn't seem angry. She didn't know what was going on inside him, but it wasn't anger. There was no heat behind his words. No bite. She had been on the receiving end of his anger often enough to recognize the difference.

"Forgiveness isn't something you deserve," she said softly. "God forgives everyone who asks to be forgiven, as long as they ask sincerely. You don't have to earn it. God *will* forgive him if he truly repents of the things he's done, and he should know that. Some people believe it's too late for them to go back once they've done something wrong, but that's never the truth. You can always repent. You can always begin again."

"This is what you believe?" His voice was hoarse. Was it the cold, or was something else affecting him?

"It's what I know," she said firmly, surety radiating through her. "God shows me the truth of this every day." How many times had she felt His forgiveness for her own transgressions? She might not have done anything as egregious as Duvall had, but there had certainly been times she'd had no right to expect forgiveness. It had always come to her anyway, a cleansing wash of divine healing. A second chance. "It's for everyone who wants it," she told him firmly.

His jaw worked. He said nothing.

Isabelle could see that something she'd said had impacted him. She didn't know what it was, and right now she thought it might be a mistake to ask. But as they made their way toward the bookshop, where she hoped to intercept Eloise rather than waiting on the steps of the bank, she was filled with a certainty that she had said something right today. Something important. Her words were going to linger with Cameron, and their message was going to make a difference to him.

She hoped he would tell her, eventually, why that was.

Chapter Twenty-Two

"Should you be doing that in this wind?" Adam asked, pausing to look at Cameron. He held the saddle he'd been cleaning against his hip and regarded Cameron through narrowed eyes.

Cameron barely spared him a glance before turning back to the work at hand, which was fixing the damaged top rail on the fence of the horse paddock. *Not that it matters now.* The horses were a little bit better, the poison having begun to work its way out of their systems. He hadn't allowed them to drink from the river since the discovery of what had happened. But they were still too weak to run free in the pasture, especially in the cold weather, and Cameron wasn't confident they would make a full recovery at all.

"It has to get done," he said around the nail he held in his teeth.

"It doesn't have to get done today," Adam countered. "We're not going to be using this pasture for anything for a little while."

That was true, but even so… "If we're going to keep the ranch, we ought to put in the work," he said. "I need to prove to myself that I'm up to the task."

"You really think we're going to be able to keep it?"

"Isabelle's plan is a good one." He hung his hammer by its head on the fence rail, took the nail out of his mouth, and turned to face his friend. "And it's working. The bank has delayed the foreclosure. We'll have the ranch at least until the new year, and by that time I'll have thought of something else. We'll come up with the money, or… something."

"That's a lot of money to come up with in a couple of weeks," Adam said grimly.

"Maybe the sheriff will be able to arrest Duvall for his crimes," Cameron countered.

Adam shook his head and rested the end of the saddle on the ground. "I don't think that would make a difference, now that the bank is involved," he said. "They still want to reclaim their asset, and proving that our losses are Duvall's fault wouldn't erase them."

"He might have to pay for them, though," Cameron bit out stubbornly. "That's what should happen. Our horses wouldn't be sick if not for his meddling. He should pay for their treatment, and for the replacement of any who don't make it." His jaw clenched. He hated speaking about it as if one horse was just as good as the next. You couldn't replace a good horse simply by buying another one. Even if Duvall was forced to replace Cameron's stock, he would have taken a heavy loss, and he would never forgive the other man for that.

Isabelle would forgive him, though.

No. That wasn't what Isabelle had said. She had said that *God* would forgive Duvall.

And for all I know, she's right. She's an amazing woman. I have to admit that part of the reason I'm so desperate to keep the ranch is that… I don't want to see her go.

Isabelle thought that God would forgive Duvall. Did that mean she also believed that God would forgive *him*?

That was the thought on his mind as he put up his gear and left Adam to the business of cleaning the horse tack. He made his way back toward the house, pondering what had happened to his family and the fact that he hadn't been there to save them. It was a knowledge that turned his stomach, something he physically turned away from every time it entered his mind.

Now, he forced himself to face it.

What he'd done—it burned like a coal in his heart. It would never go away. The results had been catastrophic. But now, he forced himself to consider it from the outside.

I didn't do anything evil, the way Duvall did. I didn't set out to hurt anyone. I didn't even neglect a promise. I just… wasn't there when they needed me.

God knows how I wish I had been.

If Isabelle is right—if forgiveness is for everyone who wants it, and I want it so badly it aches—could I be forgiven?

The turmoil inside him was almost more than he could bear and for a moment he didn't realize he was seeing anything out of the ordinary. But then it registered.

Cyrus Pike.

The gunslinger who followed Russell Duvall around. He was here on the property now. He had directed his horse down off the road and was stalled on the far side of the house, neck craned forward as though peering in the window.

Watching something.

Isabelle!

Cameron's heart clenched. How could he have been sitting out here thinking about forgiveness for leaving his family on their own when all the while Isabelle was being spied on by that rotten man? He hurried forward, his hand flying to the gun at his side and loosening the strap that kept it secured in the holster. At the first sign of Pike's weapon, he would be ready to draw.

"Pike!" he yelled. "Cyrus Pike!"

He'd gotten the element of surprise, somehow. Pike's head whipped around, and the horse reared back in shock. Pike reached for his gun, but Cameron's was already in his hand. "Don't," he snapped. "Don't you dare draw on me. What are you doing on my land?"

Pike made no attempt to mimic the saccharine air that Russell Duvall so often presented. Cameron suspected he couldn't have managed it even if he'd wanted to—this man was no charmer. Instead, he wrinkled his nose like a rat and showed his teeth. "Cameron Mercer," he said.

"All right," Cameron growled. "So you do know whose property this is. What do you want with me?" He found himself wishing that he hadn't left Adam back at the stable. Two against one would be better odds.

"Who says I want anything at all with you?" Pike gathered the reins in his hand and patted his horse's neck, encouraging the beast to settle down. "You're not the only one who lives on this land, Mercer." He cut his gaze briefly back toward the house and added, "She's a very pretty girl, isn't she?"

Cameron saw red.

For a moment, he was out of his own control. His body started forward, his fists coming up in front of him. Even though it was unwise—it wasn't what he would have done if he had been thinking at all clearly—he dropped the gun. He didn't want to shoot this man. That wouldn't be enough. He wanted to hurt him intimately. He wanted to extract every ounce of suffering Pike would experience intentionally, piece by piece.

Pike backed his horse up a few paces, laughing. "Seems I touched a sore spot," he said.

"You can't come onto my property and threaten a member of my household, Pike." Cameron's voice was a snarl. With enormous effort, he stopped himself from dragging Pike off his horse.

"Threatening?" Pike repeated. "Who said anything about threatening?"

What a ridiculous response. It had obviously been a threat. Pike knew it was a threat. Even now, he was grinning maliciously. He had said that specifically to anger Cameron. Cameron didn't want to give him the satisfaction of seeing his tactics work, but hearing this man talk about Isabelle after watching her through the window without her knowledge…

"You'd better leave," he growled. "You'd better get off my land right now." He eyed his gun on the ground and estimated how fast he would be able to grab it and get a shot off. Letting it out of his hands had been a dire mistake, but even so, he was fairly certain Pike would underestimate what he was capable of. He could probably do it.

Pike threw back his head and laughed. "You aren't going to do anything," he snorted. "Besides, she doesn't even belong to you. You might have fooled the banker, but Russell and I know the truth. You brought her all the way up here to be your wife, and then you didn't marry her. You've got no claim on her at all. Well, don't worry. I'll take her off your hands, and then you won't have to worry about it anymore."

Cameron dove for the gun.

He rolled up onto one knee, leveling it at Pike's face. "This is your very last chance to leave my land," he snapped. "One more word out of your mouth and it'll be the last you ever speak, so help me."

His finger quivered on the trigger. He'd never shot a man before, but it didn't even seem like an extreme response right now. The anger flowing through his body was so violent, so intense, that it almost *had* to lead to bloodshed. He wanted Pike in the dirt.

Pike held up his hands in mock surrender. The cocky smile on his face dipped, but only slightly. He had the good sense not to try to speak again. He grabbed the reins of his horse, jerked its head around, and galloped off.

As Pike made it back up onto the road and disappeared toward the horizon, the rage slowly left Cameron's body. In its wake, he was overcome with a wave of exhaustion and nausea, and he slumped to the ground.

He's targeting Isabelle.

It had been bad enough when Russell Duvall had come for Cameron's livestock, but this was a new level of horrendous. He wanted to pack Isabelle and Abby into his wagon right here and now, drive them out of town, and never look back.

If anything happens to them, it will be entirely my fault.

He knew it was true. In fact, if anything happened to Isabelle and Abby, it would be even more his fault than when Ruth and Philip had died. He had spent years regretting the fact that he hadn't been at home with his wife and child when the fire had caught, wondering if he might have been able to help them, but at the very least, he knew that he'd had no way of knowing there would be a fire that day. There had been no warning, no signs that he could look back and say he had ignored.

This was utterly different.

The threat was clear and overt. If he ignored what Pike had said and done today and something went wrong, he would be entirely to blame.

Isabelle says God forgives everyone, but that they have to want it.

For the first time in his life, he was acutely aware of the fact that he did want it.

He wanted forgiveness badly. He yearned for his slate to be wiped clean. It wouldn't mean that his grief was at an end—that would never stop, he knew—but if he could remember Ruth and Philip without guilt, he would be much better off.

He wanted that almost as much as he wanted Isabelle's safety.

He struggled to his feet, his whole body trembling in the aftermath of the confrontation with Pike. He knew he would have pulled the trigger if Pike hadn't backed down. He would have shot the man rather than let him get close to Isabelle or Abby.

Slowly, he made his way back toward the house.

I can't let Isabelle know what just happened. The truth would terrify her.

He would keep it to himself for now.

But he would also do all he could to make sure she was safe. He wouldn't let her out of his sight. Not until he was certain the threat had passed… or she was leaving Wintervale, and putting all this far behind her for good.

That might be the safest option left to them, and he knew it.

But the thought of it opened a chasm in his heart.

Chapter Twenty-Three

"Come out to the barn," Isabelle told Edith, stepping out of the house to meet her guest on the porch. "Eloise is already there. I can't wait to show you everything we've been working on these last few days."

Edith bent down to say hello to Abby, who was strapped to the front of Isabelle's body. She placed a hand lovingly on the baby's back. "I feel like this one has gotten bigger since I saw her last," she said, straightening up. "Good morning, Abby! Are you excited for the fair?"

Abby cooed happily at being talked to and waved a fist in the air.

"I think it's going to be a big success," Isabelle said with a smile. She walked down the steps of the porch and Edith fell in alongside her. "Cameron and Adam have put a lot of work into building booths for the people participating to use. Eloise is painting them right now. She's adding the names of everyone who has agreed to participate. We even went around and asked the different shopkeepers what colors they wanted to see used on their booths. Some of them didn't mind, but others had preferences. I think it's going to look fantastic when it's finished."

She was suffused with pride at all they had accomplished, and how quickly it had come together. It seemed not long ago—it *hadn't* been long ago—that this had been nothing more than a wild idea in her mind. It had seemed impossible at first. Now, it was coming together as if she had dreamed it into reality. As if the ideas in her mind had sprung to life and begun to take shape around her. It was magical.

Christmas is always a little magical.

This Christmas was more magical than most. And Isabelle was sure she would never forget how wonderful it had been to realize at last that she had people she could depend on, and that the community was truly going to rally to her side.

They aren't just doing it for me. They want this fair to happen for their own reasons, too. But so many people had shown kindness. There had been offers to make hot cider to share with thirsty patrons of the fair and offers to come and help set up. People had begun convincing their friends and neighbors to participate—word was spreading without Isabelle even having to do it.

The fair was going to be a success. She could feel it in her bones. Cameron would have so much goodwill within the community that no one would want to let his ranch be sold out from under him. The bank would simply have to acquiesce to the will of the people. She was sure of it.

They went into the barn. Eloise was on her feet, brushing dust and hay off of her skirts. "I was just finishing up," she said. "How does it look?" She held out an arm to the booth she had been painting.

The words *Grimes' Pies* were painted in careful blue script across the top of the booth. On the bottom section, Eloise had painted pictures of several different pies—blueberry, apple, pumpkin—each with the trademark festive crust pattern Isabelle had noticed on the pies when they had gone to visit Grimes. "It's perfect," she enthused, hurrying over to embrace Eloise, careful not to crush Abby between their bodies. The baby shifted happily at the newfound warmth. "Everyone is going to love this, Eloise."

"Well, it was your idea," Eloise said modestly. "You're really the one to thank for all of this, Isabelle."

"Eloise is right," Edith said earnestly. "If it weren't for you, none of this would be happening. You brought the Christmas fair back to Wintervale. Just think, if you hadn't been here this year, we wouldn't have had a fair at all." She smiled warmly and took the hands of both of the other women. "You know, I've always been thrilled to have you as part of this community, Isabelle, right from the moment you arrived among us. But I have to say, I never imagined you'd make a contribution like this. It means the world to me, truly. It will to everyone. We're all so glad you came to live here with us."

Isabelle caught Eloise's eyes at those words, and both of them looked away quickly, neither speaking. She didn't want to spoil the moment by mentioning the fact that her stay here wasn't going to be a permanent one. She had delayed the moment of her departure by arranging this fair, but that didn't mean she would be able to stay with Cameron forever, and she knew it. That had never been the plan.

A day would come when it would finally be time for her and Abby to leave. When that day arrived, she would have to accept it with good grace.

Every day that went by made that harder. Because it wasn't just Cameron holding her here. She had fallen in love with him, yes, and to leave him behind would be to leave a part of her heart. But as she stood here with Eloise and Edith, looking at all the fine work they had done together, she knew with a pang that it would be just as difficult to leave them—and to leave the rest of this community, too.

Wintervale had become a home to her.

She didn't want to say goodbye.

***

When Edith and Eloise had returned to their homes, Isabelle sat in the kitchen with one of Eloise's buckets of paint, working on a poster to hang on the outside of the barn during the fair.

It wasn't really *necessary*, she mused as she dragged the brush along the paper, to have a poster that read *Wintervale Christmas Fair*. It wasn't as if anybody wouldn't know where they were. But it would add cheer to the event. She carefully outlined a holly berry, wishing she had Eloise's talent for this sort of thing. People would probably understand what she had been trying to paint, but it didn't look as good as what her friend had done.

That's all right. The painting will be a way for Eloise to shine. The door banged open.

Her head darted up in surprise.

Cameron had come storming into the kitchen. Abby gurgled at the sight of him—she'd come to recognize Cameron as a friend—but Isabelle's heart leapt into her throat. She knew that furrowed brow, those clenched fists. He was angry again. *Now what?*

"Is everything all right?" she asked him, putting down her brush and rising to her feet.

He didn't answer. He didn't even look at her. He strode past her with great purpose, eyes fixed forward. A moment after he'd left her sight, she heard the door of the study slam closed.

Isabelle settled back into her chair, her hands shaking. His anger had such a terrible effect on her, much as she wished it didn't. It had always been the precursor to fights, and to the empty pit she got in her stomach when she knew that there was nothing she could do to help a situation.

"What do you think that was all about?" she asked Abby, mostly in an attempt to quiet her own nerves by acting normal. It didn't work. Her voice trembled like a plucked string. She folded her hands in her lap, closed her eyes, and took a deep breath to calm herself.

He just does this sometimes. He just gets angry and nobody knows why. Something must have happened outside to upset him. Maybe he's worried about losing the ranch again. But whatever it is, I know it's nothing to do with me. It can't be anything to do with me, so I shouldn't worry about it.

If only it was that easy. If only she could dismiss her worries as easily as she could tell herself to do so. But Cameron was the sort of man who projected everything he was experiencing. His anger radiated from him like heat from the sun. It was impossible to tell herself not to be affected by something like that.

With a deep breath, she got to her feet again. The only way this was going to be resolved was by confronting it directly. She picked Abby up and made her way down the hall toward the study. She'd talk to him and find out what had happened. No matter how angry he got, there had never been a time when a conversation hadn't been the solution. The same thing would be true this time, she was sure.

That confidence didn't make it any less difficult to knock on the study door. She only managed to make herself do it after several minutes spent standing there, talking to herself silently about what needed to be done. She was grateful to Abby for not making noise and giving her away while she wrestled with the decision. At last, she reached out and knocked on the door.

There was a long silence.

Maybe he wasn't going to answer. Maybe he would ignore her. He'd done that kind of thing before. *It isn't me he's angry at,* she reminded herself. *Whatever this is, it has nothing to do with me. How could it? I don't even know what happened.*

She was about to knock again when his voice called out. "Come in."

He sounded so gruff. It was with the greatest hesitance that she edged open the door and stepped inside. "Cameron?"

He didn't look up at her. He was writing something on a piece of paper, his hand moving quickly back and forth as if the words were too urgent to wait for anything. "Hmm?"

"I... you seemed distressed when you came in just now. Did something happen?"

"Nothing happened."

He wouldn't have snapped that way if he was telling the truth. "You can tell me, whatever it is."

"Did you look out the window just now? While you were in the kitchen?"

Meaning that if she had looked out, she would have seen something.

"No..."

If she had looked, she would have understood what the matter with him was. How she wished she had! "Cameron, you can't tell me that nothing happened."

"Nothing that concerns you. Go back out and finish what you were working on. You need to have your signs ready, don't you?"

"I have a few days. Cameron…" She hesitated. "This fair means a lot to me. I don't want you to be unhappy when the time comes. I want us to do this together."

"We're going to do it." His voice had dulled. The anger had faded. But the tired neutrality that replaced it seemed even worse to her. She was staring into a chasm.

"What are you writing?" she tried. Whatever it was, he seemed to find it urgent.

"A letter," he told her.

"To whom? About what? Does it have something to do with the bank?" Maybe that was why he was in such a dark mood.

With a long sigh, Cameron set down his pen and looked up at her.

Isabelle was shocked at the sight of him. The way his eyes narrowed, the way his jaw clenched and his lips pressed together so hard they were white—this was beyond even his normal anger. This was something new. Whatever had happened outside just now, it had clearly been serious.

"Cameron," she said, "you have to tell me things. We have to be able to confide in one another. Was it Duvall again?"

"No, it wasn't." His mouth snapped shut. He looked away.

Wasn't he going to say anything else? Was that really all he was going to tell her?

She leaned forward, trying to read the letter he was working on. If he wouldn't tell her what was going on, maybe she would be able to find something out that way. It was intrusive and wrong for her to do that, and it would probably only serve to make his anger worse, but she couldn't just be kept in the dark like this. She wouldn't.

He twitched the paper away from her and heaved a sigh. "Isabelle... once this week is over, you and Abby are going to have to leave the ranch."

Her blood froze. "What?"

"I'll let you stay through the Christmas fair." There was no emotion in his voice. It was empty, as if he was reading the words from a book he didn't care very much about. "You've put a lot of work into it, and you deserve the chance to see it through. But once the fair is over, you'll both have to go."

"Go where? I don't understand." It came out as a whisper. Her head spun. This had to be a bad dream. "We don't have anywhere else to go."

"I'm going to make an arrangement for you. We're going to find someplace you can go—someone who can take you for the short term, until something more permanent becomes available."

"But the ranch is already the place I'm staying until something permanent becomes available." A shudder passed through her. "If you're worried about losing the place, Cameron... I don't care. Truly. If you have to move into a house in town, I'll go with you. Whatever we have to do is all right with me. I don't want to have to start over somewhere new."

I want to stay with you. Don't make me leave you.

"No," Cameron said. "I don't think I'm going to lose the ranch." A hint of emotion broke through. Not anger. Pain. His voice cracked. "Your idea to have the Christmas fair here was a good one. I think it will make the difference."

"Then why…?"

"I can't have you here anymore," Cameron said. "I never wanted a family, Isabelle. You know that. I never wanted a woman and a child here. I've let you stay as long as I could, but it's time for us to go our separate ways. I'm done with this arrangement."

"You're making me leave because…" she forced herself to form the words. "Because you don't want me here anymore?"

He didn't even look at her. "I'm sorry," he said in that same empty voice.

He isn't sorry at all. He doesn't care. He has never cared.

She turned and fled the room before he could see her cry.

Chapter Twenty-Four

Adam sat back with a groan as he and Cameron pulled the foal they were delivering free of its mother. "That was the toughest birth we've had in a while."

Cameron nodded in agreement. He couldn't remember a horse struggling this much since he'd bought the ranch. She seemed all right now, thankfully, and as she turned to tend to the newborn, he too leaned back against the door of one of the stalls.

"Do you think it's the poison?" he asked, tipping his head back to rest against the wood and closing his eyes. "Could it have impacted the delivery?"

"I'm sure it did," Adam agreed. "We'll have to keep a close eye on that one in the coming days to make sure it's healthy, although the fact that she carried to term is certainly a good sign."

One of the other horses in the stable neighed, as if in agreement.

Adam let out a chuckle. "At least we didn't lose any," he said. "I was sure we were going to. They were so sick. It's fortunate we caught it when we did and stopped them from drinking at the river. If we hadn't done that, I'm sure we'd have lost most of the stock."

"Which only means Duvall will try something else," Cameron said heavily. The thought hung over his head like a storm cloud. He wished he could shake it off, but in the wake of Cyrus Pike's latest visit to the ranch, that felt impossible to do. Telling Isabelle that everything was going to be fine was one thing, but in his heart of hearts, he couldn't feel sure of that. No matter what he did, no matter how many things he tried, Duvall would just keep coming. Unless he made a mistake and got himself caught, there wouldn't be anything Cameron could do about it. There was no evidence that would allow the sheriff to intervene, even though they knew Duvall was the one behind the poisoning.

It was like ants crawling over his skin. He wanted to scream with the frustration of it. But screaming wouldn't achieve anything.

Nothing would achieve anything.

Adam looked over at him, sitting up straight so that he was no longer leaning on the stall door. "We're going to get him," he said. "We're going to find something, and we'll stop him. He's not that smart. It's only a matter of time before he makes a mistake and lands right in our laps."

His voice was full of confidence, but it wasn't reassuring. If anything, it only made Cameron angrier. He clenched his fists and gritted his teeth, breathing deeply to stop himself from snapping at his friend. Adam was only trying to help. But he couldn't understand this. He didn't have anything on the line, here. If they lost the ranch, he would just go find somewhere else to live and work. No one he cared for was going to be taken from him by all this.

That isn't fair. He cares about Isabelle too.

Yes, he did.

But not the way Cameron did. Not with an intensity that made his head spin at the very thought that something might pose a threat to her. Cameron couldn't control the way he felt when Isabelle was around. It was frightening.

Adam was looking at him. "All right," he said. "What's going on with you? You look like you're going to hit something." He knocked his fist against Cameron's bicep, and only then did Cameron realize how he'd flexed his arms in his anger. He forced them to relax.

"I'm not going to hit anything," he said.

"Well, that's good, because Russell Duvall isn't here. At least save it for him." Adam gave a forced laugh.

Cameron shook his head, his gaze fixed on his hands. "He's not even the one I'd like to hit."

"What do you mean?" Adam frowned, his brow furrowing.

"It's the other one," Cameron grunted. "That right-hand man of his. Cyrus Pike."

"That little weasel?" This time Adam's laugh sounded genuine. "I don't think we need to worry about *him*, Cameron. He looks like he'd blow over in a stiff wind."

"Yeah. Except he was on the property the other day, and I caught him looking in the window. Looking at Isabelle." The rage spiked in him again at the memory, and his arms flexed all the way up to the shoulder.

The smile dropped off of Adam's face. "What are you saying? He's been lurking around the property?"

"I don't know if he's been doing it regularly, but he certainly did that time."

"He could have spied on Eloise, too." Adam jumped to his feet. "You should have told me this."

Cameron shook his head, climbing to his feet as well. "I would have if that was a concern. She's my sister. I'd never have let anything happen to her." He swallowed. "He didn't get that far. He rode in as far as the main house, not your house or Eloise's on the back of the property. It was only Isabelle he was here to... to threaten."

Adam shook his head. "You still should have told me," he murmured. "We could have done something about it. Taken him out."

"I almost did," Cameron said through gritted teeth. "I mean, really. I had my gun in my hand. I almost shot him. I don't know why I let him ride away."

"Well, we should report this to Sheriff Grayson immediately," Adam said firmly, starting toward the door of the barn. "This could be the evidence we need to do something about these men."

"It isn't evidence," Cameron said wearily. "Technically, he didn't break any laws."

"Trespassing?" Adam demanded, incredulous.

"All right, maybe that. But I threatened to shoot him."

"You know Sheriff Grayson will take your side in this!"

"He has to follow the law, Adam." Cameron felt sick. "Trespassing won't send Pike to prison. He'll be fined, and that will just anger him more."

"What about threatening Isabelle?"

Cameron wasn't a cursing man, but he could have let one slip in that moment. He ground his teeth together. "He didn't actually say anything concrete." If only he had! If only there was something he could hold up and say, *This is what he did wrong. This is why he's dangerous.* "He said Isabelle was pretty. He saw her through the window, but it wasn't as if he was skulking in the bushes. He'll say he just happened to notice her. He'll lay it on thick, say he'd never have meant to make her uncomfortable…" He clenched his fists so tightly that he was sure his nails were going to dig into his palms and draw blood. "You know that's what will happen. If we report it, nobody will do anything, and he'll just be all the angrier. All the more determined to lash out at us—at Isabelle!"

His voice rose in pitch and volume as he spoke, and by the end, he was shouting. His whole body trembled with the effort of controlling his anger.

Adam's shoulders dropped. He regarded Cameron quietly for a moment.

"You really care for her," he said at last.

"What?" Cameron's stomach dropped. How had the conversation ended up here?

"You can admit it, Cameron. It's all right," Adam said quietly, taking a step closer. "I can tell. I like her too, but you… you're losing your ability to keep calm over this. You're out of control. Of course you are." He paused, turning away slightly, and his next words were barely above a whisper. "I felt the same way when I thought Eloise had been threatened."

Cameron had noticed the way Adam looked at his sister sometimes. There was certainly a conversation to be had on *that* subject, but his thoughts about it were very distant right now. "Isabelle is too good for me," he bit out. "She's too good for any of this." He wrapped his arms around his torso.

"Cameron, we're *all* too good for this. Duvall and Pike are low, criminal men. None of us deserve the things they're doing right now. That doesn't mean we don't stand together. You know that. We always stick together, no matter what. Isabelle would say the same. And..." He hesitated. "So would Ruth."

It was the worst time to bring up that name. Cameron flinched as if he had been struck.

Adam didn't back down. "You know how kind Ruth was," he murmured. "And you know she loved you more than anything in this world. All she wanted was to see you happy. You deserve to have love in your life again. If you feel something for Isabelle, you should tell her. You should make the most of it. You deserve that."

Why does everyone keep telling me what I deserve? It was like acid in a wound. First God's forgiveness, and now this?

No. That wasn't what Isabelle had said.

He *didn't* deserve forgiveness, she had said, because nobody deserved it. God offered it anyway.

Love didn't work that way.

You did have to deserve someone's love.

He had to be worthy of Isabelle. He knew with sickening certainty that he wasn't.

He turned and walked out of the stable without another word.

Chapter Twenty-Five

Outside, the snow had begun to fall again—just lightly now, not as blindingly as it had been a week ago. Cameron was sure the weather would clear by the day of the fair, so that was one thing, at least, that was going right.

Nothing else was.

Adam's words rang in his head as he walked with his hands stuffed into his pockets. His friend was right. He couldn't deny that. He did have feelings for Isabelle. Perhaps he might even have fallen in love with her—but his mind flinched away from that thought.

It wasn't only that he was unworthy of her, though he knew he was. It was also Ruth. He still loved Ruth. He would never stop loving her. How could he love her and love someone else at the same time? That shouldn't be possible. He was an abysmal husband for even entertaining the thought. It was like spitting on Ruth's grave. His heart was in ribbons at the thought of betraying her like that.

But...

He heard Adam's voice in his mind once more, telling him Ruth would want him to be happy. That she had cared for him, that she would want him to find love again.

Is there a chance he's right about that? Would she approve?

He thought of the day he had given Isabelle Ruth's Bible. He had been horrified to see her with it when she had first pulled it out, but then something inside him had changed. The thought had come to him, clear as a bell. *She would rather see it put to use than going to waste. She would rather see it with someone who loves it than packed away in a box.*

What if the same was true of him? Of his heart? What if Ruth was up in heaven hoping for him to let someone into his life so that *he* wouldn't go to waste?

It couldn't be true.

And yet... it made too much sense to ignore.

Without meaning to, he'd bypassed the house, walked up to the road, and started toward town. He had been so lost in his whirling thoughts that he hadn't kept track of what he was doing or how long he had been walking. Now, he realized that he had come to a halt in the middle of downtown.

The streets were empty. The weather had clearly driven everyone indoors. In the brightly lit shop windows, he could see people moving around with smiles on their faces, laughing and showing one another their purchases. Everyone was getting ready for Christmas.

It was fitting that Cameron was on the outside looking in. He wasn't a part of this joy. He couldn't be. Christmas had held no joy for him since Ruth's death.

Except that, this season, it had. Like a rooted plant that couldn't be killed, joy had begun to creep its way back in and take hold of his heart. It frightened him. If he could feel this, it could be destroyed again.

If I let myself care for Isabelle—for Abby—and something happens to them, it will destroy me. I won't survive that kind of pain twice.

"Cameron?"

He looked up, the voice breaking through his thoughts.

Edith Calloway stood in front of him, a shawl wrapped around her head, shivering slightly in the cold. "Are you going to come inside?" she asked him.

"Come inside?" he repeated blankly.

Then he realized where he was.

Without meaning to, without even knowing where his feet were directing him, he had walked straight to the church.

She must have seen him standing here from the window and come out to find out what was going on. Now, she rested a hand on his arm. "It's cold out here," she said softly. "Come inside."

He hadn't been inside the church in four years. Not since Ruth had died. "I—I don't think…" he stammered, unsure what he wanted to say. It felt wrong. He shouldn't go in. This place wasn't for him anymore. He had abandoned it. He couldn't just have it back now. That wasn't the way things worked.

"It's all right," Edith murmured. "Just come inside and get warm." She hooked her arm through his and led him up the steps and into the building.

He'd worried that he would be confronted by people once he stepped inside. Perhaps the ladies of the town would be having one of their prayer meetings, or maybe Pastor John would be working on next week's sermon. But the place was empty apart from himself and Edith.

She noticed him looking around the room. "I came to do a little tidying up today," she said. "I didn't expect that anyone would come by."

"I'm sorry."

"No. Don't apologize. I'm so glad you're here." She smiled warmly. "We've all longed to see you come back to church, Cameron. You know you're always welcome here. Would you like to sit down?"

She pointed to a pew. He hesitated, but the prospect of going back out into the snow was tiring. Besides, being here had reassured him in a way he hadn't expected. It was like coming home after being on the road for a long time.

He sat down and slumped forward, elbows on his knees. Edith sat next to him and waited.

She wants me to speak first. But how could he? How could he possibly unburden his heart when it was full to bursting with so many different things? How could he begin to explain what was going on right now?"

"Is this about Isabelle?" Edith asked him softly.

He darted a look at her.

She smiled slightly. "It's not such a guess as you might think. I've been around, watching you two get ready for the Christmas fair. I see the way you look at her when you think she isn't going to notice. Like she hung the stars in the sky."

Cameron winced. He hadn't realized it was so obvious. "She's a very special woman," he said gruffly.

"She certainly is. And a welcome addition to our community… though I know it's not your intention for this to be her permanent home."

"She can't go on living with a man she isn't married to. It's not proper." Cameron rubbed his hands on his knees, trying to center his thoughts.

"You don't see any other solution to that besides sending her away?" Edith's voice was mild, but her gaze was fixed on him, as if she was trying to etch an idea into his mind.

"I can't marry her." The words got harder every time he said them.

"You could, though," Edith murmured, pivoting slightly so that she was facing him even more directly. "You really could, Cameron. She's an unmarried woman. You are an unmarried man. And the two of you are very fond of one another. People have married for much less than that."

Cameron hung his head. That was true, of course, and yet it didn't come close to alleviating his concerns. "I don't know what Ruth would say," he managed. His voice broke.

"Ruth loved you."

Cameron turned away slightly. "Of course she did. And I loved her. I love her still. What would she say if she saw me with another woman? Falling in love with another woman? Raising another child?"

"I think she would be happy," Edith said softly. She sat very still. Cameron was reminded of a hunter trying not to spook a prey animal. "I think she'd be glad to see you living your life to the fullest."

"But you don't know!" Cameron exploded. He restrained himself from jumping to his feet, but he gripped the back of the pew in front of him so hard he was afraid it would splinter. "You don't know what she would say, and neither do I. We can't know. I can *never know.* Anything I tell myself about what she would want is just a story, nothing more. I could be lying to myself. I could be making it up to give myself permission to do something I want to do, when the truth is that I would be breaking Ruth's heart. And how could I ever do anything that would hurt her? She—she died because I wasn't there!"

A single sob burst forth on those final words, and he buried his head in his hands.

For a long time, Edith didn't speak.

Cameron was aware of every breath that passed through his lungs. They were stolen breaths, and they ached. He shouldn't have them. Ruth should have been the one to live. He should have lost his life in the fire and she should have survived to raise their son. That was what was right. He was the husband and father, and that was what he should have done for his family. If he'd had the choice, he would have done it. He had thought so every day since.

Finally, Edith spoke.

"They didn't die because you weren't there, Cameron," she said, resting a gentle hand on his shoulder. Her voice was slow and even, steady like a river. "They died because there was a fire. It was a terrible tragedy."

"I don't know if I can ever forgive myself," he whispered.

"You don't have to forgive yourself. God forgives you," Edith said. "That's His gift to us."

The words were so kind. Her voice was so warm. He wanted nothing more than to accept what she was saying. To sink into it and forget all his worries.

But I can't know if that's true, either. Maybe it's another story we're telling ourselves because we want it to be true. I can't know what Ruth would say, and I can't know what God would say, either.

The thought came in like a chill wind, disrupting the warmth he'd felt when he'd entered the church. "I'm sorry," he whispered, rising to his feet once more. "I shouldn't have come here."

Edith looked stricken. "Cameron, don't go. It's a miracle that you made it here today."

But I don't know if I believe in miracles. If miracles are real, where were they when the fire caught? If God forgives everyone, why didn't he get Ruth and Philip out of that house? Where was that miracle? That was the one I needed—not getting me to walk into a church.

He couldn't stay. He regretted coming into town in the first place. It had left him in more turmoil than ever. "No," he said. "I have to go. Thank you for talking to me." He all but choked on the words. He didn't know if he meant them or not. It had been kind of her to try, but was he really any better off?

Maybe he never would be.

If that was true, there was no question that it was best for Isabelle to leave as soon as possible. Even if it hadn't been for Cyrus Pike, getting away from him—from all this anguish and turmoil—would have been the right thing for her.

Shame swamped him as he hurried toward the door, pulling it open and rushing back out into the snow before Edith could stop him.

This is good.

This is for the best, this stinging wind in my face, this inescapable ache in my heart.

This is exactly what I deserve.

Chapter Twenty-Six

Isabelle had been walking through a fog for days, unable to believe that everything had gone so wrong so fast. The Christmas fair was only three days away, but she couldn't bring herself to do any work toward bringing it to life. She had gone out to the barn earlier today to look at the booths the men had built, but almost immediately she'd had to turn around and run back into the house, heart hammering, palms sweating. It was so recently that those booths had been evidence, in her mind, of Cameron's care and regard for her. He'd built them because he respected the plan she had come up with and wanted to see it be a success.

Looking at them now, she remembered the way he'd spun her around in his arms the day they had gone to the bank. She remembered feeling sure that he was going to kiss her, and that she was going to let him.

She couldn't possibly have been any more foolish.

So she would stick to the house. There was no need for her to go out to the barn. The preparations for the fair were far enough underway that they would be able to continue without her involvement.

I'm not needed.

It was all she could do to continue with the chores inside the house, knowing that Cameron no longer wanted her here and would be sending her away at the earliest convenience. She had thought about giving this up, too. What difference did it make now? She owed him nothing, and she wouldn't convince him to let her stay.

And yet, some small, stubborn part of her was determined to carry on anyway. To show Cameron that she had been of use to him, and that when she was gone, there was something he would miss. Even if he didn't realize it until after she left, that would be something. She imagined him wandering about the house as the dust and clutter started to accumulate, forced to notice that—if only in this small way—his life was worse with her gone.

I'm being petty, she told herself. *It's selfish and wrong to want him to be sad after I'm gone. I don't want that. I want good things for Cameron.*

It was true. But she also wanted to know that she'd made an impact on his life. She wanted to be able to tell herself that he would remember her after she was gone. Maybe the house no longer being clean was one small way to make that happen.

So she cleaned with fire in her heart, the anger and determination fueling her to work more quickly than she would have done in the past. And for the first time, she dared to go into Cameron's bedroom.

She held the dusting rag like a weapon as she stepped into the dim space. It was by far the most untidy room in the house, thanks to the fact that she had never touched it. Clothes were strewn everywhere—clearly his habit was to cast them aside after taking them off. She was surprised anything ever made it to the laundry. With a sigh, she set the dusting rag on the table next to the unmade bed, thinking she would gather the clothes. Let him come back to a properly cleaned room. Let him see what he would be missing.

But as she set the rag down, something caught her eye.

It was a photograph.

Before she had even thought about what she was doing, she picked it up, studying the subjects.

The man was obviously Cameron—but a very different Cameron from the one she knew. He was several years younger, his face less lined than it was now. But the most significant difference was the expression on his face—an unguarded smile that tugged at her heartstrings. *So much joy! He used to be happy. He has never looked like this since I've known him.*

It was an agonizing realization. She had known, of course, that losing his family had changed him, but there was a difference between knowing it and seeing it for herself. To really understand the change in him nearly broke her heart. Tears came to her eyes, and she lowered the photograph for a moment, unable to bear looking at him while he was so unguarded.

Then she gritted her teeth and looked at the photograph again.

Ruth.

For that was who the woman in the picture had to be. She was sitting in a chair in front of Cameron, a radiant glow on her face, peace shining from her eyes. He had his hands resting on her shoulders. In her arms was a tiny bundle that could only be baby Philip.

To put a face to the woman whose name had been such a part of her life since she'd arrived here in Wintervale made her short of breath. It made Ruth seem real in a way she hadn't before now. She had been a powerful character from Cameron's past, but now she was a flesh-and-blood woman—

smiling eyes, gentle hands, and a laugh that burst forth from her even as she was having her photograph taken. It was as if her personality simply couldn't be contained.

Isabelle couldn't look away from the photograph. She was captivated.

This is what he lost. This is what he mourns—the reason he can't move on.

Seeing it—seeing *them*—made it impossible to fault him. She wouldn't have been able to let go either.

"What are you doing?"

She whirled around, photograph still in her hands. The air in her lungs seemed to freeze at the realization that she had been caught snooping.

Cameron stood in the door, hands on his hips, glowering at her. "Why are you in my room?" he snapped. "You're not supposed to be in here."

"I...I came in to dust..." Her voice was barely a whisper. She'd known he would realize she had been in here, but she was mortified to be caught in the act. Her body temperature seemed to rise several degrees. She cleared her throat and tried to speak again. "I was trying to help. I've never cleaned this room."

"For good reason. This is my bedroom, Isabelle. This is *private*." It was a low growl, and it left her feeling much smaller than she was.

She took a step back, and her hip bumped the bedside table. Her hand went out to brace her against it, and she saw his eyes dart to the photograph she still held.

His eyes went wide, blazing with fury. He strode across the room and snatched the photograph from her hands. "Who told you that you could come in here and disturb my things?" he demanded, voice rising. "What made you think you had the right to touch this?"

Isabelle had nothing to say in her own defense. Cleaning was one thing, but this… "You're right," she murmured, unable to make eye contact with him. "I shouldn't have come in. I certainly shouldn't have touched the photograph. I… forgive me." She pushed past him and hurried toward the door, tears of humiliation stinging her eyes.

He let out a sigh. "Wait."

She stopped in her tracks but didn't turn around. She couldn't face him.

"I have to apologize to you," he said, his voice low and gruff.

She shook her head. She didn't want an insincere apology. "You don't have to do anything. I was in the wrong."

"Let me say this," he insisted hoarsely. "Please."

She gritted her teeth. This wasn't going to be anything she wanted to hear.

He swallowed audibly. "I shouldn't have shouted at you for looking at the picture. I know you were only curious."

Now she turned around. His eyes were closed, his hands in his pockets. The photograph sat on the bedside table once more, restored exactly to the place it had been when she'd picked it up—he had clearly set it down with extreme care. He looked more sheepish than she had ever seen him.

She didn't want this. She didn't want to feel sorry for him. That was too difficult. She wanted to be able to push away everything she was feeling, and she couldn't do that while she could see how sad it was making him.

"I shouldn't have been in here," she said. "I knew you didn't want me in this room, and I came in anyway. I have no excuse. You don't have to say anything else."

She turned and started to leave again.

His hand on hers stopped her. He pulled her back around to face him, making her gasp. His grip was gentle. She could have broken it if she'd wanted to. It was that very fact that stopped her. If he had tried to force her to stay, she would have fought that much harder to go. But with him giving her the choice like this…

She looked up into his narrowed eyes.

Torment.

Pain shone from them, as brightly and clearly as the sun in the sky. It scorched her. It was in the wrinkles between his eyebrows, the hard press of his lips together, the set of his jaw—but more than any of that, she realized, she simply knew him well enough to see that he was hurting. If it hadn't been Cameron, she would have flinched, tried to pull herself back from the intensity of what she was seeing.

But in spite of everything, she still wanted to ease his suffering. Seeing him like this made her long to draw closer, to put her arms around him and soothe him. To take on some of his burden, even if she couldn't rid him of it completely.

"You understand, don't you?" he croaked. His gaze searched hers, and his hand gripped hers tightly. "I have to send you away because of them."

"Because you haven't gotten over your wife's death," she said gently. "Of course you haven't. You don't have to apologize to me for that."

"I'm not apologizing for that," he said sharply. "You're right. I haven't gotten over losing her. I never will. But, Isabelle… the reason you have to go is that I can't protect *you*."

She blinked. "Protect me?"

"From the men who want to take my ranch. The men who poisoned my horses." He raked his free hand through his hair in clear frustration. "They'll do anything to make me feel unsafe. Anything to run me off this land. And if that means you and Abby are at risk, well, that's a chance I'm just not willing to take. I can't have you here if you aren't going to be safe. If I lose even more people I care for…" He shook his head, released her hand, and turned away. "I don't deserve the good things that come into my life," he murmured. "They're always ruined. Being too close to me is dangerous, and I'm not going to let the same thing that happened to Ruth happen to you."

Isabelle's heart skipped a beat.

He does care.

He's sending me away because he cares. It's not because he doesn't want me here.

Her self-control snapped. She moved forward and positioned herself in front of him. He avoided her gaze, but she reached up and rested a firm hand on his cheek, giving him no choice but to look at her.

"I want you to let me stay," she said softly. "I'm asking you to let me stay."

He gripped her wrist. To her shock, he didn't pull her hand away from his face. Instead, he turned toward her, leaning into her touch for just a moment, allowing her to almost cradle his head. Her heart ached with compassion for him. She wanted to wrap her arms around him, to pull him close and find the words to convince him that everything would be all right. If only she knew what to say.

"I can't," he groaned. "I can't do it, Isabelle."

"You want to." She held her breath.

For a moment she thought he was going to deny it, but he only shook his head once. "That doesn't matter."

"Yes, it does. It matters more than anything," she told him firmly. "You want me here. I want to be here."

"It isn't safe."

"*Life* isn't safe. We still have to choose a path to take, even when all the paths available to us feel perilous," she said. "You worry far too much, Cameron."

"I worry the right amount." He tipped his head forward. Their foreheads were nearly touching now. Isabelle's heart was about to burst from her chest.

"Come to me, all you who are weary and burdened," she said softly. "And I will give you rest."

"What is that?"

"Matthew 11:28," she said. "My mother's favorite, when she was alive. She used to quote it to remind me that when things felt most dark, God was by my side. It's all right to lay down your burdens, Cameron. It's all right to let someone care for you. You *do* deserve that."

"The last person I allowed to care for me lost her life," he bit out.

"And that wasn't your fault." She stroked his cheek. "You didn't set that fire, my love."

He sucked in a breath at the term of endearment. Isabelle felt she was at the edge of a precipice, but she couldn't regret letting the word come out. However he responded, it was good to have said it aloud. It was good to have finally spoken honestly.

"You're a good man," she murmured. "You're a good companion to me, and you would be a wonderful father for Abby. I want to stay here. I want you to let me love you, Cameron. And if it means we face danger, let's face it together."

He turned his head ever so slightly, and his lips pressed against her palm.

A shiver of longing, more powerful than anything she had ever felt, passed through Isabelle. His lips were warm and tender, firm and gentle all in one. She ached to pull her hand away, to close the distance between them and kiss him properly, even though it startled her to want such a thing so fervently. She was on the verge of losing control, and it was enough to make her wish that she had never had control in the first place.

"Isabelle," he breathed.

"Let me stay with you," she repeated. It was a plea, but there was no supplication in her voice. She made the request as firm as she could. It was almost a demand. That was what he needed. He had to hear her strength right now, to know that she understood what she was asking and that she wanted it wholeheartedly.

"I..."

Before he could answer, though, the moment was shattered by a loud crash.

Isabelle was so startled that she sprang back from him, though she instantly regretted ending the contact between them. Her fingers longed for his face, her palm for the warmth of his lips. She shook away her desire. "What was that sound?"

Cameron's whole body had gone rigid. "Someone's in the house."

Panic surged through Isabelle and choked her. *Abby!*

Chapter Twenty-Seven

Not the baby. Please don't let any harm come to the baby.

Cameron couldn't breathe as he ran toward the room Abby shared with Isabelle. His heart threatened to beat its way right out of his chest. Terror gripped him in a vice.

I should have sent them away the first time Duvall came onto my land. I should have known right then how unsafe this was. I let this go on because I like Isabelle so much. I've been unforgivably selfish. If anything has happened, it's entirely my fault.

He ripped open the door of the bedroom and burst inside.

The first thing he noticed made his blood freeze in his veins.

The secondhand cradle Abby had been sleeping in lay in the middle of the room, tipped over on its side. That had been the crash they had heard. The baby herself was lying on the floor, staring up at the ceiling. She wasn't crying.

Isabelle let out a dismayed wail and hurried past him, dropping to her knees beside Abby. She rested a hand on Abby's chest and another on her head. "She fell? Is she all right? Why isn't she crying? What's the matter with her?"

A cold calm descended over Cameron as tears welled up in Isabelle's eyes. He strode into the room and looked around. "I'm not sure that's what happened," he said slowly. "She couldn't have landed in the middle of the room if she'd just fallen out of the cradle."

"What do you mean?" Isabelle seemed to decide it was safe to pick Abby up. She lifted her carefully and cradled her, and at long last, Abby began to cry. Perhaps the shock had worn off. Isabelle murmured to her and kissed her head.

"I think someone took her out of the cradle and put her on the floor," Cameron said. He lifted the cradle and set it back upright. "Look at the distance between it and where she was placed. She didn't fall there. Someone moved her."

Isabelle made a choking sound, her eyes wide. The color drained from her face, and her mouth opened and closed soundlessly a few times.

Cameron understood. The thought of someone coming in here and taking Abby out of the cradle… it was unthinkable. Horrifying.

It was bad enough to think of an accident in which the cradle had tipped over and Abby had fallen. But this was far worse. Someone had done this deliberately to try to frighten them, he was sure—and it had worked.

"Is she all right?" Cameron asked. He knelt on the floor and laid a gentle hand on Abby's back. He could feel the tiny flutter of her heart beating against his palm. It should have been a relief, but nothing could soothe the mounting rage within him. Someone had dared to come into his home and hurt this little baby. "She's crying—is something the matter with her? Should I call for a doctor?"

"You don't need to," Isabelle said, rather breathless.

"Are you sure?" He leaned back and regarded her carefully. Had she thought that through, or was she reacting out of emotion?

"That's not how she cries when she's in pain," Isabelle said, sitting back on her heels and holding the baby close. "Remember the way she sounded when she wasn't getting enough food? How sharp her cries were? If she was hurt, she would sound like that. This cry just means she's upset and needs comfort."

How could she doubt that she's a good mother? Knowing what every sound Abby makes means... That's exactly what a good mother would do.

He wanted to stay with them, to continue monitoring Abby himself, but he resisted the temptation. Instead, he got to his feet and went to the window.

"This isn't latched," he murmured, pressing his fingertips to the glass and feeling it give way. "It's open."

Isabelle's head darted up. "It's *open*?" She shook her head. "I wouldn't have left the window open…"

"No, I don't think you did," Cameron agreed darkly, his fingers now moving over the latch. "It was forced. The latch is broken. Someone yanked it open from the outside."

"So you're right. Someone *was* in the house." Fear spiked through her voice, making it rise in pitch. "Someone did this to Abby."

"We're lucky they didn't take her," Cameron growled.

A soft whimper escaped Isabelle, and Cameron turned to see her curl her body protectively around the baby. "We almost lost her," she whispered. "Why would anyone come into the house just to do *this*? Was anything taken?"

"There's nothing in here. Only your things. Is anything missing?"

She looked around the room. "The Bible."

Cameron's heart turned to stone.

His face must have changed, because she spoke quickly. "No—it isn't gone," she assured him. "It's there. It's on the floor in the corner. But I would never have left it there, Cameron. I always keep it in the drawer of the bedside table. I read from it each night before I go to bed, and then I always put it away. It's important to me to take good care of it. I know how precious it is. I might have forgotten to put it in the drawer, but I would *never* have allowed it to end up on the floor."

Cameron strode over and picked it up, gripping it tightly. The Bible hadn't been damaged at all. It was easy to imagine his enemies ripping out pages, glorying in destroying this sacred book, but maybe they had been in too much of a hurry to do that. *Thank goodness for small mercies.*

"It had to be Duvall or his right-hand man, Pike." The words ground their way out through Cameron's teeth. He set the Bible down on the bedside table and paced back and forth across the room, needing to do something, not knowing what he *could* do.

Isabelle climbed slowly to her feet, still cradling Abby against her, and watched him, waiting. Her eyes were wide.

He stopped pacing and faced her. "You see it now, don't you?" he asked. Each word was a knife to his heart—he didn't want to be saying these things. More than anything, he wished he didn't have to. "You understand the danger."

She must have heard the weight in his words. Her gaze dropped. "What about the fair?"

"I should never have agreed to it." He hated to say it, but it was the truth. "We'll go ahead with it, but if you can find somewhere else to go—or if I can find somewhere for you—you might have to leave before it takes place."

Her eyes widened. She stepped back, stricken. "You'd make me leave before the fair? It's only days away."

"Look at what happened here!" The tension in his body bled through to his voice, and he could hardly keep from shouting. He clenched his fists and resumed pacing. "We almost lost Abby, Isabelle. We weren't even far away from her. We were in the other room. She should be safe taking a nap in her own cradle, and she isn't. This house isn't safe for her, and it isn't safe for you."

His voice broke under the weight of his failures. He couldn't provide a safe refuge for the people who mattered to him—was there any more powerful way for a man to fail? He choked on his own self-loathing and turned away, unwilling to let her see his face.

"You have to go as soon as possible," he said. "This is just going to keep happening. You know I'm right. You don't want Abby to be in this situation any more than I do."

She was silent. He longed to know how she was responding to his words—a part of him yearned for her to argue, as she had before. He wanted her to insist that they were in this together, and that she would stay with him no matter what.

If it was just her, she might. But I know she won't put the baby at risk. What happened here is going to change everything, and it should.

He couldn't look at her. It was excruciating to imagine the resignation on her face as she finally gave in. He couldn't force himself to witness it.

"All right," she whispered, and Cameron's heart dropped as the last shred of hope was ripped away. "I'll look for something else. I'll ask Edith and Pastor John to help me. Maybe I can stay with them in town until I find something."

So she really would be leaving right away.

Making the decision that she had to go had been so difficult that, somehow, he hadn't even allowed his thoughts to come to the point of wondering what it would be like after she was gone. Now, though, he was forced to consider it. It would happen so soon. Tomorrow, maybe. There would be no reason for her to remain here if the pastor and his wife agreed to take her in while they made other plans.

And yet, he couldn't face it. Even knowing it was the right thing, that it was for the best, he couldn't accept it.

"Don't go into town," he said, turning back to face her at last and carefully controlling the expression on his face so he wouldn't give anything away. She had tears in her eyes. They were beginning to slip down her cheeks, and the sight of it almost broke him. He forced his heart to turn to stone. "You should stay here until you figure out where you're going."

"But if it isn't safe here... I can't risk anything happening to Abby." She buried her face in the baby's downy hair.

"Nothing will happen. We can protect you both for a few days," he said. "It's not safe in the long term because eventually something will slip. But you're safer with me and Adam around you than you would be in town, where Duvall and Pike might easily find you. You'd be far less protected there than you will be here." He moved closer to her and allowed himself to rest his hands on her shoulders.

She leaned forward slightly at his touch. Even now, even as they were trying to separate from one another, she wanted to be close to him, and Cameron could no longer ignore that. The tension between them was pulling them together all the more now that they both knew they needed to be apart. In a moment, something was going to snap, and he could only imagine how painful that snapping would be.

I'm making it worse by allowing her to stay here longer. If she left right now, tonight, we could both start to move on.

But he really did believe she would be safer here than she would in town. The problem with going into town was that everyone would know what had happened. Duvall would find out right away. He would still be able to get to her, to use her to hurt Cameron. The only difference would be that Cameron wouldn't be able to protect her.

She has to stay on the ranch until we get her out of Wintervale altogether. It's the only safe way to manage this.

He allowed coldness to settle over him like a blanket. It was the same protection from emotion he'd reached for after Ruth had died. If he could keep his focus on practical things and away from matters of the heart, he would be able to get through the days.

"I'm going out," he said sharply. He turned away from her. "Stay in this room. Stay away from the windows. Close the curtains and don't let anyone inside. I'm going to look around the grounds and make sure there's no one out there, and then I'll be back in."

He didn't wait for her to respond. He didn't look back to see what her reaction was. He strode out the door, down the hall and into the kitchen, where he pulled his gun off the wall and checked to make sure it was loaded.

If one of them is out there, I swear, I won't hesitate this time. This time, I will pull the trigger.

The cold in which he had cloaked himself protected him from the intensity of that thought. He forced himself not to think about the expression on Isabelle's face when she'd seen the baby on the floor and the cradle tipped on its side. That expression—the horror she had felt—would melt his icy exterior, and he would lose the ability to focus on the task at hand. That couldn't be allowed.

He fixed his eyes on the barn and jogged forward. The yard was empty, that much was easy to see, but it was more than possible that the culprit had gone to the barn. Maybe to attack the horses again, or maybe even to lure Cameron out and force a confrontation—and if that was what Russell Duvall wanted, he would get it.

Cameron ripped the door of the barn open. It took a moment for his eyes to adjust to the darkness, and in that time, he knew he was at a disadvantage. It would have been easy for someone hiding in the shadows to lash out, to pull a gun or strike out with a fist and end his life.

He should have been cautious, but he wasn't. His determination overrode caution.

In the end, it didn't matter. There was no one in the barn. The place was empty. As his eyes adjusted, he saw the horses blinking sleepily at him, none of them remotely distressed. They seemed mildly surprised at his appearance, but that was all.

He walked in anyway and went to the back of the building, peering into the farthest corners. He looked over the doors of the stalls one by one to make sure nobody was crouching there, but he quickly satisfied himself that the stable was empty.

I should have known. Of course whoever broke into the house wouldn't linger.

He wished they had. He wished he could take advantage of this moment to force a confrontation between himself and Duvall. *I would be justified in anything I did to him right now, after he broke into my house and put his hands on the baby. If I could put an end to this, one way or another, then Isabelle would be able to stay.*

Fire rose within him, melting the cold exterior he had drawn around himself, as he realized how badly he *wanted* this to turn violent. He wanted to pull the trigger on the gun in his hand and end the turmoil he was going through. He wanted to stop Duvall once and for all.

If anything happens to Isabelle or Abby because of the two of them, I'll never forgive myself.

He had been living with the pain of what had happened to Ruth and Philip all these years, but now he faced the threat of compounding that agony. It was terrifying, but he couldn't shrink before it. He had to rise. He had to face this challenge and ensure that the people he cared about would be unharmed.

He left the barn and walked around the property a little longer, just to be sure that there was nobody there. The cold didn't seem to touch him today. He was aware of it, but only on an intellectual level. It was as if he was reading about cold in a book—he couldn't really feel it.

He couldn't feel much of anything. Only his anger, slow and simmering deep within his chest, growing more powerful with every passing moment. That was the only thing that fueled him now.

He would do whatever it took to protect Isabelle and Abby.

And as soon as he could find a safe way to do it, he would muster the strength to send them far away from here.

For their own sakes, he would never see them again.

If he could make that sacrifice, maybe he could finally begin to be forgiven.

Chapter Twenty-Eight

Two days later, Isabelle found herself still under strict orders to remain inside the house at all times, and for once, she was not at all inclined to disobey.

She sat in the bedroom she shared with Abby, nervous even to light a candle. She was on pins and needles, a feeling that had been with her from the moment she'd become aware of the intrusion into the house. Every few moments, she would spin around, convinced by the prickling at the back of her neck that someone was watching her.

She knew it was impossible. She'd kept the curtains drawn all day, even though it meant the room was dimly lit. She sat on the edge of her bed now, fingers digging into the mattress as she tried to settle her thoughts. Cameron and Adam were outside, and so was the sheriff. They were keeping an eye on the house and the surrounding land. No one would get by them. She was safe. Abby was safe.

Except that we aren't. Cameron was right here in the house when that person—whoever it was—broke in and took Abby right out of her cradle. And if he believed he could do anything to make us safe... well, then he wouldn't be sending us away.

She believed that now. She was confident that he wouldn't have resolved to send her away from the house if he'd thought she would be safe here. If she hadn't doubted it, she would have fought harder to stay. But having seen Abby in danger, everything was different. She stared at the cradle. Abby had, in the past few months, become her child just as much as she was Vivienne's. Isabelle wasn't only caring for her out of loyalty to her friend. She loved this baby as her own, and it would destroy her if anything were to happen to Abby. She knew now that she would go to the ends of the Earth to make sure Abby was safe.

"Oh, Abby," she said softly, looking over at the cradle, still unable to rise from her seat on the bed. She was frozen—movement felt impossible. "What are we going to do? How are we going to get through this?"

Abby cooed in response, unaware that anything was wrong.

"You and I will be together no matter what," Isabelle murmured, more for her own sake than for Abby's. "That's one thing no one will take away from us, sweetheart, I promise you."

Abby kicked her feet against the bedding.

"And there is still the Christmas fair," Isabelle said, though the words were like swallowing rocks. "Maybe that will be… fun."

It was almost impossible to believe that the Christmas fair was happening tomorrow. She had spent so much time planning, so much time looking forward to it, that now it felt as if it was a part of someone else's life. It belonged to someone who had been happy and excited about the future, not someone who had been filled with fear and despair. Everything else had fallen apart, so how could the fair still be happening?

But it's good that it is. It means so much to the town.

Yes, that was true. But the purpose of the fair, the reason for having it here in the first place, had been to help Cameron keep the ranch. To thwart the things Duvall was trying to do to him. Now, after the break-in, it seemed that they'd only managed to make Duvall angrier and more determined. The Christmas fair no longer seemed like a sign of hope or triumph. Instead, it was a sign of everything that had gone wrong.

I can't just sit here on the bed all day. Already, she had been here for hours, numb and unmoving, unable to force herself into action. But she had to get up. There were things to do, and it wouldn't do to give in to the heaviness of her heart.

She got up and walked over to the cradle. Abby was awake and had been for some time, kicking her feet merrily in the air, unaware that anything at all was wrong. Isabelle lifted her out and changed her, dressing her in one of the beautiful new Christmas outfits she'd made. She'd had such hope when she had sewn this outfit that it was painful even to hold it in her hands now, to remember the fantasies she'd had of dressing Abby up for Christmas morning. She couldn't picture celebrating Christmas anymore. She had no idea what the holiday was going to look like.

She carried Abby into the kitchen, sat her in her chair, and prepared the morning bottle, surrounded by fog, as if she was in a dream. She was so lost to the world that the knock on the door didn't even register as something odd until it came the second time.

She froze, though, when she heard it again, panic rooting her to the spot.

Is this Duvall? Has he come to finish what he started?

He couldn't have, could he? It was supposed to be relatively safe right now, with the men on patrol outside the house. But had Duvall slipped past them somehow? She hurried to Abby's side, about to pick her up and run, to hide under the bed if she had to.

"Isabelle? It's me."

The tension drained from Isabelle's body at the sound of Eloise's voice. She hurried to the door and opened it to let her friend in.

Eloise crossed the threshold, a smile on her face and a pie in her hands. "Did I scare you?" she asked. "You're white as a sheet!"

"I—" Suddenly, it was all too much for Isabelle. While she had sat frozen in her bedroom, she had been able to keep her emotions at bay, but now they crashed over her like a wave. She let out a sob.

"Oh, Isabelle." Eloise enfolded her in a hug. "It's all right. Everything's going to be all right."

"I don't see how it can be," Isabelle cried. "I know I shouldn't give up hope. I know I should have faith in the future. But... I really thought it would work out. I thought that, somehow, I would be able to stay here."

"Come and stay at my house," Eloise said. "I have a spare room. You and Abby would be comfortable there. You don't have to leave town."

"Yes, we do. You know we do. After what happened... Abby could have been hurt. She could have been kidnapped." Isabelle pulled free of Eloise's embrace and sat down at the kitchen table. Then she looked up. "Oh no—I didn't even finish preparing the milk."

"Stay there. I'll do it," Eloise instructed. She went to the stove and began to work on getting Abby's bottle ready.

"If it was just me, I would stay," Isabelle said. "I would come to your house, force Cameron to see that I'm committed to him—to this arrangement. But it isn't just me, and I can't have Abby in danger. I can't let any harm come to her. It's not worth the risk. Nothing is worth that." Tears streamed down her face. "I just don't want to go. Being here has meant so much to me, and I don't want it to be over. I hate that an evil man like Russell Duvall gets to take this from us."

"You don't think you would feel safer at my house?" Eloise asked, testing the temperature of the milk against her arm. "You know that Duvall wouldn't come looking for you there."

"It's the first place he'd look when he realized I wasn't here," Isabelle countered. She picked up an apple that someone had left on the table and fidgeted with the stem, spinning it in her fingers. "I don't even like the idea of you being there, Eloise. If Duvall can't reach me to hurt me and use me as a weapon against Cameron, he's going to look for someone else to do it to, and I think you'll be the very first person he'll target." A shiver ran through her at the thought of Eloise, left behind and in danger when she was gone. "I know I can't make you do anything you don't want to do, Eloise, but I would feel better if you weren't here anymore either."

She folded her hands in her lap and looked down, shame creeping over her. It was right to take Abby away, but it was wrong to run from the people she cared about. It was wrong to ask Eloise to leave Cameron.

There aren't any right answers. There's nothing that would be right to do.

Eloise lifted Abby from her chair and sat down next to Isabelle, bottle in hand. She began to feed Abby. "You know I'm not going to leave," she said softly.

"I know you won't." Eloise would never leave her brother. Isabelle ached for the freedom to show that strength and loyalty. She would never have left either. Not if she hadn't had to.

"Listen," Eloise said, leaning forward across the table. "I know everything feels awful right now, but don't despair. The Christmas fair is happening tomorrow, don't forget."

Isabelle laughed bitterly—she couldn't help it. "I don't think a few hours at the Christmas fair is going to help me now," she said. "I don't even want to go anymore."

"Oh, Isabelle, you have to. Everyone wants to see you there, to congratulate you on all the hard work you did to make this a reality. The whole town is excited, you know, and everyone recognizes that it's all your doing."

"It isn't all my doing. Everyone worked together." Isabelle's heart was hollow. She stared at the wood grain of the table, getting lost in the pattern. Tomorrow, everyone would be festive and joyful and happy. Everyone would want to come up to her and tell her what good work she had done.

Isabelle quite simply didn't want to hear it. It would be salt in her wounds to have to listen to those words. If she could have spent tomorrow in bed with the blankets pulled over her head, she would have done so. If she could have left Wintervale tonight, she thought she might have done that, too. Better to move along, to put this behind her and end the whole thing so she could finally start to recover.

Eloise glanced out the window. "Adam is coming up to the door," she said. "Can I let him in?"

"I'll do it. You have the baby." Isabelle rose to her feet and went to the door. She opened it and saw Adam approaching the porch, and she left the door open and went back to her seat. The winter wind blew in while they waited for Adam, a fact Isabelle noticed with only mild interest. The cold didn't make her shiver. It didn't seem able to touch her.

Adam entered the house and closed the door. Eloise sat up a little straighter, pink coming into her cheeks. "How are things out there?"

"We haven't seen anyone," Adam said. "I came here to check on the three of you." His gaze fixed on Eloise. "I saw you walking over. Are you all right?"

Eloise clearly couldn't keep the smile off her face. Isabelle saw her fighting it, but it was a losing battle. "We're just fine," she said. "I thought Isabelle might be in need of some company, and it seems I was right."

"I thought the same," Adam said. "Well, I thought you both might be." He spoke awkwardly, something Isabelle had never heard Adam do before. In response, Eloise's cheeks went from pink to deep red.

"You should join us," Eloise said. "It *is* good to have a man in the house at a time like this. Until Cameron comes back, you should sit with us. If he can spare you, I mean."

"I think it'll be all right," Adam said, glancing over his shoulder at the door. "There isn't anyone out there, and we've made it so obvious all day that we're patrolling the property that I can't imagine anyone disturbing us now."

Eloise beamed up at Adam. "You're awfully brave, you know."

He grinned back at her, showing his teeth.

He's the reason she won't leave. It isn't because of Cameron, not really. It's because she doesn't want to be away from the man she loves, even if they haven't admitted their feelings to one another.

Jealousy rose up in Isabelle like a tide as Adam sat down next to Eloise. The two of them began to talk, their heads tipped together, their voices low. Both of them were smiling. Even in the face of everything that was happening, being together made them happy.

She closed her eyes, forcing herself not to react. She was happy for her friend, and for Adam. She had known Eloise long enough to know that she wasn't truly happy being on her own, and at her age, she must worry that she would never find someone. This thing between her and Adam was so real. It was powerful. Their lives held such potential. The only obstacle they faced was their inability to confess their feelings to one another, but they must have seen the truth that was so obvious between them. Eventually, it would come out. Eventually, they would be together. She was sure of it.

And Cameron and I never will be. We have more than our share of obstacles.

It was like someone had tied a boulder to her heart and cast it into a river. She was sinking into despair. Through the depths, she could look up and see Eloise's joy, and reaching for it made her own pain that much worse.

Adam held out his arms, offering to hold Abby for a while. Eloise glanced at Isabelle for permission. Isabelle nodded, and Eloise passed the baby over. Adam's eyes shone as he held her, and Eloise looked at him as if he was the most magnificent thing she'd ever seen.

Don't be like this. Don't be jealous. It's good that Eloise is happy. It's good that she's found someone, that she won't be alone.

Isabelle would have given anything to be able to stand by Cameron's side the way Eloise was standing by Adam's.

Well—no. That wasn't true.

She would have given *almost* anything. Anything but the one thing it would cost her.

Nothing in the world was worth Abby's safety.

Chapter Twenty-Nine

Isabelle looked out the window first thing in the morning on the day of the Christmas fair.

She'd wondered from the day she had come up with the idea of the fair what she would see on this morning, and she held her breath as she drew back the curtain. If the weather was foul, the whole thing would be ruined. It was a surprise to realize she still cared about that—but she did.

The sky was clear. There was snow on the ground, but none in the air.

Perfect.

To her surprise, the weather didn't lift her spirits. If anything, her heart felt heavier. The world was bright and beautiful, and it contrasted sharply with the dark and dismal way she was feeling.

She forced herself to get out of bed and dress herself and Abby for the day ahead. She had laid out clothes the night before—the most festive new garments she'd made for them, in bright red and green. She placed Abby on a blanket on the floor to play while she stood in front of the mirror, carefully combing her hair and arranging it in a neat bun.

While she pinned it up, she thought about the day ahead.

This weather… it's a blessing from God. God wouldn't give us beautiful weather for no reason. He certainly wouldn't do it to try to make me feel worse about my plight. I have faith in His reasons. This is something else.

There was only one thing that could justify the good weather. God wanted the fair to go well. Even though everything was coming to an end, He must have wanted Isabelle to have one last beautiful day here. One last good memory to take away with her when she went.

That was a gift. Isabelle would accept it. She would be grateful for it.

"Are you ready for the fair, Abby?" she asked, injecting as much merriment as she could into her tone. It was up to her to try to be cheerful today, to make this a positive experience for Abby. Also, it might be the last truly good day she and Cameron had to spend together. She wouldn't allow that to be soured by her dread of what was to come next.

God, give me the strength to make this a good day for everybody. That's all I want to do.

The prayer centered her, and she did feel stronger. She adjusted Abby in her arms and made her way down to the kitchen.

Edith and Eloise were already there, bustling about, removing cookies from the oven and putting new ones in. Both women were covered in flour. She stopped in the doorway and stared at them. "What's going on?"

"A last-minute decision," Eloise said breathlessly, turning to face Isabelle. Her eyes shone with excitement. "We thought we'd make cookies for everyone. At first we were going to sell them, but Edith suggested it would be more in the spirit of the season to just give them away."

"Well, it didn't seem right to charge people," Edith said modestly. "If they're going to spend their money, let them do it with the vendors who have gone out of their way to bring their wares here. But even people who don't have a dime to spend today should be able to enjoy the event, and cookies are something I can offer."

Isabelle smiled. "I think that's great," she said. "I'll make some lemonade." She put Abby in her chair and got out the pitcher.

The three women worked in companionable near-silence for a while. What little conversation there was centered around Abby, who was easy to talk about. Isabelle didn't want to discuss the more serious issues looming over her, and she was grateful that neither Edith nor Eloise wanted to do so either. After three more batches of cookies had been prepared, people started to arrive and set up their booths in the yard, and Isabelle decided she ought to go out and greet them.

"Can you two finish up in here?" she asked, wiping her hands on her apron. "I'd like to get outside."

"Of course," Eloise said with a smile. "Do you want to leave Abby with us so you'll have your hands free?"

"No, I should bring her." She lifted Abby from her chair. "Everyone will want to see her." *And this might be their last chance to do so.* The unspoken words were a knife in her heart.

Slowly, she walked out the door and down the porch steps into the yard.

Everything was just as she had envisioned it. The vendors had set up their wares at the stalls that had been prepared for them. Everyone in town seemed to be here, milling about from one booth to the next, admiring crafts, making purchases, and generally enjoying the occasion. She heard snatches of cheerful conversation drifting from various groups of people. She could smell the baker's fresh pies and the evergreen of the wreaths and garlands some of the women had brought to sell. The cinnamon of the mulled cider permeated everything. It looked, sounded, and smelled just like what Christmas ought to be.

Cameron, though, was nowhere to be seen.

She was sure he was still patrolling the property, making certain Duvall and Pike didn't show up and ruin the day. She knew that was important, but at the same time, a lump grew in her throat. Even though the fair matched her imaginings, it could never be what she'd dreamed it would be without him here.

"Oh, Isabelle!" Ginger Hargrove, one of the women she knew from church, came hurrying over. Ginger was a tiny ball of energy. She never seemed to stop moving, and today was no exception. She bounced up and down on her toes as she spoke. "It's perfect! Look at all this! I was so devastated when the fair was canceled. We all so look forward to it. And I have to admit, though I was grateful you offered to step in, I did have doubts. You were at such a disadvantage, you see, because you weren't here for last year's fair." She took hold of Isabelle's arms. "But you've done a *magnificent* job."

"I agree." Blonde, blue-eyed Melody Strasser joined them. She was the one who usually organized the fair, and Isabelle was relieved to see the warm smile on her face—she'd worried that Melody might resent her for taking over the fair. "I felt terrible when I realized I was too ill to put this together this year."

"We're just glad you're feeling better!" Ginger enthused. "It's so good to see you up and about and able to attend the fair, even if you weren't up to putting it together."

"Yes, the doctor says I'm on the mend," Melody agreed warmly. "Just a bad bout of the flu. But even so, I knew everyone would be so disappointed. Having you step in was truly such a gift, and looking at what a great job you've done... well, I have to say, I hope you and I can work together on next year's fair!"

Isabelle's stomach twisted into a knot. "I don't think I'm going to be here next year," she admitted in a low voice. She didn't want to be overheard by anyone else—she hadn't planned to bring the day down by sharing this news. It felt wrong to lie about it, though.

Melody frowned. "What do you mean, you won't be here? Of course you will be. Where else would you go?"

"It's never been a permanent arrangement, me staying here," Isabelle said softly. "Cameron and I always knew I would move on eventually."

"Well, eventually doesn't have to be *now*. We need you here, Isabelle! You've been such a splendid addition to the community. This fair is only part of it. You're part of the church now. And everyone loves Abby." Melody rested a hand on Abby's back.

"Melody is right," Ginger said fervently. "You can't go now. If you don't want to stay with Cameron, I'm sure there's a spare room at the church you and Abby could move into. We want you with us. You're a part of Wintervale. Don't go!"

Her tone was so earnest that Isabelle couldn't bring herself to argue. It was wonderful to realize that someone wanted her here so badly—wonderful, but excruciating at the same time. She *did* belong to this town. She had found a community for herself here. Losing Cameron would be horrible, but there were other losses too, and each and every one of them would cut like a blade.

She pulled back from the two women in front of her. "I should go check on the other guests," she said. "See if anyone needs anything… greet everyone…"

"All right, well, make sure you meet back up with us in a while," Melody said, her brow furrowed. "We need to discuss this matter of you leaving town, Isabelle. If you need help—a place to stay, anything—we'll help you. Friends do that sort of thing for one another, and we consider you a friend."

"That's right," Ginger said. "Whatever you need. You've put in so much work for this town. You should let us help you in return now."

Isabelle ached to tell Ginger yes, that she would love the help. She wanted to stay in Wintervale. Even if she and Cameron couldn't be in one another's lives, she still wanted that.

But she wouldn't risk anything happening to Abby.

She couldn't explain that. She couldn't find the words.

Instead, she turned and hurried away.

***

Hours later, the fair was still going strong. Some of the booths had packed up as the sun had started to fall in the sky, and the merchants had come to find Isabelle and thank her for all her hard work. Isabelle had fought her way through every interaction, her heart growing heavier and heavier as the day went on.

She had given Abby to Eloise and Edith when they had come out with their cookies. Separating herself from the baby allowed her to take a few moments to herself, to sneak behind the barn and dab at her eyes when the tears started to come. No one should see her cry. Not today.

"You look lovely," a familiar, deep, steady voice spoke from behind her.

She turned. Cameron had appeared as if from nowhere. "You missed the whole fair," she accused, biting the inside of her cheek to keep the tears out of her eyes. She didn't want him to see her cry. Not right now.

"I didn't miss it," he said. "I've been around."

"I haven't seen you." She raised her eyebrows, suffused with indignation. That was good. It was easy to control herself while she felt like that. It was easy to keep her emotions off her face. "I've been walking around, greeting everyone, making a good impression on people, thanking them for coming, and I've had to do it all by myself."

"I've been watching the perimeter. You knew I would be doing that today," he said. "You wouldn't want me to relax in my guarding of this land today. Just because there are people here, that doesn't mean there's no danger. In fact, a crowd would provide the perfect cover for Duvall to sneak in… where is Abby, by the way?"

She couldn't help feeling touched that he'd thought of Abby so quickly. The words lit a spark at the center of her chest that threatened the cool exterior she was fighting to maintain. "She's all right," she assured him. "She's with Eloise and Edith, helping them serve cookies to people. Perfectly safe."

Cameron nodded slowly. "In that case... would you like to dance?"

She couldn't have been any more shocked if he'd asked her whether she'd like to jump off the roof of the barn and fly away. "Would I like—what?"

"To dance," he repeated, pointing toward a commotion behind him. "It looks like Pete Harper is going to start playing his fiddle."

Sure enough, the strains of fiddle music rose up from somewhere behind Cameron.

Isabelle met his eyes, unsure of what to say. As always when she faced him directly like this, the eye contact didn't help. Instead, she felt as if she was tumbling downhill and he was the only person with a prayer of catching her, and she had no idea whether or not he was going to do it. "Do people usually dance at the Christmas fair?" she managed.

"It's been a few years since I've been to one." She was aware of the warmth of his hand in hers. He pulled her a step closer to him, and she didn't resist. *Oh, God help me.* "Seems to me I remember dancing happening at the end of the night," he said. "But then, I don't care so much what other people do. I want to dance with you, Isabelle."

"But we... you and I..." she swallowed. "We aren't... involved like that."

"I know we aren't," he murmured. "But it's only a dance. It's one night, and it's one dance. We can have that, can't we? One dance?"

One dance.

She nodded and allowed him to pull her into his arms.

At once, the rhythm of the music entered her body, and she began to sway against him. He held her closer than was strictly necessary, arms curled protectively around her body, close enough that he could have pressed his lips to her forehead if he'd wanted to do it. She wished he would—she couldn't help longing for a touch like that—but at the same time, she knew that she would be lost if he did. She would never be able to pull away from him. She would lean into his chest, try to convince him to hold her tightly, and she would be bereft when he walked away.

Stay strong. Enjoy it while it lasts, but know that it has to end.

If only Cameron wasn't so lost in his grief over what had happened to his family.

If only Russell Duvall wasn't threatening everything they held dear.

But there was no way to put a stop to those things. All she could do was wish, and wishes like that didn't come true.

She would look for a seamstress position, she'd decided. Someone would hire her—someone who wouldn't mind her bringing her daughter along, someone who wouldn't ask too many questions. Edith would help her find a position like that. She wouldn't look for another marriage situation. She had never imagined that being a mail-order bride would have the potential to break her heart like this, and now that it had, she wouldn't put herself in harm's way again. It would be better to be on her own.

Cameron was looking down at her with a scorching heat in his eyes, and suddenly she was sure that the fact that this was the last time they would ever be this close to one another was not lost on him. She was sure he was on the verge of taking advantage of this moment.

He's going to kiss me.

She was putty in his hands. It would drive the knife in her heart even deeper if he kissed her now. She would be that much more painfully aware of what she was losing. Even so, she wasn't going to be able to stop him. She wouldn't resist.

She had always been helpless to resist him.

Her eyelids fluttered closed. *Just remember that it doesn't mean anything,* she told herself firmly. *Even if we both give in now. It doesn't change anything. It doesn't mean love. It doesn't mean I can stay.*

With her eyes closed, she saw nothing, but she was still aware of the distance closing between them. She could feel the heat coming from him, could smell the manly musk of his body as he drew close to her. She imagined the press of his lips—they must be so close. It would happen any moment now—

Bang!

The sound of a gunshot ripped through the night air.

Isabelle's eyes flew open, and she found herself staring into Cameron's, now mere inches away from her face, stricken with horror.

Chapter Thirty

Screams ripped through the night.

Cameron pulled Isabelle against his body without thinking, his hands roaming up and down the plane of her back. For a moment, he didn't even know what he was doing, and then he pieced it together. *Searching for a gunshot wound. I need to feel for myself that she hasn't been hurt.*

"I'm all right." She pulled back from him. Her chest rose and fell raggedly, her breathing uneven with fear. "Abby."

Before he could stop her, she had turned and sprinted away.

No. Someone here had a gun, and Isabelle couldn't be on her own. Anything might happen. The thought of it coursed like acid through his veins—he would die before he'd lose her like that. He tore after her, determined to put himself between her and any danger that might emerge.

She broke through the chaos of the panicked crowd with Cameron on her tail and ran to a table where Eloise and Edith had clearly been sitting handing out cookies. Both women were on their feet now, looking around frantically. They seemed to notice Isabelle and Cameron at the same moment. Both of them came around the table and ran over, and the four of them huddled together.

"What was that?" Edith demanded shrilly, hands clasping and unclasping in front of her. She seemed unable to focus on what was going on. She kept turning to look this way and that, looking for something. Cameron couldn't blame her. He wanted to do the same thing. It was difficult to keep from breaking free of this conversation and running around, looking for evidence of who might have fired a gun. Looking for Duvall.

"Is Abby all right?" Isabelle's voice was high-pitched and frantic. She reached out for the baby in Eloise's arms.

Eloise passed Abby over to her. "She's fine," she said. "She slept through it, if you can believe that."

Sure enough, Abby's eyes were closed, her breathing deep and even. Isabelle accepted her and turned toward Cameron, leaning into him, sheltering Abby between the two of them.

Adam came running over. He stopped before Eloise, gripping her shoulders. "Are you all right? What's going on?"

"I'm all right," Eloise said shakily.

Adam seized her in an embrace and turned to Cameron. "That was a gunshot."

Cameron wrapped his arms around Isabelle and held her. He couldn't resist, and in that moment, he didn't want to. "Eloise, what happened? Do you know?"

His sister's face was pale, but her jaw was clenched with determination. "I doubt I know any more than you do," she said. "We heard that sound. It *was* a gunshot, wasn't it?"

"I think so," Cameron agreed.

"Well, I think we'd better get inside—maybe get everyone into the barn or something," Eloise continued, looking around once more.

"No," Cameron said sharply. "We don't know what happened yet. Packing everyone into a confined space isn't a good idea. I want you three and Abby to go into the house. Do you understand? Adam and I will deal with things out here."

Isabelle pulled back and looked up at him, her gaze searching his. Her eyes darted anxiously. "I don't want you to stay out here," she said. "Anything might happen." Her voice trembled.

"I'll be all right," he said. "You need to protect Abby right now."

She nodded. He had known she would agree with that.

"Go inside," he said. "I'll be with you soon."

He pushed her gently into his sister's arms, then turned and strode back into the crowd before his worry over her could compel him to look back.

Everyone was in shambles. People were running around hollering at one another, clearly trying to figure out what had happened and what they ought to do about it. Cameron would have given anything to shove all of them into the barn. It was going to be impossible to figure out what was going on with all this mayhem.

"Spread out," he told Adam. "We need to figure out who's shooting. Find them and disarm them."

Adam nodded. "I'll see if I can find the sheriff, too, although I'm sure he's already aware of what's going on." He disappeared into the crowd.

Cameron hurried toward the house. Maybe he could climb up to the roof and get a better view. Doing so would expose him, but if that was the only way to figure out what was happening here, he would do it. It was worth the risk.

It didn't turn out to be necessary, though. As he pushed his way past two young men who were still in their teens, the situation became clear.

Cameron would never have said that he knew everyone in Wintervale by name. He was not a social man. But it was a small town, and he did know them all by sight. The group of men clustered in front of his house now was unfamiliar to him. He'd never seen any of them before.

They all looked to be in their twenties, and each man had a gun, answering at once the question of who had been shooting. It had to have been one of them. The one at the front of the group—the tallest, with dark, curly hair and a mean smile—was the clear leader. The others all watched him as if waiting for cues as to what they should do next.

"Who are you?" Cameron stepped in front of them, hands on his hips. He was acutely aware of the fact that he was unarmed, and he couldn't believe his own foolishness. He had taken such care to make sure he *always* had a gun at his side over the last few days. But today had felt different somehow. Even as he'd patrolled the grounds during the fair, he hadn't believed that anything would actually happen. Too many people were here. Duvall wouldn't choose a day like this to make trouble. It would be too easy for him to be seen. Too easy for him to be caught.

If these men were affiliated with Duvall, though... well, that explained a great deal, because of course he would have no fear of sending someone else to do his dirty work for him. That was exactly what a cowardly man like Duvall would do.

Rage boiled through Cameron. *He couldn't leave us alone for even one day. Even soldiers stand down for Christmas! But I suppose soldiers fight with honor, and Russell Duvall wouldn't know honor if it came up and bit him in the face.*

The leader of the strange men smirked at Cameron. "We're just trying to enjoy the fair," he said. He snapped his gun arrogantly.

"Well, weapons aren't welcome on my property on a day when women and children are present," Cameron said acidly. "You're going to have to go someplace else."

"Isn't this fair for everyone? We were to understand that this was a community event. I don't think you can tell us to go." The man showed his teeth.

Blinded by rage, Cameron started forward.

The man fired a shot in the air, and Cameron stopped where he was as the gun was leveled at the middle of his forehead. "I don't think you want to do *that*," the man said, his voice low and dangerous. "I'm not a very good shot. I was aiming at the sky, but next time I might miss."

"What's going on here?" Sheriff Grayson's voice barked, and Cameron was both relieved and disappointed to see the man in his peripheral vision. Relieved because this situation certainly called for a little backup, and because the sheriff was armed. Disappointed because he needed to do something with the anger shuddering its way through his muscles, and he would have given anything for a fight right now. The urge to lash out and strike the man standing in front of him was so powerful that it overrode good sense—he'd have done it, even though the man was armed.

"You boys get off the property," the sheriff barked.

The one in charge laughed. "You're going to make us?"

"That's right," the sheriff said coolly. He unholstered his gun and pulled it out casually, though he didn't aim it at anyone. Still, Cameron saw the men's eyes go to it. "I think you were sent here by someone to cause a ruckus. Is that about right? Maybe you're getting paid for your time. But none of you actually want to see this come to bloodshed. You aren't being paid that well. None of you want to risk going to jail for shooting an officer of the law, so you won't shoot me." He took a step closer to them. "And I know you don't want me to shoot you. Time to wrap it up and go on home."

He'd struck a nerve. The men looked uneasily at one another, and the one in front lowered his gun slightly.

The sheriff cut his eyes toward Cameron. "Get in the house," he said.

"I'm not leaving," Cameron growled. "If Duvall sent these delinquents, I'm heading over to his place right now to confront him. He's not getting away with it this time."

"Don't do that," the sheriff said sharply. "You need to cool down, Cameron. You're a tinderbox right now, and if you confront anybody, this whole thing is only going to get worse. I know you want to call Duvall to account for this, but remember, we still have *no* evidence of his involvement. You're not going to get anywhere with him tonight. Go home, make sure your family is all right. I'll deal with things here, and you and I will discuss this further in the morning." He waved a hand at the men, who were looking completely deflated. The sound of Duvall's name had done something to them, made them realize that they didn't have any protection after all and that everyone knew exactly how they had come to be here. They were on the verge of slinking away with tails between their legs. They were no threat now.

Cameron took a breath and nodded. "Fine," he said through gritted teeth, taking a step back. "But I'm going to confront Duvall *tomorrow*, and I guess it's up to you if you want to come with me or not."

He turned and jogged away without giving the sheriff a chance to answer. If Grayson didn't agree, he would only be able to argue, and he didn't want to get drawn into a debate right now. Things were handled out here, and it was more important to get back up to the house.

All around the property, people were packing up their things as quickly as they could and running toward their wagons. The fair was obviously over, and everyone was in a rush to get home. Voices were high-pitched and loud as people called out to one another, organizing their retreat. No one took note of Cameron as he made his way toward the house. He glanced around, hoping to see Adam, but his friend was out of sight—probably checking behind the barn to make sure no one else was back there stirring up trouble.

Cameron climbed the porch steps and opened the door.

Eloise and Edith were sitting at the kitchen table, each with their hands wrapped around a cup of tea. They looked up when he entered, and Eloise rose quickly to her feet. "Where's Adam?" she asked, a spike of fear in her voice.

"It's all right," Cameron told her. Exhaustion was beginning to creep in now that the worst was over, and his eyes felt suddenly heavy. He wanted to drop into a chair beside them and rest his head on the table. "We found the men responsible for the disturbance. Sheriff Grayson is handling them now. Everything is going to be fine. Adam will be along as soon as he finishes checking the grounds."

Eloise looked ill at ease, but she sank back into her chair all the same. Edith rested a hand on her arm.

"Where's Isabelle?" Cameron asked. "And Abby?"

"They went to the bedroom," Edith said. "She said she needed some time to herself. I think she wanted to lie down. She looked so upset…"

Cameron didn't wait to hear more. He left the women in the kitchen and made his way down the hall toward Isabelle's bedroom, his heart pounding hard enough to drive back the exhaustion he'd been feeling. What if something was wrong with her after all? She hadn't been shot, but fear could do things to a person. He shouldn't have let her go off on her own after all the excitement tonight had brought…

He knocked on the bedroom door.

"Come in." Her voice was miles from the usual energetic tone he'd come to expect from her. She was quiet. Meek. *Defeated*.

For some reason he couldn't explain, it sent a chill of fear through him.

He opened the door.

Isabelle was standing in front of the bed, her back to him. Cameron glanced over and saw that the baby was lying in the cradle. "Are you all right?" He stepped into the room, hesitated, then closed the door behind him.

She turned to face him, and he saw past her.

Her suitcase lay open on the bed. She had been folding clothes, putting them inside. Packing.

"What are you doing?" he breathed.

"I'm going to be leaving soon," Isabelle said. Her voice was steady, but she didn't look at him. "I might as well get ready. In fact... I know we said town wasn't safe, but I think I should go and stay with the pastor and Edith until I figure out where I'm going next. I'm going to look for a job as a seamstress. I'm sure I'll find something quickly. But until I do, this isn't a safe place. Not for Abby. I have to get her out of here."

She made eye contact with him for the first time. "I'm so sorry," she said. "This isn't how I wanted things to end."

There were tears in her eyes.

He wanted to disagree. He wanted to beg her to stay. But he couldn't.

Because she was right.

"It was always going to end like this," he said, numbness creeping over him. "I can't protect you. I know that. You're right to go."

The words grated at his heart. Speaking them was painful, and his chest seemed to cave in as they left him. He turned away from her, ready to leave.

"Cameron," she said softly.

He stood still, waiting, but he didn't turn back.

"Please don't forget what I told you," she said. "The things that have happened to you are not your fault. You don't deserve to be unhappy. I hope you can forgive yourself one day for all the things you believe you caused. I hope you know that God has nothing but love and forgiveness for you right now, even if you aren't ready to accept it. I hope one day you will be. If you can only keep one aspect of our time together in your heart, I hope it's this. I hope you understand how loved you are, and what a good man you are, and I hope you find a way to let those things in."

Her voice broke on the last sentence, and he knew she was crying.

He wanted to turn back to her, to tell her that he would try to accept everything she was telling him, but the truth was that he didn't know if he could do it and he didn't want to lie. Not to her.

He hurried from the room without another word.

God...

God, please help me hear the truth in what she says. Help me believe it, for her sake.

And please, wherever she goes, whatever she does... keep her safe. Let her be happy. If I can believe she's all right, I can survive everything else.

Chapter Thirty-One

"The snow is awfully heavy today," Isabelle murmured, peering out the window of her bedroom at the whirling flakes. "Are you sure it's going to be all right?"

"I can drive through snow," Eloise reassured her. "It was snowing the night I picked you up from the train, remember?"

"It wasn't like this." The snowfall had been light that night. This was a blizzard. It was lucky that the weather had missed yesterday's Christmas fair. They'd probably have had to cancel if it had been this bad. At least the fair had gone well. At least there was a good memory to go out on.

"We don't have to leave today," Eloise said quietly, walking over to stand beside Isabelle at the window. "You know how much we're all going to miss you around here. If you want to put this off, you can. A couple of days aren't going to make any difference."

"That isn't true," Isabelle countered. "We don't know when Duvall might come back. I wish I could stay, Eloise. You know I do. But I truly think we'll be safer in town, with Edith and the pastor. I can't keep Abby somewhere so dangerous, and Duvall isn't going to stop."

Eloise sighed. "I suppose I would make the same choice if I had a baby to think of," she murmured. "I'm just going to miss you so much, and I know that Cameron will, too. This isn't going to be easy for any of us."

Isabelle swallowed hard. She wished there was something to say—something that *would* make it easier. "I'll just be in town," she said. "We'll still see each other."

"Only until you find a seamstress position somewhere else. I've seen your embroidery." Eloise touched the sleeve of Isabelle's dress, the careful stitching there. "I know you're good at what you do. You're going to find a job in no time, and once you do, you'll be gone from our lives forever." Her eyes filled with tears. "Our friendship will be over."

"Our friendship will never be over." On impulse, Isabelle leaned over and hugged Eloise. "You will always be someone who was there for me during one of the darkest times in my life, Eloise. I'll never forget that. I'll carry your friendship with me no matter what comes next for me. I hope you'll do the same."

Eloise took her hands. "Of course I will," she said, smiling through her tears. "I'll never forget you. I'll always think of you as a sister. I wish…"

She trailed off.

Isabelle didn't need her to finish the sentence. She wished it too—that they could have been real sisters to one another. That the marriage Isabelle had come here for could have happened. She'd caught a glimpse of that other life, and her heart ached for it. She grieved deeply, knowing it could never be hers, as if a gulf had opened up within her.

"I'd better go say goodbye to him," she said quietly.

Eloise nodded and released her hands. "I'll get the wagon ready."

She went out to the living room. Cameron had taken Abby out there to allow Isabelle a bit of time to finish packing. She found him sitting on the floor with the baby lying on her back in front of him, shrieking with laughter as he tickled her belly.

Abby's laughter was a dart directly to Isabelle's heart. It should have been a good thing to hear the baby so happy, but it wasn't. She was about to separate Abby and Cameron for good. It wasn't likely they'd see one another again after today.

She cleared her throat. Cameron looked up at her, eyes squinted with emotion. "I'm going to miss her," he said quietly.

"She'll miss you, too." She was sure it was true. There was no way to explain to Abby what was happening, and she had noticed the way the baby lit up every time Cameron came into a room. Abby loved Cameron. It was deeply unfair that she was going to lose him.

She's the most innocent victim in all of this, the one who deserves it the very least. And yet, she's the reason I have to go.

Cameron swallowed audibly and got to his feet. "I want you to take this with you," he said, holding out a milk crate.

She looked down into it. It was the mobile, the one he had made himself. He'd placed a blanket inside and arranged the mobile carefully on top of it.

Her heart melted. "Are you sure?" she asked, voice trembling. "I know you gave it to her, but... that was when you thought we were going to be living here a little longer. If you don't want to let go of the mobile, I understand. I know it was meaningful to you."

"It is," Cameron said, meeting her eyes. "It means a great deal to me." His tone was husky, and she sensed the emotion he was holding back. "I can't put it back in a box in the attic. Seeing it used was like a tiny part of Philip had come back to life, and if I pack it away now, I'd be burying him all over again. Besides..." He took a deep breath and closed his eyes briefly.

"I want Abby to have something of me. I don't want to disappear from her life as if I was never there."

"You won't," Isabelle said, her voice thick.

It was an empty promise and she knew it. How could she say that Cameron would leave any mark on Abby's life? Abby wasn't going to remember any of this. In all honesty, it was probably better that she wouldn't. Abby had lost her mother already. She didn't need to carry the loss of a father figure. It was for the best that she wouldn't remember any of the people who had entered and left her life while she was young.

Isabelle wished she could believe that.

The truth was that there was no benefit to Abby that she could see in having Cameron out of her life. Isabelle desperately wanted Abby to have a father, especially one as loving as she now knew Cameron was capable of being. She didn't think she would ever find someone else who was such a good father for her baby. She certainly didn't think she would ever find someone she was able to feel this way about.

This had been precious, and now they were losing it.

"Will you bring this out to the wagon for me?" she asked Cameron, indicating the crate. She bent down and picked Abby up. "We're about to leave."

Cameron nodded.

Neither of them said another word as they made their way out of the house. It seemed to Isabelle as if there were simply no words to be said. It was all too sad, too weighty. All she wanted now was to get it over with, to get in the wagon and drive away so that the worst of the pain would be behind her.

Eloise was waiting beside the wagon. Cameron paused as they drew near. "You know, maybe you shouldn't go," he said. "In this weather, I mean." His voice was gruff, and he wasn't making eye contact with anyone. "Maybe it would be best to wait until the snow clears. The roads would be safer then."

Isabelle shook her head. "That's what we said at the start." Her throat was so tight that the words were barely audible. "We can't keep putting it off now that... now that we know what we're going to have to do."

"It's all right, Cameron," Eloise said quietly. "You know I'm a good driver, and the horses are strong. I'll get us into town just fine."

"Well, don't try to get back if the weather is too bad. If the snow gets deep, stay in town tonight," Cameron said. "They can put you up at the church."

Eloise nodded. "I won't try to get back if it doesn't seem safe." She paused. "I'd better make sure the horses are secured."

She was giving them a moment alone, Isabelle guessed. Letting them say a private goodbye. She wished she could tell Eloise that it wasn't necessary. It was making things worse. It filled this last moment with a weighty significance that she didn't want it to have. The thought that this was the most important interaction she'd had with Cameron in all their time together... it simply wasn't true. It wasn't the most important. It was only the last.

Cameron puffed out a breath of air, which turned to fog in the cold. "All right," he grumbled. "Travel safe."

That was it. There was no embrace. There was no talk of what their time together had meant to either one of them. Just a parting comment he might have made to anybody at all. Isabelle couldn't have felt less significant to him if he'd stayed in the house and not bothered to come out and see her off at all.

She passed Abby to Eloise while she climbed up into the wagon, then reached down to take the baby back. Eloise handed Abby up. Then she turned and faced her younger brother.

Words were exchanged. Isabelle could make out the sounds of their voices—Isabelle's strident, Cameron's low and ponderous. But she couldn't hear the words they were saying, and she didn't want to. She could guess. Eloise would be trying one last time to convince Cameron to let her stay and Cameron would be refusing. Or perhaps it wasn't that at all. Maybe they were in agreement that she should leave. Either way, she couldn't imagine there was anything in that conversation that would feel good to hear.

Eloise turned away and climbed up into the wagon. She took the reins in her hands without looking at Isabelle. "Are you all right?" she murmured out of the corner of her mouth.

Isabelle couldn't speak. Her throat was swollen with unshed tears, and if she tried to say anything, she would break. This was probably the last Cameron would ever see of her. She didn't want to cry. Not right now. She wanted to be strong. Even if it gutted her to do it.

The wagon began to move.

Don't look back. Don't let him see you look back.

If she looked back, she would never be able to set her eyes forward again. She would be staring over her shoulder, fighting to keep him, until distance ripped him from her. She would leave her heart behind on the ranch. The only thing to do was to keep her gaze on what was ahead, to remind herself that she had chosen this.

"I didn't think he would go through with it," Eloise admitted. "I thought he would change his mind at the last minute. He does care for you, you know. I think..." She took a deep breath. "I think he's making the wrong decision here."

"I decided too," Isabelle managed.

"Well, I think you're both making the wrong decision," Eloise said darkly. Isabelle had never heard her sound so much like her brother. That opinionated growl... she was just like Cameron. It was no wonder Isabelle was so fond of her.

I love them both. They're my family.

But they were a family she couldn't allow herself to have.

Chapter Thirty-Two

"Cameron, for heaven's sake, stop pacing. You're going to wear a hole in the floor."

Adam was on the settee in the living room, his hands clasped tightly in his lap as he watched Cameron stalk back and forth in front of the fireplace. He might be putting on a show of calm, but Cameron wasn't fooled. The white color of his knuckles gave him away. He was just as tense and distressed as Cameron was.

"I shouldn't have let them go out into the snow," Cameron growled. "I should have made them wait." It had been three hours since the women had left. That was more than enough time for Eloise to have gotten Isabelle into town, turned around, and come back.

She should have been back by now.

In the time since they'd left, the snowfall had gotten heavier and heavier. It had been thick hours ago, but now it was blinding. If they were still on the road, they wouldn't be able to see more than a foot in front of them. He stopped, staring out the window for a moment, then resumed his pacing.

Any moment now, Eloise is going to come through the door and make me feel foolish for worrying about this.

But she didn't. The door remained empty, and Cameron's worries mounted like a tightened string on a fiddle, ready to snap at any moment.

"You should have told me to take them," Adam said. "I thought Isabelle and Abby were leaving tomorrow. I didn't know they'd go this fast. You shouldn't have kept that from me." His voice was spiked with anger. "Why didn't you tell me?"

"You would have tried to stop me from letting them go if I had told you," Cameron said, turning and pacing back the way he'd come. "I didn't want another argument about it."

Adam slapped his hands furiously on his thighs. "You're right, I would have!" he barked. "You should have stopped yourself. Letting a couple of women go out alone in this snowstorm? I can't fathom what you were thinking!"

"Well, the snow wasn't this bad when they left!" Cameron snapped, rounding on his friend. This was bad enough without Adam giving him a hard time about it. "I thought they would be able to make it. I did tell them they didn't have to go. I encouraged them to wait."

"You shouldn't have *allowed* it." Adam's hands curled into fists.

"I can't force them not to do things. You know that." Cameron was sick to his stomach. Adam was right. He should have guessed that the weather would get worse. He should have held them back from leaving. He should have insisted they wait a day. He could have gotten them to listen if he had really fought for it, but he hadn't because he'd known that Isabelle wanted to leave. She'd barely been able to look at him since the Christmas fair. Since he had caught her packing in her room, and she had told him that he was right—that this place wasn't safe.

He had known this place wasn't safe. He'd known she was in danger because she was here. But hearing *her* say it had been different. It had made all his worst fears real, had confirmed for him that what he believed was true. He *was* a danger to the people around him.

Nothing is safe. No matter what I say or do, I am putting her in danger. She's in danger because I let her leave, but she would have been at risk if she had stayed, too. I had no options. There were no good choices, no way for me to protect her.

The moment she met me, her life was in danger, and the only way she can be safe again is to get as far from me as possible. Then the curse that hangs over me like a storm cloud won't be able to touch her. But not until then.

The knowledge sat like a stone in the pit of his stomach. He stalked to the window and whipped open the curtains.

"They made it to town," he murmured. "They must have. Eloise is just staying there for the night, that's all. She's being responsible, waiting until the weather clears before she tries to come back. We agreed she might do that."

"You can't be sure." Adam got to his feet and joined Cameron at the window. "Is it a risk you're willing to take, Cameron? Because I'm not. Eloise is... too important to me."

His voice cracked slightly.

Cameron turned to look at him, taking in the furrow of his brow and the clench of his jaw. He had never seen Adam so on edge in all their years of knowing one another.

"You love her," he said.

"You know I do," Adam ground out through gritted teeth.

"Well, you can say it."

He meant to sound magnanimous, to give his friend permission to speak about his feelings, but Adam growled in frustration. "I'm not the one who needs to say it," he said. "What about you and Isabelle? You *know* you're in love with her. We *all* know it, Cameron. It's as clear as sunshine on snow, and you won't admit it for some reason I'll never understand. You're so stubborn, and you're going to lose her because of how stubborn you are. Do you understand that? You are losing her!"

Cameron turned his back on Adam. This was too cruel. It was as if his friend had his heart in a vice and was tightening it mercilessly, doing what he could to inflict as much pain and torment as possible. "Stop it," he said, his voice low. "Just stop it." He couldn't even manage to sound angry. The hurt went too deep. "If you're not going to help then just go back home."

Adam slammed the side of his fist against the wall. "You're not thinking," he said. "I know what you believe, Cameron. I know you believe that being close to you puts people in danger."

The bowstring finally snapped. Cameron whirled. "Because it *does*," he yelled. "Aren't you paying attention? Just look at what happens to everyone who gets too near me! Look at what happened to Ruth and Philip! And if Isabelle had stayed— Duvall has already attacked Abby, Adam! How could I leave them at risk like that! They had to go. They had to go before anything terrible could happen to them, and that's why it had to be today."

"No, *you* look." Adam grabbed him firmly by both shoulders, his grip so hard that it almost hurt. "I'm sorry about what happened to Ruth and Philip, Cameron. It's a terrible tragedy. But that did *not* happen because they were too close to you. It happened because *there was a fire*. You've said yourself that if you had been there, you might have been able to get them out."

Cameron flinched, turning his head away and closing his eyes. Adam couldn't have hurt him any more if he'd struck him in the face.

Adam's voice softened, and so did his grip on Cameron's shoulders, though he didn't drop his hands. "I'm sorry," he said. "I know you don't like to hear it. And I don't agree with you blaming yourself for any of it. But it's also true that they might have survived if you'd been a little *luckier*. If it had happened when you'd been there to help them. It's not your fault you weren't. You couldn't have known. But Cameron... you *do* know this time. You know she's in danger. From the snow. From Duvall. You love Isabelle. Your choice should be easy here. Just keep her by your side."

Adam's words hit Cameron like a bolt of lightning to the heart. He thought he might burn where he stood. A shiver passed through him and his knees grew weak. If his friend hadn't been holding onto him, he might have dropped to the ground.

He's right. I love her. And I let her get away.

There was *no* danger they could face which they wouldn't be stronger against together. If Isabelle and Abby had been here right now, he would know they were safe. He would know everything was all right.

He should never have warned her away. He should have reassured her. He should have told her that he would keep them safe.

Cameron pulled free of Adam's grip and hurried to the door.

"Where are you going?" Adam rushed after him.

"I'm going after them. I'm going out to find them and bring them back." Cameron barreled through the kitchen and flung open the door. Immediately, the swirling snow struck him in the face, but he didn't care. He snatched his coat from the peg by the door and hurried out into the bluster.

Adam was right behind him. "Don't think for a moment that you're going without me," he called into the howling wind. "It should have been me taking Isabelle into town in the first place, not Eloise."

No. It should have been me. She was my...

Cameron's thought trailed off. She wasn't his anything. He had no claim on her. She'd come here to be his wife, but he had rejected that. She belonged to him no more than she did to Adam.

She does, though! There is something between us that makes her mine in a way she isn't his. When she was ready to leave, I should have been the one to take her. I shouldn't have let Eloise do it, even if I did believe my sister could make it through the snow. Even if there was no snow at all, I should have been the one to do it!

He had allowed himself to be so preoccupied with his belief that nearness to him was an inherent danger that he had unwittingly put Isabelle in *more* danger by sending her off with only Eloise to protect her.

Adam is right. They should never have been allowed to go away alone. I let my fear blind me to that. But Isabelle should never have been allowed to go in the first place, and that's my fault more than anything else is.

He wasn't to blame for the things Duvall had done.

He *was* to blame for letting Isabelle get away from him.

If he didn't bring her back now—if he was too late—that was one thing that would forever be his fault.

He opened the door of the stable and ran to the stall of his fastest horse. He'd wasted so much time in figuring out how he felt, figuring out what he needed to do, and right now nothing seemed fast enough. He pulled the horse out, on the verge of madness, his mind a sudden storm.

"I'm sure she's fine," Adam said as he saddled up his own horse, moving quickly and with a skill born of years of experience. "I'm sure they're both fine."

Cameron could tell by the distance in his friend's voice that Adam was trying to reassure himself more than anything. He didn't respond, merely continued what he was doing. It was a matter of minutes to secure the saddle, and when he had done so, he mounted the horse without looking to see whether Adam was ready to go and kicked it into a gallop.

Adam pulled even with him as he reached the road. Or rather, where he knew the road to be. The road itself was obscured by the snow that had piled up on it. The tracks Eloise's wagon would have left were long since covered up. The horse had to take high, careful steps to get through the drifts— it was impossible to go at a speed Cameron would have liked.

He clutched the reins so hard that the strength of his grip made his fingers hurt.

God, if you're listening—help me. Let me reach them quickly, and let me find them safe.

Chapter Thirty-Three

They had been on the road for only about five minutes when Eloise decided that Isabelle should get into the back of the wagon. "You can't have that baby out here in the snow," she'd said, gesturing at the blizzard that was growing noticeably worse by the minute. "Both of you, get inside."

Isabelle had been only too happy to comply. Eloise was right about shielding Abby from the weather, of course. But also, Isabelle needed a quiet moment to herself, a respite from trying to carry on conversation. She needed to mourn what she was leaving behind.

In the back of the wagon, with Abby cradled in her arms, she finally let her tears flow freely. For the first time since all this had started, she didn't even try to hold back. Her sobs choked her, and she wondered whether Eloise could hear. But the worry over being heard was, for once, not enough to stop her. Her pain was like an infected wound, and it needed to be drained for healing to begin.

Right now, healing seemed a long way off. All she could think about was her last exchange with Cameron and the way the two of them had hardly been able to look at one another. Was that really the end of everything that had happened between them? Could it have been only yesterday that they had been dancing in the moonlight at the Christmas fair? Could it have been mere days ago that she'd hoped he might kiss her? Now it was all gone, ripped from her hands as though it had never existed.

The warmth of Abby's body against her chest was the only measure of reassurance she had. She wrapped her arms around the baby. "We're going to be all right," she whispered through her tears. "It's you and me now, Abby. You and me against the world, and we'll always have one another, no matter what happens."

She didn't doubt it, but it didn't hold a candle to the future she had glimpsed with Cameron. It would take her a long time to forget that vision and to fully accept that it could never be. Right now, it still seemed within reach, as though if she only shouted to Eloise to turn the carriage around, she would be able to go back and claim it.

I wouldn't. He doesn't want that future. He doesn't want us there. Even if I decided it was worth the risk, he would never let us come back. Even when I begged him to let me stay, he was resolved that we should go. I won't put either one of us through that again now that the choice has been made. I'll respect it and go.

The carriage came to a stop.

For a moment, confusion fogged Isabelle's mind. Had she called out to Eloise in spite of her determination not to? Had she asked her friend to stop?

Even though she was sure she hadn't, she couldn't quell the sudden burst of excited anticipation that exploded within her. Maybe something had changed. Maybe they were going back after all.

Maybe I'll see Cameron again.

No. Don't hope for that.

"Eloise?" she called out, fighting to keep the quiver of hope out of her voice. "What's going on? Why have we stopped?"

There was no answer.

She peered toward the driver's seat, where Eloise had been. It was impossible, in the darkness, to see what was going on up there. "Eloise?"

Suddenly, the canopy of the wagon was yanked back, exposing her to the cold night air. She gasped and clutched Abby more tightly against her.

"She's back here," a voice called out, sending a shiver of pure terror through Isabelle.

Then a hand reached in, closed around her arm, and yanked her violently forward.

She couldn't fight back. Not with Abby in her arms. The best she could do was to stagger along with the person who had grabbed her, doing her best to keep from falling so that Abby wouldn't be injured. The fear turned to acid in her mouth as she was dragged from the wagon and onto the ground, barely managing to land upright on her feet.

She looked up. She was staring into the coal-black eyes of a man she had seen only once before, standing in front of the bank that day she and Cameron had pled their case to the banker.

Of course it was him. She should have known. Surely there was only one person who would stop their wagon on the road, who would search specifically for her.

"Russell Duvall," she choked.

The howling winter wind stole her words and swept them away, and she couldn't be sure he had heard. He didn't answer. He turned instead toward another man, who stood a few yards away. The second man was both leaner and meaner to look at. He wore a hooded cloak, though the hood had been blown back by the wind. He held Eloise at arm's length in front of him, a pistol against her temple.

"Pike," Duvall barked at the second man, "don't you get too happy on that trigger. We're not shooting her here, understand? That doesn't gain us anything."

"You said—" Pike began to object.

"I know what I said. This is what I'm saying now. Hold your fire. We don't shoot them like dogs in the road. We're doing this differently." He turned his gaze to Isabelle. "Give me that baby."

Fury surged up within her. Fury was good. It warmed her against the cold and drove away the fear. She spat in his face.

His eyes narrowed. He raised a hand slowly and wiped the spit away, flicking it onto the snow. "You're going to regret that, little miss," he snarled.

She regretted it already. Her breath came hard and fast, and she struggled to maintain her composure. A large part of her was tempted to start screaming. But that would do nothing. There was nobody who would hear her out here on the road, and if she made too much noise she would only aggravate Duvall and make matters worse.

But she would die before she let him take Abby.

Humility might work with a man like him. She took a small step backward. "I'm sorry," she said. *Yes. Let him feel in control. That's what he wants. He* is *in control, but he needs to see that I realize it.* "Please let me hold on to her. Please. I'm begging.

There's no need for her to be frightened, and if I give her to you, she'll just start crying." She held her breath, her heart about to burst through her ribs. Surely he didn't want to risk Abby crying. He wouldn't want that. It would be too disruptive.

He ground his teeth together, turned to look at Pike, then turned back to Isabelle. "Fine," he barked. "You hold her. But if I decide I want to take her and you try to fight me, it's not going to end well for you."

A shiver of fear pierced through Isabelle's anger. Her teeth chattered. She wished desperately that she had listened when Cameron had offered to let her stay with him until the weather had cleared. Maybe leaving at a different time would have yielded a different result.

The one thing I can say for sure is that I was safer when I was with Cameron. Her heart ached with regret. Her stomach churned. *I was frightened when I was there. I knew I was in danger. But the danger there was always less, because he was by my side. If he was with me now, he would protect us. He wouldn't let Duvall hurt Abby. We would be safe.*

How could she have been so blind as to think she was better off without him? To run away from him? Of course she should have stayed. It was so obvious now that she couldn't believe she'd made the choice she had.

"What do you want?" she asked Duvall.

He looked her up and down slowly. "I don't want anything from you," he said.

His voice was colder than the winter air. She believed he meant it. There was nothing she could offer him that would satisfy him. "Then... let us be on our way," she suggested without much hope.

"I don't want anything from *you*," he repeated, emphasizing the word this time.

She understood his meaning. "I can't make Cameron sell you the ranch," she said. "He's made up his mind about it."

"It's too late for that, anyway," Duvall growled. "I don't want to buy the ranch anymore. He had his chance to sell it to me, and he refused. Now we're doing things my way. No profit for Cameron Mercer. Only pain."

Isabelle thought she might vomit, the horror and fear were so strong. "What do you mean?" she breathed.

"He could have sold the ranch to me. He didn't. Now I'm going to take it from him. But before I do, I'm going to take everything else he cares about and leave him with nothing." Duvall unholstered a gun of his own and raised it slowly, aiming it directly at Isabelle's heart.

And directly at Abby.

Isabelle froze. Her whole body turned to stone.

"No," she gasped.

"He's going to lose everything," Duvall hissed. "He deserves to lose everything, after the chase he's led me on."

"Not the baby," Isabelle begged. Tears gathered in her eyes. "Please, not my baby. She's innocent. She's done nothing."

"But you refused to give her to me," Duvall said. "You didn't want me to take her from you. So she stays with you." His lips parted in a menacing grin. "She *dies* with you."

"No, please—" Panic rose like a wave in Isabelle. Her words came too fast, a disorganized babble, but she made no effort to stop them. There had to be something she could say, some right combination of words that would convince him to spare Abby's life. "You can keep me," she said. "You can do what you want with me. You're right. That will destroy Cameron. That will hurt him. But he doesn't care about the baby." A lie, she knew, but a good lie. "Let Eloise take her into town and give her to Pastor John and his wife. None of this has anything to do with her. I'll do whatever you want me to. You... you can kill me if you want to. But let my baby go."

"She's a mother," Eloise called, her voice cracking. "You can't take a baby from its mother. Can't you see that Cameron sent her away because he doesn't want her anyway? Can't you understand that he isn't going to care what happens to her now? You want to unhinge him, but this isn't going to do it. All it will do is put a death on your conscience."

Isabelle's stomach turned over. She was sure that was a futile argument. Men like these weren't bothered by conscience. That wasn't going to stop him.

Sure enough, Duvall shook his head. "It's too late for these theatrics," he said. "If you wanted to convince someone of something, you should have tried to talk Mercer into giving me his land. But you told me yourselves that you couldn't persuade him to do that, so the only use you have to me is this." He leered at Isabelle. "He might not care about you, but everyone knows Mercer blames himself for the deaths of his wife and child. No matter how he feels about you, of course he's going to be damaged when he hears what his stubbornness caused. I think it will be enough to make him give in."

He gripped the gun with both hands and cocked it.

Hope left Isabelle like a tide receding from the shore, leaving her stranded.

She turned her back to him, shielding Abby with her body, knowing it wouldn't be enough to protect the baby.

God, if you've ever been with me—be with me now. Forgive me for my failure to protect her.

She took a deep breath and waited for the sound of the gunshot.

Chapter Thirty-Four

The wind was ferocious, and it beat Cameron and Adam back with every step they tried to take forward.

They had departed at a gallop, but that had proved impossible to maintain. They couldn't see where they were going, and neither could the horses. The snow grew deeper and deeper, and before long each step was a chore. More than once, the horses stopped where they stood and had to be coaxed to go on.

More than once, Cameron considered jumping down and continuing on foot.

It wouldn't be a good idea. He would be less able to fight the wind and the drifts than his horse was. But he was more determined to get there. Under his own power, he would never stop. Not until Isabelle was back in his arms.

The journey seemed interminable. He lost track of how long they'd been on the road. It might have been fifteen minutes or an hour after leaving the house when Adam reached out and grabbed his arm. "There," he called over the roar of the wind.

Cameron looked in the direction his friend was pointing.

There *was* something in the distance. At first it was just a dark shape, and then, as he squinted at it, it came into sharper focus.

It was the wagon.

And there were figures moving around outside.

Two women. Two men.

The men were holding guns.

No.

It was happening again. Horror opened like a chasm inside of Cameron's heart, and for a moment he thought he might tumble right in and never find his way out.

I'm going to lose them. And this time there won't be any argument that it wasn't my fault. This time I'll know forever that it was. Not because they were too close to me, but because I let them leave.

Adam's hand came to rest on his arm. His voice was as tight as a bowstring. "Don't."

"Adam..."

"Don't you go charging in there. The moment Duvall sees you, he'll shoot. He'll either shoot you or he'll shoot one of them and *then* you, and either way, we all lose."

"You want me to stand here and watch this? He's going to kill her!" His body was ablaze with furious energy. He needed to do *something* or he was going to start screaming. "What about Eloise? You told me you loved my sister, and now you just want to stand by and..."

"Stop," Adam said sharply. "*Think*, Cameron. They haven't seen us yet, all right? That means we have the upper hand on them. Take a breath. I know you don't want to. But if we play this right, if we use our heads, we can all get out alive."

He gripped Cameron's arms hard, just above the elbow, digging his thumbs into the flesh. It hurt, and the pain centered on Cameron. Slowly, he came back to himself.

Adam was right. If they were reckless, the shooting would start. Caution was the only choice that made sense.

"All right," he said, lowering his voice as much as he could in the wind. "I'll go that way." He pointed to the right. "They'll see me, but if I'm careful, it won't happen until I'm pretty close. They're distracted. You flank around to the right. Get behind the wagon if you can and cover me from there. If you get a shot, take it. I'm tired of Duvall. He can't keep doing this to us. When he put the women and the baby at risk, he crossed the line."

"I agree." Adam's voice was dark and dangerous. "Be careful."

The men separated. Cameron crouched low as he cut a path to the left, creeping closer to the wagon and the people gathered around it. As he drew nearer, a voice rose over the wind, and he recognized it as belonging to his sister.

"Can't you see that Cameron sent her away because he doesn't want her anyway? Can't you understand that he isn't going to care what happens to her now?"

His gut clenched so hard it hurt.

He didn't think Eloise really believed that… but what about Isabelle? What would she think of Eloise's words?

Well, he couldn't worry about it now. He would correct whatever wrong impressions she had when the two of them had a chance to talk. When this was over. Because they *would* be together when this was over. They would both live. Anything else was unthinkable, so he didn't allow himself to think it. He crept closer.

Duvall was facing away from him. He said something—Cameron didn't catch it in the wind—and brought his free hand up to grip the gun in his hand. He leveled it at Isabelle's heart. She turned away from him, curling her body over the baby in her arms.

Cameron was out of time.

He let out a roar, dove forward, and tackled Duvall to the ground.

Duvall yelled as he was taken down. He put up a fight, shoving his body back against Cameron's, but the righteous anger that poured through Cameron lent him a strength he'd never had before. It was easy to hold Duvall down, easy to keep him from throwing Cameron off. For a moment, he wondered how he had ever allowed himself to be intimidated in the least by this man—why hadn't he done this from the start?

Pike was somewhere, he knew, but he couldn't think about that now. He couldn't think about the fact that he might be outnumbered. He would have to trust that Adam had gotten into position. And if he hadn't, well, Cameron would just have to try to handle this on his own.

He heard a gunshot, but the energy pouring through his body was so intense that he registered nothing more. No pain. Even the weakness that spread from his calf seemed somehow unrelated. He locked his hands around Duvall's neck and pinned him to the ground, slamming him down so hard that the gun shook loose from his hands. It disappeared into a snowbank.

"Everybody freeze!" a familiar voice yelled, and relief poured through Cameron.

Sheriff Grayson.

There were voices all around. He didn't let go of Duvall, though—he couldn't. Only now was it occurring to him that he had his pistol at his side, that he could have shot Duvall. He hadn't. He'd sworn that he would if they were ever in this position again, and yet he hadn't. Why?

"Cameron." Grayson was kneeling beside him. "Let him go. The deputies have him. We're going to lock him up, it's all right. Do you need help getting up?" He frowned. "Is that your blood or his?"

"What?" Cameron looked down. Sure enough, the snow was stained red around his leg.

The pain came all at once, dull and throbbing and horrifyingly deep in the muscle of his calf. He groaned and allowed himself to be rolled away from Duvall.

"We're going to need a doctor," the sheriff called.

"No we don't," Cameron grunted. "I'm all right."

"You're not all right. You've been shot. And don't argue with me." In spite of the harsh words, the sheriff's tone was gentle and reassuring. "You've done enough foolhardy things for one day."

"Don't worry about me. Where's Isabelle?"

"She's fine," Grayson reassured him. "The pastor is talking to her now."

"Pastor John is here?"

"He's the one who came to get me when the women didn't arrive at the church on time," Grayson said. "He was sure something was wrong. And he was right. We got here just in time. Don't let me hear you say that you had this under control. You didn't even pull your gun out. I don't know what you were thinking."

Cameron was spared having to address that question. Isabelle had suddenly appeared and dropped to her knees in the snow beside him.

"Cameron," she breathed, her hands hovering over him as though she wanted to touch him but wasn't sure how to do it without hurting him.

He tried to sit up, but his head spun and he fell back in the snow. Isabelle let out a soft, pained cry.

"Don't," the sheriff said. "Don't try to get up, or you'll make that worse. Isabelle, can you make sure he stays down until the doctor arrives?"

"Yes," Isabelle said firmly, placing a hand on Cameron's shoulder. "He isn't going anywhere. You don't need to worry about that."

The sheriff turned and walked off, presumably to deal with Duvall and Pike.

"You are without a doubt the most stubborn man I have ever met," Isabelle said, her eyes filled with tears. "I'm begging you to stay down. He shot you. You're bleeding."

"It isn't that serious." But he didn't fight her. He'd lie here forever if it meant looking into her eyes and reassuring himself that she was safe. That everything was going to be all right.

"You're losing blood, Cameron. That is very serious. You could die." Her voice pitched up on the last word, as if it physically hurt her to say it.

He found her hand and gripped it. "I'm not going to die," he said softly. "It's a leg wound. It's not going to kill me."

"Just... please don't risk it? If anything happened to you, I couldn't bear it. I love you too much."

She sucked in a breath. Her eyes met his, and then she quickly looked away.

"I shouldn't have said that," she whispered.

"Look at me." It cut him deep that she had been the first to speak the words, and that she was sitting there regretting them. But he would make that right. "You say whatever you want to say, whenever you want to say it," he told her as her eyes met his. "But I love you too. That's what brought me out here today. I should never have let you go. I'm just sorry I let things get this far. I'm sorry it took the threat of losing you to make me see that I would be destroyed if that ever happened. I know now that I couldn't bear it."

"Oh, *Cameron*."

"My love." He reached up and touched her face. "Thank God you're safe. And Abby?"

"She's with Eloise. They're both fine." Tears were spilling down Isabelle's cheeks now. "I just had to get to you, Cameron,

I couldn't stand not being with you, not being able to see for myself that you were all right. Not knowing..." She ducked her head and a sob escaped her.

"Sweetheart..." He ached to sit up and put his arms around her, but if he tried to move he'd frighten her more. He wanted to pull her down to him, but not into the snow. *Just a little bit longer. Just a little more time until we can finally be in each other's arms. I'll never let anything come between the two of us again as long as I live. And as soon as I'm able to, I'm going to wrap her up in an embrace, and I think I'll never let her go.*

Whatever happened now, he swore to himself, the two of them would be together. He'd let go of the pain of the past and embrace the future with her. They would build a life together. They would be a family. Never again would Cameron allow his fear to stand in the way.

He still had doubts. He probably always would. But doubts no longer seemed insurmountable.

With Isabelle beside him, anything—everything—was possible.

He let his head fall back in the snow.

"Hold on, Cameron," he heard her say, her voice laced with taut anxiety. "A doctor is coming. Stay with me."

I'll stay with you. You never have to worry about that again.

Thank you, God. Thank you for opening my eyes. Thank you for helping me find my way to her in time. I will never squander the gift I have been given. I'll be grateful every day for the rest of my life.

Chapter Thirty-Five

"You've been working all day," Cameron called out from the living room as Isabelle hurried past. "Stop for a moment. Come in here and see me and Abby. We miss you, you know."

"I'm sorry," Isabelle laughed, detouring into the living room. Cameron sat in a comfortable chair beside the fire, his leg propped up on an ottoman. "I was going to come in soon to check the bandages. It's almost time to change them."

"It's been a week," Cameron said with a chuckle. "You don't still have to change my bandages every few hours, you know."

Isabelle lifted her chin primly. "It's better to be safe than sorry."

The two of them grinned at one another. It was a good-natured dispute they'd been having for days now. The truth was that Isabelle knew Cameron was probably right, but she didn't want to stop tending to him. She enjoyed having the opportunity to inspect his healing wound for herself and to see, moment by moment, that he was all right.

More to the point, she liked being able to put her hands on him. Once he was healthy, she didn't know if the two of them would have any sort of physical relationship anymore, and she'd miss it.

She knelt before him and began to unwind the bandages, pulling out a fresh set from the basket that sat beside him on the floor. He watched her as she worked. Though he wouldn't admit it, Isabelle was sure Cameron enjoyed this time as much as she did. He liked being cared for.

"Everything smells amazing," he told her. "I wish I could be in the kitchen helping you."

"Well, next Christmas, you will be." It gave her a surge of joy, like an explosion in her heart, to be able to talk about next Christmas and to feel confident that it was something the two of them were going to share. *I'll still be here next Christmas. I have a future here.* She cleared her throat. "But this year, your job is to entertain our guests while I deal with serving the meal."

As if on cue, there was a knock at the door.

Isabelle put the finishing touches on the fresh bandage she had been wrapping and gathered up the old one. "I'll be right back," she told Cameron, resting a hand briefly on his shoulder. "Don't go anywhere."

She hurried from the room, pausing only to deposit the bandages she held in the laundry basket. The knock on the door came again as she was crossing the kitchen, and a smile broke across her face. There was only one person who would be so impatient.

"It's about time," Eloise said, her voice mock-cross, as Isabelle opened the door and ushered her, Adam, Edith, and Pastor John all inside at once. "Adam and I saw Edith and Pastor John crossing the yard and decided it was time for us to come over too."

"Yes, I'm glad you did," Isabelle assured them. She'd told Eloise and Adam to come over at any time, but if they hadn't arrived within the next hour she would have gone looking for them. Dinner was going to be ready soon. "Why don't you go into the living room and sit down? That's where Cameron and Abby are. I'll get the food ready."

"I'll stay and help you," Edith said, smiling at her. "Many hands make for light work."

And so they did. In no time at all, the food was laid out on the kitchen table. Isabelle had done what she could to make the place especially homey and festive, lighting candles and placing them at intervals on the table as well. Now the candles were joined by a turkey, roast potatoes, buttery vegetables, and freshly baked bread. Several pies cooled in the windows, waiting for the assembled group to be ready for dessert.

The men helped Cameron into the kitchen. Eloise came behind them, carrying Abby in her arms, and placed her in her chair. "Does she need to be fed?"

"I just fed her an hour ago," Cameron said, pride in his voice at having been the one to care for Abby. "She'll be all right while we have our meal."

Everyone sat down at the table and Pastor John led them in a prayer. When he was finished, he left a moment of silence so they could offer up their own quiet thanks to God.

Isabelle was grateful for that moment. She had a lot to be thankful for.

Thank you for bringing me to Wintervale in the first place, she thought, her hands folded before her. *Thank you for giving me the strength to stay when things felt uncertain. I know now how wrong it would have been to leave. Thank you for bringing all of us safely through the struggles we faced, so that we can now live here together without fear. Thank you for my home, and for my family. The way we came together might be unusual, but I wouldn't trade what I have here for anything in the world.*

She felt the answering warmth she associated with God's presence and was assured He was listening. He had heard her prayer of gratitude, had received it, and had blessed her.

As though her life could possibly be any more blessed than it already was!

**

"Thank you so much for everything," Edith said as she and Pastor John stood in the doorway hours later. "Are you sure we can't stay and help clean up?"

"Nonsense," Isabelle said with a warm smile. "To tell you the truth, I don't know how much cleaning I'm going to do tonight anyway. I'm pretty tired."

"Of course you are. You must have worked so hard to put everything together!" Edith embraced her. "Dinner was magnificent."

"Thank you so much for the quilt," Isabelle enthused. "I'm sure that must have taken a very long time. It's gorgeous. And Abby's hair bows!"

"She'll have enough hair to wear them before you know it," Edith grinned. "All right. You two stay warm."

"We'll see you in church on Sunday if the weather stays clear," Pastor John said. His gaze lingered on Cameron for a moment, but he didn't ask the question.

You'll see him too, Isabelle thought. *It might not be this week, but eventually Cameron will return to church. All the walls around his heart are finally starting to come down.*

Edith and Pastor John left. Eloise and Adam were saying farewell to Abby, passing her back and forth between them, looking up into one another's eyes at intervals.

Isabelle stood back and watched them for a moment. The warm smiles on their faces. The sparkles in their eyes. The way they both looked down at the baby they held between them, then back up at one another.

They're in love.

She didn't know what they might have said to each other in the privacy of one or the other of their own homes. She didn't know if they'd confided their feelings. But it was clear that it was only a matter of time, and that was one of the best Christmas gifts she could have received. What a blessing it was to know that Adam and Eloise were going to find love at the same time she was finding it—that everyone was going to be happy.

They gave Abby back to her. Both of them hugged her, and then they were out the door and on their way back to their respective homes. She watched through the window as they paused to say a private goodbye to one another in the light flurries.

"I think he's giving her a gift," she said as Cameron joined her at the window. "But I can't tell what it is."

"He made her a carving of a horse," Cameron said. "He's been working on it for weeks. He showed it to me."

"Did he?" Isabelle's heart soared. "That's such a thoughtful gift. I'm sure she'll love it. And he must have put so much work into it!" She clasped her hands in front of her. "I wish they had stayed to exchange gifts here so I could have seen it."

"Well, to tell you the truth, I asked them to leave," Cameron said.

There was a spark in his voice that she didn't recognize. She turned to face him, shifting Abby from one arm to the other. "Are you tired?" she asked with a frown. "You shouldn't be on your feet, you know. Maybe you should go lie down."

"Don't fuss," he said with a warm smile.

"You like it when I fuss," she smiled back.

"All right, yes, I do. But don't *worry.* I'm all right." He held up the walking stick he'd been using to support himself when he'd needed to get around for the last week. "As long as I don't stay on my feet for too long or get too far away from the stick, I'm fine."

"Why did you ask Adam and Eloise to leave, then? Just tired of having company?" That would have made sense, she supposed. Cameron was beginning to open up to people once more, but he was a quiet, private person, and he probably always would be.

He shook his head. "I asked them to go so that I could give you *your* Christmas present," he said.

"My present?" They'd exchanged gifts before their guests had arrived. They had agreed to keep things small this year, given the events leading up to the day. She had gifted him some more embroidered handkerchiefs and some knitted socks, and he had given her a couple of books she was excited about reading. "You gave me my present already."

"Put Abby in her chair," he said, hobbling away from the window. "I've got one more gift for you before we're done."

Frowning, she put Abby down and turned back to face him. "You didn't have to do that. We agreed to keep things small."

He gave her a smile that seemed to hide some sort of unspoken joke. "Don't worry," he assured her, his eyes bright with mirth. "This is small."

He reached into his pocket and pulled out one of her handkerchiefs, folded carefully around something. Laying it flat on his palm, he held it out to her. "Go ahead. Open it."

She unfolded the handkerchief slowly and gasped.

A ring.

It was a beautiful diamond—not too big—set on a golden band. She looked down at it, then back up at him, her head buzzing. "This... Cameron..."

"Adam picked it up for me in town," Cameron explained. "But I chose it. He drew pictures of all the ones he saw that fit the description of what I was looking for, and I chose this one. I hope you like it."

"It's beautiful," she breathed, touching it gingerly with one finger. Her heart raced. "But..." She was afraid to accept it. This was Cameron, after all. Could he possibly mean what this seemed to indicate?

"I want you to marry me, Isabelle," he said. "I want you to be my wife. I want to complete the journey we started when you came here. I think that's what Ruth would want... to see me happy in a new family. She wouldn't want me to isolate myself and give up on love." His voice grew thick. "And I love you. I thought I would never be able to love again after I lost my family. I was determined *not* to let myself love you. But in spite of all that, I do. There's something so special about you, about the way you touch my heart, that I couldn't resist you no matter how hard I tried. All I want now is to keep you beside me for the rest of my life."

He picked up the ring and held it out to her.

"Will you marry me?" he asked, his voice low and husky with emotion.

She pressed a hand to her mouth, controlling the swell of love that rose up within her. Lowering her hand, she whispered, "Of course I will."

He smiled, took her hand, and slid the ring onto her finger. "I'm sorry I couldn't get down on one knee," he said softly. "I'd have liked to. Another time."

"You could ask me to marry you any way at all and I'd say yes," she assured him. "You're all I want, Cameron. You and Abby—this family. This is what I've prayed for."

He pulled her into his arms and she went willingly, and this time she had no doubt that the kiss she anticipated would come.

When it did, she rose up onto her toes to meet it, relishing in the warmth of his arms and the yield of his lips against hers, the knowledge that this kiss was the first of many, and that they were taking their first steps along a road they would travel together for the rest of their lives.

Epilogue

One Year Later

The weather was mild, the snow thin on the ground, and Cameron was thankful. This winter looked to be much more pleasant than last year's.

At the very least, it had made it possible for everyone to gather in the barn. The doors stood open to admit light, and a bit of a chill came in because of that, but the number of people in the barn and the lanterns positioned all around the place made it warm enough for dancing.

They had come back to the ranch from the church, and it seemed as if everyone in town was here. The decision had been made to hold the Christmas fair at Melody Strasser's home again this year, so the booths were all gone. In their place were assorted mismatched tables that people had brought over, encircling a clear space that was serving as a dance floor.

It was in that space that Cameron now rotated slowly with his new bride in his arms.

She stared up at him, her eyes shining, radiant with the joy of the day. He'd never seen anything more beautiful. The dress she wore was simple enough. It was white, with sleeves that flared and some of Isabelle's signature embroidery on the neckline. It fit her perfectly, accentuating her figure in a subtle way. She wore a crown of holly on her head in honor of Christmas. Cameron could have watched her dance in that dress all day, and the fact that he got to hold her in his arms made it all the more special.

The assembled guests applauded as their dance came to an end. They lingered in one another's arms, faces close together. "I don't want to stop," Isabelle murmured, a smile on her lips.

His heart pounded. "I don't either," he whispered. "But... we should give some attention to our guests. They came all the way out here to celebrate with us, after all."

"I never thought I'd see the day you would be choosing to socialize," she teased him.

"You bring it out in me." He raised a hand to her face and cupped her cheek. "You bring all the best things out in me."

Abby came toddling out onto the dance floor. "Papa!" she cried, flinging her arms around Cameron's legs.

Isabelle laughed as Cameron bent down to scoop her up. "She's such a Daddy's girl." She poked Abby's nose gently. "You love your papa, don't you?"

Abby nodded, biting one of her fingers.

"Do you want to go say hello to Sheriff Grayson?" Cameron asked Abby. "Maybe he'll let you try on his badge."

Abby bounced up and down eagerly in Cameron's arms, and Cameron laughed. "She wants to become a sheriff when she grows up, I think."

"If there's any little girl I'd ever think was capable of such a thing," Isabelle said fondly, meeting Cameron's eyes, "it would be ours."

***

After they had greeted Sheriff Grayson, Isabelle took Abby and went to sit with Pastor John and Edith for a while. Cameron remained with the sheriff, speaking in low tones. What he had to discuss was serious enough that he didn't want to risk being overheard and bringing down the festive atmosphere of the day.

The two men sat at a table in the far corner of the barn, watching as the guests danced. "Have you thought about what we talked about?" Grayson asked. "Opening up your stream to prospectors? You could make a lot of money. I think we have to acknowledge now that it's likely there's more gold in there. That nugget you found last summer was a sight to behold."

It was true. Cameron had been down at the water fetching a drink for his horses when he'd seen the nugget glistening at the bottom of the riverbed. He'd waded in to get it and discovered, after pulling it from the muck, that it was as big as his fist. The profit had been enough to pay off his debt to the bank. He owned the ranch free and clear now. And ever since that day, there had been plenty of talk around Wintervale about what else might be in that stream.

Cameron shook his head, kicking his feet up to rest on an empty chair. "Absolutely not," he said firmly. "No prospectors." He had thought this through and come to a decision he was very happy with. "I don't need any more money. I have enough now to last me the rest of my life."

"But with a little more, you could expand the ranch. Buy more land, create a new pasture…"

Cameron waved a hand. "I don't need any of that," he said. "I'm more than happy with what I have."

His eyes focused on Isabelle. She was leaning forward, a bright smile on her face, and though she was too far away for Cameron to hear what she was saying, he recognized the expression she wore when she found something funny. It made him long to go over to her and find out what the joke was. He didn't like the idea of missing out on anything she had to say, no matter how small. Even though he had the rest of his life to listen to her jokes, each one was precious.

"Well, if you're sure that's how you feel about it," Sheriff Grayson said, leaning back in his chair. "I suppose I can't blame you, as long as you've thought things through."

"I have," Cameron said, rising to his feet. "And I don't want to discuss business, today of all days."

"Well, I certainly won't fault you for that," the sheriff said, a smile breaking over his face as he got to his feet too. "I don't even know what you're doing with me right now, given that you have that beautiful woman to spend time with."

Cameron had to laugh. "I don't know what I'm doing with you, either," he said. "You'll excuse me, I'm sure?"

"Of course." Grayson clapped a hand on Cameron's shoulder. "Congratulations. Everyone in town is happy to see a smile on your face again, Cameron. I mean it."

Cameron inclined his head gratefully and turned toward Isabelle. As he crossed the room in her direction, he saw Eloise and Adam on the dance floor. They were moving more slowly than the music called for, their heads bent close together, and a surge of warmth welled up within him.

They're going to be next, he thought. *We'll be dancing at their wedding in no time.*

The thought put a smile on his face, and he turned his attention back to his own bride.

***

The next year passed blissfully. Abby grew stronger every day, and before long she was running around the yard and doing her best to help with the chores. Her favorite thing to do was to gather the eggs from the chickens, though she broke as many eggs as she successfully put into the basket.

Today, the family was unpacking Christmas ornaments. For the first time since they had known one another, Cameron had cut down a Christmas tree and brought it into the house. It was a blessed reminder of a long-gone past. As he stood and watched Isabelle hang ornaments on the tree, he lifted a hand and pressed his fingertips to the cross that had once belonged to Ruth. It hung permanently around his neck now, a reminder of her and of his gratitude to her.

She would love all of this. I believe she's looking down on us right now, and that it brings her joy to see it.

Isabelle turned to face him. "I have a gift for you," she said, picking up one of the smaller packages under the tree.

He laughed. "Christmas is still a week away!"

"I know it is, and I meant to wait, but I can't." She bounced up and down on the balls of her feet, as she so often did when she was excited, and held out the box. "Please open it now."

Cameron laughed. "Of course I will, if it means that much to you."

"Presents?" Abby asked hopefully. She was sitting beneath the tree, picking up each box in turn and shaking it gingerly—Isabelle had instructed her not to be too rough when handling the presents in case something inside was fragile, and Abby had taken that very seriously.

"Not yet," Isabelle told her with a smile. "This present is just for Papa. You get yours on Christmas Day."

Abby nodded seriously and returned to the business of investigating the packages.

"It seems cruel to make her wait while I get something right now," Cameron observed, taking a seat on the settee.

Isabelle sat down beside him. "Trust me," she said. "This is really a gift for the whole family. Abby will get as much out of it as you will."

That piqued Cameron's curiosity. He tore off the paper and opened the box.

It was a silver baby rattle.

He took it out, frowning. "This… is beautiful," he said slowly. What did she mean, Abby was going to get as much out of it as he would? How would either of them get anything out of it? Abby was too old for a toy like this. It would only be useful for…

He gasped.

Isabelle's eyes were shining. Her hands gripped one another the way they did when she was nervous, but she had nothing to be nervous about. Not now. He took her hand and unwound her fingers. "Isabelle… how long have you known?"

"Only three days," she said. "The doctor confirmed it. We're going to have another baby. I wanted to tell you as your Christmas gift, but I realized I couldn't wait."

Her lip quivered, and she looked as if she might cry with happiness.

As for Cameron, the joy that bloomed within him was like carrying the sun inside his chest. He could hardly bear this happiness. He had never believed it would find him again.

But it had, of course. It had found him when *she* had found him. He hated to think about the life he'd been living before she had come into it.

"Oh, Isabelle," he breathed. "Thank God for you."

He pulled her to him and kissed her with everything he had.

THE END

Also by Chloe Carley

Thank you so much for reading "**The Woman Who Saved His Christmas**"!

I hope you enjoyed it! If you did, here are some of my other bestsellers:

#1 A Surprise Bride for the Cowboy's Christmas

#2 Finding Forgiveness in the West

#3 A Godsent Governess for the Reserved Rancher

#4 Shedding God's Light on his Broken Heart

Here are my inspiring Boxsets, too:

#1 Three Unlucky Brides on their Miraculous Paths

#2 Three Faithful Heavenly Brides

#3 Three Brides' Praying Misfits

#4 Three Daring Matches Made in Heaven

My full Amazon Book Catalogue is available at:

https://go.chloecarley.com/bc-authorpage

Your heartfelt support is my blessing! ❤

Made in United States
Troutdale, OR
11/14/2025